$2.25

"What you done, bitch?" Larry asked.

His hand reached inside his plaid shirt and came out holding a straight-edge razor. "You're dead, you murdering slut!"

In the confined space, Krysty knew that the man's bulk and raw power could tell against her.

The steel edge began to weave a lightning pattern of hissing death in front of Krysty's face, pressing her back a half step at a time. Larry was breathing hard, sweat glistening on his forehead and around his open mouth.

Mildred was sitting on her bed, ready to use her blaster if things went far enough against Krysty. Suddenly, out of the corner of her eye, Krysty saw the black woman tear open the front of her blouse, revealing her breasts.

"This is for you, boy," she called. Larry Ballinger's gaze wandered to the black woman's chest. It was the opening that Krysty had been hoping for. Taking advantage of Larry's inattention, she stepped forward, flexing the powerful muscles in her thighs. She swung her right foot upward with all of her strength.

Larry Ballinger's numbed fingers released the razor. He opened his mouth to scream and yellow vomit dribbled down his chin. His hands were reaching for his groin to try to stem the terrible pain, but the blackness came surging up and washed him into unconsciousness first.

Also available in the Deathlands saga:

JAMES AXLER

DEATH LANDS

Latitude Zero

A GOLD EAGLE BOOK FROM

W RLDWIDE

TORONTO • NEW YORK • LONDON • PARIS
AMSTERDAM • STOCKHOLM • HAMBURG
ATHENS • MILAN • TOKYO • SYDNEY

I'm grateful every single day for the miraculous
luck that brought us together.
Now and for always, this is for Liz.

First edition April 1991

ISBN 0-373-62512-X

LATITUDE ZERO

Copyright © 1991 by Worldwide Library.
Philippine copyright 1991. Australian copyright 1991.

All rights reserved. Except for use in any review, the
reproduction or utilization of this work in whole or in part
in any form by any electronic, mechanical or other means,
now known or hereafter invented, including xerography,
photocopying and recording, or in any information storage
or retrieval system, is forbidden without the permission
of the publisher, Worldwide Library, 225 Duncan Mill Road,
Don Mills, Ontario, Canada M3B 3K9.

All the characters in this book have no existence outside the
imagination of the author and have no relation whatsoever to
anyone bearing the same name or names. They are not even
distantly inspired by any individual known or unknown to the
author, and all the incidents are pure invention.

® are Trademarks registered in the United States Patent and
Trademark Office and in other countries.

Printed in U.S.A.

With its notorious extremes of terrain and temperature, the area of southern Texas known as Big Bend is the only place on earth where one can witness both Purgatory and Paradise in a single afternoon.

From *Water and Stone*, by
J. McKinley Thompson, 1943

CHAPTER ONE

BEHIND RYAN CAWDOR and his five companions, the apocalyptic pillar of swirling red and orange dust rose thousands of feet into the clear sky. The choking cloud contained the disintegrated ruins of a long-hidden redoubt that had honeycombed the mountain, the remains of which still towered above the friends. The complex had been destroyed by a self-terminate device placed there by some long-dead hand nearly a hundred years ago, before the brief and savage nuclear war that had ravaged the United States of America, turning it into what was now simply called Deathlands.

Within the redoubt had been one of the rare mat-trans devices known as gateways, which would have enabled Ryan and the others to make an instantaneous jump from that particular redoubt to another, maybe a thousand miles away.

With its destruction came the bitter awareness that the companions were stranded in that bleak desert land with little food or water, and no sign of any semblance of civilization as far as the eye could see.

J. B. Dix, the armorer of the group, was busily checking figures off his micro-sextant, trying to find out where they were. Ryan wiped grit from his one good eye and looked around, guessing that they could be somewhere in the Southwest.

But the nuking of the year 2001 had done more than wipe out all the cities and virtually all the people. It had also produced almost indescribable changes in the formation of the country. Half of California had slithered into the Pacific; mountains had fallen and burst up again five hundred miles away; there were monstrous steaming lagoons filled with water so acidic it would separate flesh from bone; there were forests where there had been deserts and there were deserts that had once been rolling acres of fertile grazing land.

"New Mexico, I think. Not all that far from the border with old Texas." J.B. wiped his wire-rimmed spectacles on his shirtsleeve and looked across at Ryan.

"Don't know this region all that well. We were here with Trader, ten years or more ago. There's plenty of old hot spots around here."

Out of habit he glanced down at the miniature rad counter buttoned to his coat. It was showing a pale yellow light that barely shaded above the green of safety. It showed there was some kind of radiation within twenty miles or so, or a milder area a little nearer. The rad counters weren't all that accurate or reliable.

Mildred Wyeth had been sitting on the ground, resting her head on her hand. "Sure is warm after that dank, cold dungeon. I haven't been so cold since they froze me."

The black woman had been in her midthirties when minor abdominal surgery had led to complications. She'd been one of the leading experts in the United States on the relatively new science of cryogenics and cryosurgery, and had been one of a number of people whose bodies had been frozen in the hope of reviving and curing them at some unspecified future date. Mildred had been thawed out by Ryan and the others when they'd found the cryo-center in what had once been called Minnesota.

Apart from the column of dust slowly drifting away, the sky was clear of any threatening chem clouds. Ryan glanced once at the battered comm dish—covered in stones and boulders—that had saved their lives when the self-destruct blew out the redoubt. The area for several hundred yards around was scattered with similar rocks, most no bigger than a baseball, a few of them the size of a house.

Jak Lauren, the albino teenager, caught Ryan's look. "Fucked without dish," he said, trying to brush the thick dust from his mane of pure white hair.

"We'd have been in serious trouble if it'd run away with the spoon, wouldn't we?" said Krysty Wroth, grinning.

"What spoon?"

The woman's grin broadened. "Didn't anyone ever tell you rhymes when you were young, Jak?

Mother Sonja told me that poem when I was a young girl in Harmony ville."

"Never young," the boy replied.

"I recall it," Doc Tanner boomed in his rich, mellow voice. "The dish running off with the spoon and the cat playing upon a violin and a heifer leaping across the lunar landscape. A diminutive canine that found the entire subject fit for considerable merriment. Ah, yes. I do remember it well, Krysty."

Doc Tanner was, in some ways, the oldest member of the group of friends.

He was born Theophilus Algernon Tanner in South Strafford, Vermont, on February 14, 1868, and married Emily Chandler on June 17, 1891. They had two children—Rachel and Jolyon.

In November of 1896, Doc Tanner was trawled forward as part of an experiment in time travel— Operation Cerberus, part of Overproject Whisper, which was itself a key segment of the Totality Concept. The efforts to use gateways for chron jumps were horrendously and cruelly unsuccessful. Their targets included a leading judge and a famous writer, each of whom vanished in mysterious circumstances. Subjects Crater and Bierce, as they were known on the files of Cerberus, failed to make it to the twentieth century. Though Doc's brains were sometimes a little scrambled, he arrived safely in 1998.

But he didn't prove to be a sufficiently docile guinea pig for the scientists. Eventually, to remove the disruptive Victorian, they sent him forward, pushing him nearly a hundred years into the future.

There, after some peculiarly unpleasant adventures, Doc was rescued by Ryan Cawdor, and had been traveling with him ever since.

He looked to be close to seventy, with straggling silver hair and a lined face, and wore the same old-fashioned clothes that he'd been wearing when trawled.

Ryan and Krysty had once tried to work out with Doc just how old he really was. By one count he was only in his midthirties, about the same age as Ryan and J.B. By another count he was somewhere around two hundred and twenty years old.

"Not surprising my mind becomes somewhat addled at times," he'd commented.

"North?" J.B. queried. "Looks like some more mountains. But the land should get greener up to the north."

"East's acid lagoons and swamps," Jak informed them. "And East's what was home."

Ryan spoke quietly. "South."

"Why, lover?" Krysty asked. "South looks like a lot more heat and sand."

"Remember what Rick said about there being two cryo-centers that he knew about?"

"One was where you defrosted me," Mildred said.

"The other was supposed to be someplace in the south of Texas near the Grandee. Rick called it Big Bend."

Doc coughed and tapped on the dry earth with the ferrule of his sword stick.

"I know something about Big Bend. When I was living in the nineties, I met a fine girl, Galadriel Okie, a reporter. She was a great one for what was called backpacking. She visited Big Bend several times and said it was one of the quietest of the national parks."

"South Texas, Doc?" Ryan asked.

"Indeed, my dear fellow, indeed. I recall that it took its nomenclature from the large loop of the Rio Grande, what you now call the Grandee. She also was much incensed when the government took over some of the parks in the nineties and closed them for purposes of national security."

"Including Big Bend, Doc?" Krysty queried.

"I believe so. Yes, I'm sure. Galadriel wrote an article for the *Washington Post* on the subject. 'Save Big Mac.' No! I mean, Big Bend. It did scant good, I fear."

"It fits," J.B. said quietly. "Want to go freezie hunting again?"

"Why not? Mildred worked out well, didn't she? Could strike lucky again."

Ryan was conscious that his itch to talk to survivors from the past wasn't logical, but it still nagged at him in the waking hours of the night to wonder why a civilized and reasonably affluent world would allow itself to be blown apart. Maybe someone, somewhere, would one day be able to provide the answer.

Mildred was running her fingers through the tiny, tight plaits on the top of her head. "Glad you think I worked out well, Ryan. Thanks, man. Praise indeed! Maybe next semester I'll get an even higher grade from you."

"Sorry, Mildred. You know what I mean. Just seems that if we aren't that far off from Big Bend, we should go down and take a look. Anyone else got any feelings on it?"

Jak was occupied with picking up small pebbles, flicking them in the air, and jabbing at them with the hardened edge of his palm. He caught Ryan's question and glanced sideways, shrugging his shoulders. "Don't give fuck. There's same as here."

"Guess he's right," Krysty agreed. "Long as we can get food and drink, I'll go along to Big Bend with everyone else. Like the sound of the name."

Doc also shrugged. "I was going to the store for cigarettes, but I'll go to Big Bend."

Mildred sniffed. "In some ways I'd kind of like to go back home to Lincoln, Nebraska. But... everyone's long, long dead. Children of friends are dead. Grandchildren gone. Cemeteries brimming with the descendants of folks I knew. No...never can go home like that. Sure. I'll go to Big Bend, Ryan. Thaw out a freezie and I'll have someone who can talk to me about television, books and stuff like that."

She grinned up at Ryan, but he could also see tears brimming in her dark eyes.

J.B. was the only one who didn't answer.

"We got five votes," Ryan said. "Want to make it six, J.B.?"

"No."

Ryan was surprised. He and the Armorer had known each other for so long—from the early days with the Trader—that their judgment on situations was almost always the same.

The others waited for J.B. to expand on his decision. He brushed a small, buzzing insect away from his lips before speaking.

"Little food and water. Doesn't look much in that direction. Krysty, you got the best eyes of any of us. You see anything?"

Krysty hopped agilely onto a large crimson boulder, its bright color almost identical to her fiery mane of hair. She shaded her eyes and stared across the wilderness, concentrating for a very long time before jumping down again.

"Dust. Could be the wind, but it doesn't look like it. More like animals, maybe horses. And I thought I saw a building close by, but can't be sure. It's a long ways off."

"But there's something?" Ryan asked. He shaded his good eye with his hand and looked into the distance. Though he prided himself on his keen sight, it was nothing compared to Krysty's.

"Yeah. Something."

J.B. wasn't convinced. "Gotta be close to three hundred miles, Ryan. No wags to hitch along on, no cattle to butcher, no crystal streams to wet your lips at."

"Three hundred. We'll move mainly in the dark, and there must be water along the blacktops. Soon as we find a blacktop, that is. It'll take us ten days to two weeks on foot. I just can't believe we won't find people and transport somewhere."

The Armorer nodded. "Could be you're right. Then we'll be fine." He paused and half smiled. "Then again, could be you're wrong. Still, I heard say that getting chilled from heat and thirst wasn't all that bad."

A half hour later the six friends began to walk south.

CHAPTER TWO

THE RAD COUNTER FADED into a steady green once they were a couple of miles away from the ruins of the redoubt.

The sun burned down from sky that was tinted the palest of pinks in the far west and a fiery orange in the east. Once or twice they heard the distant rumble of thunder from a chem storm over the hills off to the north.

"Gotta be way over a hundred," Mildred said, pausing to lever a pebble from her white sneakers.

"Yeah," Ryan agreed.

"We're losing body moisture at close on a pint every hour," she said. "Medical fact."

"No," Jak disagreed, overhearing her. "Not sweating."

"Wrong, son. In such dry heat the sweat's evaporating the moment it gets on the outside. Feels like you aren't sweating. That's the danger. If you dehydrate your mind goes, and it takes your body down the line with it."

"The building you thought you saw, Krysty? It should mean water."

In his heart Ryan had a nagging doubt that they'd taken the wrong option by heading south. But when you made a plan you stuck to it—unless there was some big reason to change. The Trader always used to tell him that.

"Maybe not. This trail's taking us down into dead ground. Can't make anything out from down here."

The land was barren, apart from small clusters of the delicate purple prickle-leaf gilia, its beauty almost unbelievable in the dusty heat.

J.B. brought up the rear. In the hour or so that they'd been slogging south he hadn't uttered a single word. Ryan fell back to join him, allowing Jak to take the point position.

"How's it going?"

"Warm."

"You think we've made a wrong move?"

The Armorer turned to face him, the sunlight dancing off the lenses of his glasses.

"Yeah. Could be. Then again, it could be we've made the right move." He grinned at Ryan. "Hell, you think I'm sulking back here?"

"No," Ryan replied unconvincingly.

J.B. laughed. "Thought you knew me better'n that, friend. No. It's just that talking costs, and it's too hot to spend words."

The faint trail started to wind its way upward again.

Krysty was out in front, and she beckoned to the others.

"Small spread down yonder," she called. "It's the one I saw way back."

"Best get low," Ryan advised. "Don't know what kind of folks is there."

The redheaded woman nodded and crouched. Ryan knew from experience that her flaming hair could be seen from miles off, particularly if the sun happened to catch it.

One by one the rest of the group joined her, with Doc struggling up last.

"There's a road." J.B. pointed to the right, where an undulating ribbon of ancient blacktop rolled and pitched toward the south.

"Are there any horses?" Mildred asked.

"Yeah," Krysty replied, "and the place has a well and a vegetable garden to the side. Looks a real neat place."

"Nobody's moving." Ryan scanned the land, looking for a trace of movement. In this kind of desert it would be hard to move around without leaving a telltale pillar of orange dust behind.

Ryan was conscious of a faint, high-pitched hum somewhere behind them and high in the air. Almost immediately the others heard it as well.

"Swarm fucking bees," Jak announced, looking around worriedly.

"Could be. Can't see anything." Ryan knew that the southern part of Deathlands was plagued occasionally by huge swarms of what used to be called "killer" African bees. He'd read in an old, brittle mag once, about how they'd been moving north from the forests of Brazil around the time that the world blew apart. He'd never been clear about what bees from Africa had been doing in South America. That page had been missing.

The one thing they all knew from bitter experience was just how dangerous a swarm of such mutated bees could be. Unless you could seal yourself in some safe cover, you just had to pray the swarm didn't come your way.

The sound was growing louder, a whining, like a distant electric drill cutting through the sky. But there was still no sign of the actual swarm.

There wasn't a hint of cover for a good half mile, and even the fittest of them would take at least five minutes to sprint across the broken terrain. The speed at which the sound was racing toward them made it unlikely that they had even two minutes.

"Why can't we see them?" Ryan snarled.

The noise swelled, rising to a demonic screech. Something blurred at the corner of Ryan's vision and J.B.'s beloved fedora flew from his head.

"Dark night."

The sound Dopplered away across the valley and then seemed to turn and head back toward them. Ryan felt a chill of unease at his nape. Whatever the creature was, it didn't seem like a swarm of bees. But it wasn't like anything that Ryan had ever encountered before.

"You all right, J.B.?" he asked, his eye raking the land below them.

"Yeah, but something took a damned great bite out of my hat." He picked it up and poked a finger through a ragged gash near the crown.

"It's coming again," Mildred warned. She'd drawn her ZKR 551 six-shot revolver. Chambered to take the standard .38 Smith & Wesson round, the blaster had been designed as a target pistol. Mildred had represented her country in the last ever Olympic Games in Atlanta in 1996 in the free shooting event, and had picked up the silver medal.

The shrieking closed in, then softened and seemed to swing high in the air above them. It was Krysty, with her mutie-enhanced vision, who finally spotted what they were up against.

"There!" she yelled. "Some kinda insect. Just one."

All of them, except Doc, saw it. The old man had drawn his ponderous Le Mat pistol and was waving it around. Everyone had a blaster out, but the target was tiny, hovering at least a hundred feet above them. To Ryan it looked like some sort of mutie dragonfly, but from the evidence of J.B.'s hat it was a potentially lethal opponent.

"Coming again!" Jak shouted, cradling his head to protect himself from the shrieking dive.

J.B. was the only one to try to shoot at the plummeting speck of iridescent color, the crack of his blaster sounding flat and weak in the desert stillness.

But the creature was way too fast and elusive. It's target was Krysty, possibly because of her tumbling fiery hair. The woman raised a hand then cried out in pain.

There was the hiss of the thing's passage and a high-pitched whine as it looped above them again. Krysty held her right wrist in her left hand, dark blood trickling between her fingers. Her face was pale with shock, and she turned to look at Ryan through blurred eyes.

"I'm fine, lover," she said. "It took a slice from my arm, but... Better find some way of stopping the little bastard before it takes out an eye."

For once, Ryan was totally at a loss. The insect was too small and too fast for anyone to have much hope of hitting it, and ferocious enough to present a real threat to them. As Krysty said, if it chose to go for an eye... The thought made him wince, and lift a hand unconsciously to his one good eye.

"It's getting ready to come again," Mildred said.

"Perhaps if we all shoot at once?" Doc suggested.

"No," Mildred said. "The little mother's mine."

The blaster, designed by the Koucky brothers for the Zbrojovka works at Brno, was steady in her right hand. She'd already operated the thumb-cocking hammer, and the ZKR 551 was ready to speak.

"No hope," Doc scoffed. "There's more chance of finding snow in Albuquerque in July."

"Shut it, Doc," she warned.

The creature was getting ready to blitz them again. Straining his vision, Ryan was just able to make it out as a tiny dot, wings humming as it held its position.

It looked no bigger than a grain of sand against the light sky.

The revolver fired, bucking a little against Mildred's wrist.

"Dark night," J.B. whispered. "You got it, Mildred."

There had been an almost human screech, then the dot was tumbling, over and over, growing larger as it fell.

It thudded to earth only a dozen paces from Ryan, hitting the top of a frost-shattered boulder and flopping lifelessly to the orange dust beneath it.

The six friends circled the dead creature where it lay broken in the dirt.

"Fucking bird," Jak spit.

It was a mutie hawk with a wingspan no larger than a child's hand. Its plumage was a dark coppery-green, almost black, and glistened in the sunlight. The heavy bullet had smashed its breast apart, killing it instantly. Its beak, hooked and vicious, was tipped with Krysty's blood.

"It's beautiful," Krysty said, busily tying a strip of cloth around her wrist. "Gaia! But it's *so* beautiful."

"You make me feel bad about chilling it."

J.B. was staring at the bullet wound in the falcon's body. "That has to be around the best show I ever saw, Mildred."

"No. One of the worst. I was aiming at its head."

They left almost immediately, but the scavenging ants of the desert were already picking their way around the bird's corpse.

There was still no sign of human life around the small farm. As they started toward the ribbon of highway it became easier to make out the live-stock—cows, pigs and horses, all in pens or corrals. Once they heard the sudden noise of a guard dog barking, but the sound stopped as abruptly as it had begun.

"It can't have scented us," Ryan said. "Wind's blowing the wrong way for that."

"Anyone inside should have seen us by now," J.B. observed. "We stand out on this light sand like moose shit on a christening gown."

"I have been considering that small dark bird we saw," Doc said. "And there is something that evades the edge of my memory about such a falcon."

"What's that, Doc?" Krysty asked.

"All I recall—"

The old man was interrupted by the crack of a hunting rifle, the bullet kicking up a plume of dirt a yard from the toes of his boots.

CHAPTER THREE

As Ryan dived for cover into a shallow draw a dozen yards from the blacktop, he spotted the white puff of powder smoke from one of the windows of the house. He'd already noticed that the spread was built like a small fortress.

There was a heavy studded door at the front, and all of the visible windows had stout wooden shutters, with firing holes cut in their centers. A second floor also had protected windows. It looked at first glance that it would take some serious firepower to get inside.

The first shot was followed by an irregular, scattered volley, but everyone had easily made cover. If the aggressive defenders had waited another fifty yards or so they could have caused some serious damage. There was the sound of bellowed laughter from inside the house, and then someone shouted angry orders. Silence followed.

"Want us to start blasting back at 'em?" J.B. called.

"No. Not yet."

Isolated houses most anywhere in Deathlands were desperately vulnerable to attack. There were always gangs of roaming outlanders—hired guns—riding together in killer bands, and several areas still held groups of murderous muties. Ryan couldn't altogether blame someone who'd adopted the policy of shooting first and getting around to talking awhile later. A dead man would never try to backshoot you.

"Yo, in there!" he shouted.

Nobody answered. Ryan cautiously eased his head up over the top of the ridge. Four of the front windows contained a rifle muzzle but nobody replied to his yell.

"Hey, in there!"

This time there was a response—a deep voice, ragged and harsh. "Get on your way and nobody gets hurt!"

"Need water and food!"

"Go!"

"Got jack."

Both Ryan and J.B. carried jack with them wherever they went, enough to pick up some of the basics with a little to spare. Some big villes issued their own scrip, but the ordinary jack was accepted in most places.

"Where you from?"

"Traders! Wagon blew its engine out east."

"You seen that mountain go up?"

"Yeah. We were lucky. You going to let us come in or you going to try and blow our heads off?"

There was another long silence. Ryan could hear three men's voices, and once he thought he heard a woman speaking. But the sound of a hand striking flesh shut it up.

"How many of you?"

"Six. Two of us women."

"One of the women black?"

"Yeah. That a problem?"

The answer was a heartbeat too fast. "No. No problem, mister. You got blasters?"

Ryan considered that one for a moment. J.B., a half dozen paces to his left, glanced across at him and said, "Two single-shot homemades. One's a Winchester repeater. Sounds like an M-16 as well."

If that was what the Armorer thought, then that's almost certainly the firepower they had in the house. J.B. wasn't often wrong on weaponry.

Ryan raised his voice to the listeners. "Yeah. We got us some blasters."

"Any of you ride with Skullface?"

"Who?"

"Skullface."

"Never heard of him."

The disbelief from the hidden speaker was obvious. "You been trading these parts and you never heard of Skullface?"

"We been east trading in the Glades. Never heard of any Skullface that way."

"Well, they say he hunts south of here. We ain't never seen him, but we heard tell from travelers that way. You sure you ain't with him?"

"Mister, I'm hot, thirsty and tired. So're my friends. This talk is making me powerful wearied!

You going to let us in, or..." Ryan let the sentence
dangle in the hot, still air.

"Or what?"

"Or we'll shoot the hell out of your dog-knobbing,
shit-dipping little hut!"

"Oh, yeah? You and whose army, mister?" But
Ryan's anger had sown seeds of doubt.

"We got plas-ex enough to spread you and your
kin all over the fucking desert, thin as honey on a
sour roll."

"Now, there ain't no call... Just show your-
selves, slow and easy."

"I'll stand up here. Then you come out the door.
How's that?"

"Sure. You move first."

"Careful, lover," Krysty warned. "Can't say I like
the sound of his voice."

"Me, neither. But I like the look of that well out
back."

"Like smell baking bread," Jak called from his
right.

Keeping his hand hovering over the butt of the
SIG-Sauer P-226 pistol, and pushing back his long
coat to give himself a clear draw at it, Ryan stood up.

It wasn't the first time in his life that he'd stood
out in the open, facing hidden blasters, but that
didn't make it any easier. The skin still crawled across
his cheeks, tugging at the edge of the livid scar that
coursed from eye to mouth. His finger still flexed,
wanting to grip the butt of the pistol. Every nerve
was taut as a waxed bowstring, ready for the light-

ning reflex that would probably still be too slow to save his life.

One of the rifle muzzles had disappeared. Apart from that, there didn't seem any sign of movement from the fortified house.

"Door's opening," Krysty whispered, her sharp hearing picking up the faint sounds of oiled bolts sliding across.

There was an edge of darkness against the sun-bright wood, growing slowly wider. The muzzle of a battered Winchester appeared, followed by its owner. He was a tall man, several inches over six feet, heavily built, bald with a fringe of dusty grey hair, narrow eyes and a full mustache. At first glance Ryan made him out to be in his early fifties, which was a good age for the deserts of Deathlands.

"Name's R. G. Ballinger. You and your friends are welcome to share God's repast with us. Come on in, slow and easy. Remember we got blasters on you."

"I'm Ryan Cawdor. We thank you."

There were four in the family.

R. G. Ballinger, a widower, had been farming the valley for more than twenty years. His wife, Martha, had died several years ago. He had three children—two boys, Larry and Jim, in their twenties, and a daughter, Christina, who looked close to thirty.

She was a rawboned, homely woman, with a built-up laced boot on her left foot. She walked with an ungainly, hip-swinging motion, the boot clunking on the scrubbed plank floors at every step. Her hair was a stringy midbrown, tugged back in a tight knot, and her eyes were a watery blue. There was the mark of a healing bruise on her left cheek. In the first couple of hours that Ryan and his companions were in the homestead she never spoke a word. Ryan would have figured her as simpleminded, if he hadn't glimpsed a spark of interest and intelligence when the conversation turned to outland matters.

"You ain't heard of Skullface? Son of Beelzebub? The Antichrist come to inherit with the riders of chaos?"

Ryan shook his head at Ballinger's question. "No. He some sort of raider?"

"Came down here a few months back. Got hisself a band of mean sons of bitches. Women as well as men. Brought death and pestilence, near the Grandee. But I heard tell as how he's riding north, burning the earth behind him."

Ballinger used the last of his cornbread to mop up the streaks of dark gravy off his tin plate. He clicked his fingers to attract his daughter's attention. "Bring us some more stew, slut, and stop making eyes at these men. Just like your scarlet whore of a mother. Best keep your hands on your cocks while this steaming harlot's around."

Without a word, Christina served her father from a large iron caldron. Her face was blank, her eyes not settling anywhere.

The brothers sniggered. Larry, the fatter of the two, poked Jim with his elbow. "Pa told the slut, didn't he? Teach her keep her greedy eyes off men's weenies, huh? Keep it in the family like . . ."

"A chattering tongue is an offence to the courts of the Almighty, Larry," said his father, silencing the grinning boy.

Krysty broke the uncomfortable silence. "How'd your wife die, Mr. Ballinger? Sickness?"

"Could say that, Miss Wroth. Kind of a sickness took her away from us."

Not altering the sanctimonious tone of his voice, he addressed his sons. "Wipe off the smiles, boys, or by the heavenly gaudy house I'll wipe 'em off. Clear the table, slut."

Ryan was aware of the tension around the table at the brutal way the farmer treated his daughter. But it wasn't their business. That was one of the very first rules for survival in Deathlands.

"Trade in the morning, folks," Ballinger said, leaning sideways in his chair and easing out a thunderous fart. "Guess you'd like some sleep?"

Ryan nodded. "Sure would. Seen a couple of small bunkhouses out back. You got some hired hands working the spread?"

Ballinger had risen and turned away. At Ryan's question he turned slowly back to face him, his small eyes glowing like late embers. "What have you heard, Mr. Cawdor?"

"Hey! Talking to you's like walking over eggs, Ballinger. Just a question. You got a big spread. You got bunkhouses. So, you got some hands to help you work the land?"

"Not now. Not since... not since we had us some trouble. Gimpy slut stays here, and me and the boys do the rest."

"How much land?"

Jak hadn't spoken since they'd arrived, and his question took everyone by surprise.

"How much, son? Well... By Jesus and the blood of the shroud, you sure got white hair and scary eyes. Used to have more'n we do now."

It seemed yet another touchy subject, and the teenager contented himself with nodding. Out of the corner of his eye Ryan noticed the disabled girl had been watching Jak with unusual interest.

"Now. One place got four beds, the other got three. The nigra woman sleep with you folks?"

Mildred answered, eyes cast low, voice rising into a scratchy whine. "Lordy, Mr. Ballinger, these are real good white folks and they take care of me. I sleep in with Missy Wroth. If I'm lucky I get a bed, but most nights I just get the cold, cold floor."

"Well, we got the beds. Slut'll take out some blankets. Talk business in the morning. Want to leave your blasters here with me? No? No, I guess not."

There'd been liquor offered during the meal, a raw corn spirit that threatened to take the skin off the tongue. Ryan and the others had drunk sparingly, but the two Ballinger boys had nuzzled into it like they were weaned on it. Both were red-eyed, thick-lipped and staggering by the time the meal was finished.

One of them hung on his father's shoulder and mumbled something in his ear, smiling a sloppy smile at Krysty. Old man Ballinger had shaken him off with an impatient curse, waving a warning fist in his face. He noticed that everyone had watched the exchange and managed an insincere grin.

"Boys! What the hell d'you do with 'em, huh? Least they don't bring their troubles home with 'em like sluts do."

Mildred and Krysty took the smaller of the bunkhouses. When the door was opened there was the familiar sound of cockroaches scuttling for cover. Christina Ballinger had shown them to their quarters, carrying a pile of bedding, shrugging away Jak's offer of help.

"Thanks," Krysty said. "We can manage now."

"No. Pa said for me to do the bedding. He'd not take it kindly if I didn't."

She'd put the blankets on one of the bunks and her hand rose, unconsciously, to touch the dark bruise on her face.

"Sure," Mildred barked. "We get the picture. By God but we do."

The girl managed something that came close to being a smile. "Pa's quick with his hand. But since Ma ... . I gotta do the beds. Gotta clean up the dishes and then makes the beds up for Larry and Jim."

She moved with a clumsy grace around the room, unfolding the bedding and tucking in the blankets with a practiced ease. Krysty and Mildred stood and watched her, uncomfortable that they couldn't help. Jak had also hung around, waiting silently in the corner of the room by the door.

"There," she said finally. "I did the other bunkhouse. Best get on back. You folks sleep well and…" The young woman hesitated a long moment, looking over her shoulder toward the silhouette of the main homestead. "The door bolts, but the windows don't. Sleep light and watchful."

"What's that supposed to mean, Christina?" Mildred asked. "You saying there's some danger to us?"

The door of the fortified house crashed open and R. G. Ballinger bellowed into the still evening. "Get the fuck over here you useless crip! Boys want to get to their beds."

"Coming, Pa."

They watched her limp across the yard and vanish into the house. Nobody spoke for several long seconds. Then Jak said, "Could open up bastard's throat and smile."

Krysty passed on the woman's warning to Ryan and the others.

"I trust him and those two crazies about as far as I could throw them," Ryan said. "We'll all take care."

"Fancy a walk before turning in, lover?" Krysty asked. "There's a small grove of sycamores by the creek."

"Why not?"

CHAPTER FOUR

THEY'D JUST FINISHED making love. It hadn't been one of the all-time apocalyptic earthshakers, but even when it wasn't terrific it was still real good. They'd been plagued by stinging insects coming up off the slow-moving creek, and there'd been a coyote howling too close for comfort.

Krysty was pulling up her bikini panties when she paused, looked urgently at Ryan and lifted a finger to her lips.

Ryan had left his rifle alongside his bunk, but his 15-round automatic was in his belt. Without a word he quickly fastened the belt on his pants and drew the blaster, reassured by the familiar feel of twenty-five and a half ounces of concentrated power.

Krysty finished dressing, drawing her own Heckler & Koch P7A 13, with the silvered finish, and pointing it toward the house. She made the sign for someone walking, one man, alone.

"Ballinger?" Ryan mouthed, getting a nod of acknowledgment.

They both crouched into the thick undergrowth, watching in the pallid moonlight. Unusually Ryan spotted him before Krysty. He caught the pale gleam off the homesteader's bald head.

Ballinger was walking fast, looking down at the winding path toward the narrow river. He didn't glance around, and passed within six feet of Krysty and Ryan. The man carried a squat 10-gauge sawed-off shotgun in his right hand.

They could hear his boots crunching through the dry brush, and he stopped only thirty or forty paces farther on.

"What's he doing?" Ryan whispered, his mouth so close to Krysty's ear that he could taste the sweat on her skin.

"He's knelt down. Can't see. There's something there. Like a stone."

"Grave?"

"Yeah. Yeah, it could be."

"Come on."

Moving with extreme caution, Ryan led the way among the stunted, dried trees. There was a very light breeze, and the river was murmuring over the stones, but they still didn't want to get caught creeping up on a man holding a sawed-off scattergun.

Ryan held up a hand. He could now see Ballinger, kneeling behind some scrubby mesquite. The gun was in the dirt. There was a white boulder, with something written on it in faded red lettering. The homesteader was talking to himself. Or to the stone.

"So the wheel turns, Martha. The circle is unbroken. The riders of the storm come from the east again."

The voice was quiet, conversational, and sent a chill down Ryan's spine. He'd heard of folks who drew comfort from talking to dead friends or relatives, but this was something different.

"Larry and Jim are going to do good. Help me, like they helped me with you, Martha. They're good boys. See it clear. See wrong and right. See what a woman can do. They seen it with you, Martha. Seen how you fooled me. They seen how you got dirty, you stinking slut corpse, Martha."

Krysty tugged at Ryan's sleeve, gesturing that they go back to the bunkhouses and leave Ballinger to his raging hatred.

He nodded. But the flat, unemotional voice pursued them through the trees.

"Christina knows. Knows what my fist, my boots and my whip teach her. That women are an abomination, a vessel for a man's needs. They have to work hard and do what they're told. Christina knows that. It's all she knows. Christina's world, Martha. What you fucking left behind, you whore."

Once they were out of range, Krysty turned to face Ryan. "I'd like it if you held me just a minute or two, lover. Feel in need of a bath after listening to that."

As he put his arms around her, Ryan could feel Krysty trembling.

Because of Christina's warning, Mildred and Krysty took care, dragging a ramshackle old table against the door and wedging it under the handle. The bolts that the girl had mentioned were held together by a thin film of old rust and wouldn't have stopped an angry kitten.

Windows were on three sides of the single-story building, wooden-framed, each with four panes of glass. At one time there'd been shutters, but they'd been long gone. Krysty tried to open one of the unpainted casements, wincing in anticipation of the shrieking of warped wood. But to her amazement it slid up as soft and easy as silk.

"Gaia!"

Mildred came over and looked, holding the smoky oil lamp higher to see better. "Someone's greased the sash runners," she said quietly, her face solemn. "Now why'd they want to do something like that, Krysty?"

"Like the girl said—best take care."

Krysty had some thin cord in one of her pockets and she unwound it, tying one end to a window latch, taking a turn around the top of one bed, then looping it across the room to the second window, putting another turn around the catch, and down to the other bed, making sure she kept it taut. She finished by knotting the other end around the last window.

"There. If anyone tries to open a window, he'll make one of the beds move. Best I can do. Just sleep with your blaster real handy."

Ryan and J.B. discussed whether they should keep a watch during the night. Despite her muteness, there was something about Christina Ballinger that made them agree her warning could be serious.

"It's close to eleven now," the Armorer said, checking his small wrist chron.

"Two hours on," Ryan suggested. "Can't see the main house from here, but I figure we should keep watch."

"Better to be on guard when you don't have to be..." J.B. started.

"Than not be on guard when you should have done," Ryan finished with a grin. They'd ridden long enough with the Trader to know his favorite sayings.

J.B. took first watch, then Doc came second, followed by Jak. Ryan claimed the leader's right of taking the last dawn guard.

It happened about fifteen minutes after Doc had taken over. But for some time he didn't know anything was wrong.

CHAPTER FIVE

KRYSTY HAD BEEN dreaming. Most times she could remember many of her dreams, a skill taught to her by Mother Sonja. But not tonight. They were blurred images, moments from never—a large apple, sliced through the middle, fresh and tender. Yet when Krysty brought it to her lips it was as cold as stone. A bird, bright-colored, hovering in the warm air while its long beak sipped with a fragile delicacy at the heart of a waxen lily.

None of the dreams seemed fearful or threatening to her, but something started her awake, eyes wide, the curls of her fiery hair coiled tightly to her head.

The early moonlight had gone, tugged away behind a bank of heavy cloud. The bunkhouse was in deep shadow, and it was like being inside a black velvet sack. Krysty lay still for a few moments, keeping her breathing regular and steady, straining her senses to try to remember what had awakened her.

Her hand moved slowly to touch the taut cord that linked the windows and the two beds. It was still there, but it was slack. She pulled and felt it come loosely toward her fingers.

Her mind raced. Someone had reached in through a narrow gap and cut the thin cord with a sharp blade. That meant that the greased windows could now be inched silently open.

Or worse, they already had been opened.

Mildred was also awake.

During the night she'd suffered the pangs of a migraine, the pain focusing around her left eye, a blinding, bitter pain that made her want to reach up and pluck out the eye itself. One of the things that she regretted about Deathlands was that there was a distinct shortage of aspirin.

Gradually the white agony had dulled to a crimson ache, and she'd come close to slipping back into sleep. But something had jerked her into wakefulness—the whisper of wood against wood, the fractional movement of cloth on cloth, someone struggling hard to control his breath.

Mildred inhaled slowly, catching the mixture of stale sweat and raw alcohol.

Then she knew what had awakened her.

Krysty had reached precisely the same conclusion at almost the same moment, almost tasting the smell of perspiration and liquor.

"Come courting, boys?" she asked in a loud, clear voice.

"Fuck'n shit!" one of the Ballinger brothers hissed. Krysty thought it might have been Larry, but she couldn't be certain. Nor did she much care.

"Why don't you just get out the same way you came in, boys? And don't come back again."

"Amen to that," Mildred added.

"Don't much want you, nigra," said the other brother.

Mildred spoke again, her voice cracking like a buggy whip. "I don't give a sweet damn what you redneck peckerwood dip-shits want! I want you the hell and gone out of our room."

"Or else what, slut? Or else what?"

Suddenly Krysty could put her tongue out and taste the violence that was simmering in the room. When she'd first realized that the brothers had come sneaking into the bunkhouse, she'd only felt a vague unease. Now the threat was explicit and dangerous. This wasn't going to be a clumsy attempt at touch and run.

This was for real.

She heard one of the horses in the corral whinny, high and plaintive.

"You make a move, boys, and you'll have four blasters in here quicker than goose shit off a greasy shovel."

"And your Pa'll likely give you a whipping," Mildred added, trying to keep the tension out of the air.

There was a snorting giggle from the blackness. "That's where you're wrong, nigra. Pa's got his sawed-off or the Winchester, and he's sitting out there ten feet from the door of the other bunkhouse."

"That's right, Larry. That door comes open and Pa starts blasting. Knocking cans off of a fence post!" Again the giggle, this time doubled. "Pa likes to wait till we had some funnin', then he comes in after and gets himself some sloppy seconds."

"That the way it always is, Jim?" Krysty asked, feeling the prickle of fear.

"Sure is. Ever since Ma got caught, we done had good times with harlots come calling here."

"Must be about a million by now, Jim," Larry sniggered.

"No. More like...like fifty hundred million! Yeah."

"And we get to be fifty hundred million and one and fifty hundred million and two?" Krysty said, feeling the reassuring coolness of her Heckler & Koch P7A 13.

"Sure do."

"Then what?" Mildred asked. "Go on, boys. Surprise us."

"Then you get the mallet across the temple and we butcher you, and leave out the remains for the crows and the coyotes," Larry replied.

Krysty had them placed. One was near the door and the other close to the foot of Mildred's bed. But the darkness was so total that even her mutie vision couldn't make out what kind of weapons they were carrying. They hadn't seen any handguns around the main cabin, so knives seemed the most likely bet.

It wasn't going to be easy.

Ryan came awake, hand already reaching for the blaster by his head.

"What?" he said quietly. The bunkhouse was pitch-dark. The lamp had guttered and gone out before midnight, and there wasn't the slightest glimmer of light. He couldn't work out what it was that had roused him.

He swung his legs out of the narrow bed and stood, heels rasping on the boards. The fragile sound was enough to wake both J.B. and Jak.

"What's up?" the Armorer whispered.

"Doc?" Ryan queried.

"Doc?" Jak repeated. "You fucking sleep, Doc?"

There was a certain irony to a situation that had the sentry asleep and everyone else awake, but right at that moment Ryan wasn't particularly into irony.

"Wake him, J.B., quiet."

They were still speaking in hushed tones. None of them knew why they were awake, but all of them were experienced enough in lethal fights to know that you kept quiet until it came time to make a noise.

There was a flurry of restrained movement from the corner where Doc had been sitting, supposedly on watch. Then they heard the old man's voice.

"Sorry, my friends. I am so sorry. I must have nodded off for a moment. What is amiss?"

"Keep it real quiet, Doc," Ryan warned. "We don't know. Something woke me."

He didn't reproach the old man. Doc was normally reliable and knew as well as the others that he'd put them in potential danger.

Ryan eased his way to the window at the front and squinted out.

"Hard or easy, sluts?"

The Ballinger boys had played this particular game so often that they'd gotten good at it. But they'd also gotten lazy about it.

"Will you let us go if we don't struggle or fight? We could be real nice to you both. Me and Mildred know some special tricks."

Krysty put on a narrow, whining voice, trying to base it on the girls she'd heard in pesthole gaudy houses.

Mildred picked up on Krysty's gambit and followed suit. "Yessir, I can show you fine boys a good time. Just so's you don't hurt us."

Jim Ballinger laughed, a gloating, triumphant sound that helped Krysty to pin down his position more accurately. "We won't hurt you harlots none, and we'll let you ride free tomorrow. How's about that?"

"Mildred," Krysty said.

"Yes."

"Keep still."

"What?"

"Do like I say."

"When you sluts finish chattering, we best get our show on the road."

Krysty wasn't in the same league as Jak, or Ryan when it came to hand-to-hand fighting, but she was good enough.

Hearing the sound of boots scraping on the planks, she slipped soundlessly off the side of the bed onto the floor, closing her eyes for a moment to draw on the power of the Earth Mother. "Gaia, aid me," she whispered, feeling the strength flow into her tensed muscles.

R. G. Ballinger sat patiently in the dirt, the shotgun cradled between his legs. His eyes were fixed on the door of the main bunkhouse, but his hearing was concentrated on the smaller building behind him, listening for the sounds that would tell him his boys were getting themselves some funning.

"Be having some more whores to share Hell with you, Martha," he said quietly, his lips pulled back off his rotting teeth in a satisfied smile.

The wrack of clouds parted for a scant heartbeat then closed again, but for a frozen moment moonlight had flooded across the Texas landscape.

"Fireblast," Ryan growled, seeing the hunched figure of Ballinger and the glint of metal off the scattergun. "We got some trouble."

The flicker of moonlight also changed things in the small bunkhouse.

It showed Krysty the legs of the Ballinger brothers. It showed the Ballinger brothers that the redhead's bed was empty.

"Fuck," Jim Ballinger swore.

And then died.

CHAPTER SIX

KRYSTY JUMPED OFF the floor with a truly terrifying power. She'd been sleeping in her metal-tipped Western boots, and she kicked out when she was at the highest point of her leap, aiming at the memory of Jim Ballinger's figure, trapped in that split second of bright silver light.

The hard edge of her right boot struck him across the throat, and the destructive force of the blow was devastating and final. The hyoid bone was splintered and the thyroid and tracheal cartilage crushed. The pressure smashed the air passage closed and finally snapped two of the vertebrae.

The effect on Jim Ballinger was about the same as if he'd been hanged. He had an instant erection, which was followed by a gushing orgasm. But he wasn't enjoying it, being immersed in the shock and pain of his own passing. Bowels and bladder opened simultaneously; blood came from his mouth, where he'd bitten through his tongue, and from his ears and nose.

Jim's body was already going into terminal spasm before he'd even hit the floor.

He clattered down, arms and legs flailing, kicking one of the beds so that its rusty springs jingled.

Outside, his father stood slowly, grinning at the sounds he heard. "Give it to them whores, boys," he muttered.

Krysty landed badly, slipping and turning an ankle, and jarring her shoulder against the side of Mildred's bed. But Larry Ballinger was standing paralyzed on the far side of the bunkhouse, a foolish grin sliding off his fat cheeks. There was just enough ghostly light for him to see his brother down on the planks, twitching like a gut-shot coyote, eyes wide and staring.

"I'll chill him," Mildred said, holding the cocked pistol in her hand.

"No. It'll bring in the old man. Only as a last resort." She got to her feet again, panting with the effort, her whole body feeling as if it were covered in a mesh of coiled silver wires.

"What you done, bitch?" Larry asked. His hand reached inside his plaid shirt and came out holding a straight-edged razor. "You're fucking dead, you murdering slut!"

His voice was just loud enough to reach his father outside, whose smile broadened.

In the confined space, Krysty knew that the man's bulk and raw power could tell against her.

The steel edge began to weave a lightning pattern of hissing death in front of Krysty's face, pressing her back a half step at a time. Larry was breathing hard, sweat glistening on his forehead and around his open mouth.

To draw fully on the power of Gaia took time in preparation and always left Krysty totally drained for hours after. But she'd only been able to tap the surface in her attack on the dead man. Now, she didn't have the force within her to defeat the approaching Larry.

Mildred was sitting on her bed, ready to use her blaster if things went far enough against Krysty. Suddenly, out of the corner of her eye, Krysty saw the black woman put down her ZKR 551 and tear open the front of her white blouse, revealing her breasts, nipples standing out in the tension like fresh-picked cherries.

"This is for you, boy," she called.

Larry Ballinger was way beyond his depth. He'd just seen the flame-haired woman kick the shit out of his little brother, Jim, spread him out cold on the floor. The idea that Jim might actually be dead was something Larry didn't want to think about.

And now the black bitch was ripping out one of the finest pair of suckers Larry had ever seen. Most of the women they'd raped and chilled had been either scrawny bitches or sagging old whores. But these were real prime....

Krysty took advantage of the moment of inattention and took a half step forward, flexing the powerful muscles in her thighs. She swung her right foot behind her, then kicked up and forward with all her strength.

The chiseled toe hit Larry in the center of his scrotal sac. The sight of Mildred partly undressed had produced the beginnings of arousal, but all of that was crushed upward against the cutting ridge of his pubic bone.

There was a single, stretched moment of unbelievable, sickening agony for Larry Ballinger, then the razor dropped from numbed fingers to the wooden floor. He opened his mouth and tried to scream, but nothing came out. He took two staggering steps backward and stumbled over his brother's body. His eyes had rolled up in his head, and yellow vomit dribbled from his open mouth. His hands were reaching for his groin to try to stem the terrible pain, but the blackness came surging up and washed him into unconsciousness first.

"Them boys!" R. G. Ballinger laughed, listening to what he assumed were the noises of forced sexual congress.

"We open the door and he'll blast us," J.B. said.

"Could take him out by shooting through one of the windows," Ryan suggested.

Doc had drawn his massive Le Mat. "What I do not quite comprehend is what the rogue is doing there? Is he a Peeping Tom, do you think? Spying on our female companions?"

Ryan shook his head. "No. Looks like he's waiting for something. I don't like it. Not at all. It's like he's waiting for a signal from inside the bunkhouse.

Means that mebbe those two nukeheads are trying something on."

"Safest blast fucker," Jak said.

"No." Ryan shook his head. "Suppose Larry and Jim-boy *are* inside. They see Pa chilled, and what do they do? Chill Krysty and Mildred. We gotta wait awhile."

Mildred pulled her blouse together, looking down at the corpses.

"Let me," she said.

"What?"

"Chill that bastard—if you left any breath in him after dividing his family jewels with your boot."

"What about your doctor's oath, Mildred?"

"That was then, Krysty, and this is now." She knelt down and put her right hand to Larry's neck. "Pulse is weak. Could be you might have killed him. Shock like that. But we'll make sure."

She moved finger and thumb to where the big artery still throbbed behind his ears, pressing, holding. The sound of harsh breathing became uneven and more ragged. It slowed and the unconscious man suddenly gave a huge shuddering sigh.

And became quiet.

"That it?" Krysty asked unnecessarily, because she knew that it was. You see enough death, and you never ever mistake it for anything else.

"That's it." Mildred stood. "Now all we got to do is worry about Daddy Bear."

The old man had been at the corn mash over the evening meal, keeping himself topped up from an old fruit jar he hid on a ledge by the back door of the house. The mellow feeling was rising nicely, and he knew he'd soon feel good and ready to join his boys. Not that he actually *did* anything. He just watched and maybe diddled a little. Truth was, he hadn't managed to get anything approaching a real diamond cutter of a hard-on...since Martha. Since before Martha.

It had gone real quiet.

"He's coming in," Mildred announced. "Blast him now?"

Krysty shook her head. "Wait. If we miss him he can still go and take out the others. Just wait a couple of seconds longer."

The door was jammed inside. Ballinger pushed at it and found that it would only open a couple of inches.

"C'mon, boys. Open up for your pa." Nothing happened, and the bunkhouse was deathly quiet. "Stop that screwing and open up this fucking door! Jim! Larry!"

Mildred and Krysty stood on either side of the door, flattened against the wall, each holding a blaster.

The door moved again as Ballinger leaned his weight against it.

"You boys gonna feel the buckle of my belt around your asses if you don't open this door in five seconds."

If Krysty's blaster had been a more powerful weapon she'd have taken a chance on blasting the man clean through the door.

Across the yard Ryan had his Heckler & Koch G-12 caseless assault rifle to his shoulder. The sniperscope sight was centered on the top of Ballinger's spine, just below his collar. But he'd now heard enough to be sure that the two sons were probably in the other bunkhouse with Krysty and Mildred. There didn't seem to be a right move to make. Squeeze the trigger and the two women could die. Don't squeeze the trigger and the two women could die.

Jak touched him on the shoulder, his voice in Ryan's ear.

"Me," he whispered.

"No noise," Ryan replied, lowering the blaster and turning toward the boy. Jak's hair was like a cosmic flare in the pale moonlight, his face like wind-washed bone.

"Knife," Jak said, showing one of the leaf-bladed throwing knives he wore hidden about his body. "No noise."

He opened the door slowly, glancing out toward the shadowy figure of Ballinger, calculating the distance and the rotation of the blade. Moonlight shimmered cold off the steel.

"Your time's up, you thankless sons of a bitch! I'm coming in for my piece of the action. Here I— What the fuck was . . . Shot me and—"

Ryan hadn't been able to follow the flight of the knife. He'd seen the supple whip of Jak's wrist and thought he'd heard the soft thunk of the weighted steel hitting flesh.

Inside the other bunkhouse the two women heard the gasp of shock from Ballinger and then the clatter of the shotgun hitting dry earth.

"Didn't hear a blaster," Mildred said, turning to Krysty. "Silencer?"

"Guess a knife. The kid."

The men came quietly from their bunkhouse, all holding blasters. Ballinger turned to face them, staggering slightly, one hand waving in the air like a drunk greeting an old friend.

"How'd you . . ." he began, sliding to his knees, shaking his head.

Like a child slipping into a warm river, the man slithered down onto his face. His boots scrabbled for a moment in the dirt and then he was still.

Mildred and Krysty quickly got the door open and stepped out, looking at the dead man near their feet. Jak moved forward and stooped, pulling his knife from the back of Ballinger's neck, just below the skull. He wiped it in the dust and sheathed it.

"You all right?" Ryan asked.

"Sure, lover. Thanks, Jak."

"The boys?" J.B. probed.

Mildred jerked her thumb behind her. "They're in there."

There was a faint creaking sound, and the door of the main homestead opened. Christina Ballinger stood there, holding a golden oil lamp in one hand, an ancient Winchester repeater in the other. She looked at the group of people, circling the corpse of her father. Slowly she began to move toward them, her crippled foot trailing in the sand. Her face showed no emotion.

Ryan considered shooting her on the principle of never taking unnecessary chances, but the rifle was at the trail and her finger was away from the trigger. The woman didn't seem like she was intending any threat to them.

Christina stopped a few paces from the friends, her eyes raking them, settling finally on the albino boy. "You killed my father?"

"Yeah."

"What about my brothers? What about Larry and Jim?"

"Inside," Krysty replied.

"They both dead as well?"

"Both dead."

There was a long moment of silence, the far-off howl of the coyote the only sound.

Christina nodded. "That's good."

CHAPTER SEVEN

CHRISTINA HAD insisted on burying her father and her two brothers, refusing help, though she finally accepted Jak Lauren's repeated offer of assistance. The three bodies went into the same grave, with no marker. The hole was dug deep in the soft earth, and Ryan asked Jak why that had been.

"Said didn't want 'em rising."

After a good breakfast of eggs fried over easy, smoked ham and cornbread, Ryan asked Christina to go outside with him to talk.

The hardness and tension had already begun to slip away from Christina's face, and her eyes were brighter. Twice she even smiled.

"I'm sorry about the way this turned out," Ryan apologized. "It wasn't of our making."

That was the first smile. "You think I don't know that, Ryan? You don't mind my calling you by your given name, do you?"

"Course not. I guess life wasn't easy."

Christina nodded. "Work a homestead like this and life's not easy. If you get born with a gimp leg it doesn't help none. And having someone like Pa rule your life kind of puts the lid on the kettle."

"You ever think of running?" he asked, looking around at the barren wilderness and realizing immediately the futility of the question.

It produced a second smile. "Sure, Ryan. Just set off running. North? South? East? West? I could've taken one of the horses, but they'd have caught me and Pa would have been angered. If I wasn't a lady I could show you things Pa done to me when he got himself in a righteous anger."

"You want to come with us?"

She looked at him, and he was suddenly aware of the rawboned beauty that had been hidden behind the mask of restraint and fear.

"Yes. I'd like that a real lot. You seem good folks."

"Then we can—"

But she interrupted him, holding up a warning hand. "But I won't come, Ryan. I'll stay here. Work the land."

"How can—"

"Work the land," she repeated. "*My* land. I've earned this spread, Ryan, and I'm not about to ride away without a backward glance."

"It's too big a job. It'll break you down."

"I bend, Ryan, but I don't break that easy. Never know, might get myself some help one of these fine days."

"I hope so. I truly hope so, Christina."

They agreed to a deal over six saddle horses plus a rangy pack mule. The jack had changed hands, and

Christina had tucked it into a dark green coffee can that sat over the fireplace.

Ryan and the others had gone to check on the girths and stirrups for their ride south. It was several minutes before Krysty noticed that Jak wasn't with the rest of them.

"Must be outside," Ryan suggested.

"Or in the outhouse," Mildred said.

"Probably deeply immersed with the lady," Doc offered.

"What? A kid like Jak, and Christina? She's a woman grown," J.B. said disbelievingly.

Ryan patted his bay mare on the neck, looking away from the homestead into the distant heat haze where they'd soon be heading. There was a darkening on the farthest horizon, which suggested the possibility of rain.

"I'll go get him. Don't like the look of that sky."

He walked toward the main house, seeing swirling dust devils out on the plain beyond the corral. A ball of sagebrush tore loose and rolled away, jamming itself to a halt against a fence of old, rusting barbed wire.

"C'mon, Jak!" he yelled as he stepped onto the porch.

From the cooler, shadowed gloom within the main room he caught sudden movement. But his eye wasn't accustomed to the darkness, and he couldn't be sure what he'd seen. Or what he'd nearly seen.

"You ready, Jak?"

The teenager had stepped away quickly to stand near the table, his fingers drumming nervously on the scarred wood.

"Sure, sure."

Ryan glanced across to where Christina Ballinger stood, hand patting at her hair. "Don't want to change your mind and ride along with us?"

To his surprise it was Jak who answered. "Doesn't, Ryan. Asked her. Said not."

"Oh, well, if you're sure..."

"I'm sure as I can be, Ryan. Thanks for the invitation. A big part of me wants to come along with you all, but this is home."

"As long as you can manage the stock and—"

The boy slapped his hand on the table. "Fucking said not, Ryan. Drop it!"

"Hey, come on," Ryan said, feeling a surge of anger at the boy's rudeness. "Just watch the way—"

Christina stepped between them, shaking her head. "Easy now, easy," she said, as if she were gentling a couple of spooked animals. "No call for this."

"You're right." Ryan nodded. "I'm real sorry. Sorry, Jak."

"Sure. Sorry, Ryan. Sorry, Christina."

The three of them waited, like a frozen tableau. Ryan took a couple of steps toward the open door and the dazzling sunlight, but the boy made no move to follow.

"Jak, there's a chem storm blowing up a way south. We should leave."

"Yeah. Go, Ryan. Catch up. Coupla fucking minutes is all."

Ryan hesitated, completely thrown, unable to understand what was happening. He was puzzled at Jak's determined refusal to join them.

Christina smiled gently. "Don't worry, Ryan. I won't eat him. It's just that he and I need a few minutes to talk some."

"What about?"

"That comes down to being Jak's business and my business, Ryan, and not your business at all. Sorry. He'll be out in five minutes and on the trail after you in ten. I promise."

"Fine." He turned toward the door, then stopped, swinging to face her again. "I wish you well, Christina. I mean it."

"I know you do. And may your gods go with you, Ryan." Her voice followed him into the morning. "And I'll always be in your debt."

As they rode toward the darkening sky, neither Jak nor Ryan said anything to satisfy the curiosity of their friends regarding what had gone on at the homestead.

Doc was the only one who tried to question the boy.

"You reach an understanding with that woman, Jak?"

"My business, Doc."

"She's almost old enough to be your mother, wouldn't you say?" Doc persisted.

"Say you're fucking old enough be nearly chilled, Doc."

"Guess there's some degree of truth in that, Jak. I won't argue with you. And you're right. Privacy is of prime importance."

"Yeah," the teenager said.

In front of them they could see towering thunderheads, blotting out the hazy sun and bringing an oppressive, humid gloom across the land. On either side of the highway were narrow arroyos, their bottoms deeply sculpted and eroded by rain and frost.

Lightning streaked in silver-purple daggers, bringing an almost ceaseless rumble of thunder.

J.B. hunched his shoulders and tugged on the brim of his fedora, settling it tighter on his head. "Could be bad," he said.

"Yeah," Ryan agreed.

CHAPTER EIGHT

THE STORM HELD OFF for almost an hour, but the sky boiled with the swollen clouds. Lightning slashed across the turbulent canvas, and thunder cascaded all around them.

The horses were uncomfortable, and twice J.B.'s mare got spooked and made a frantic dash along the dusty blacktop. It took all of the Armorer's strength and skill to control the frightened mare.

All the animals were edgy, and only Doc seemed able to ride comfortably.

In his early life, particularly around the ville of Front Royale, Ryan had ridden a lot. But over the past ten years he hadn't spent much time on horseback. Krysty kept leaning forward and whispering to the Appaloosa she'd picked out, trying to keep it calm.

Jak clung to the back of a tall gelding, like a burr stuck to the hide of a buffalo. His white hair glowed in the dimness of the approaching storm and he hadn't spoken a word to anyone in the past fifty minutes or so.

But Doc, on a black stallion, rode with a stately grace. His grizzled hair blew out around his head in a silvery halo, making him look like a circuit preacher of olden times.

"Best damned fun I've had in a long while," he called across to Ryan.

"Hard on the ass, Doc."

"I noticed that you have been riding tall in the saddle, Ryan," the old man cackled. "Thought you might have been stricken with piles."

"Go shove it up a skunk's ass, Doc."

There was another burst of eldritch laughter, which was quickly drowned out by a peal of thunder.

The trail wound down a gentle slope toward a valley, steep on the right and shallower on the left. On the lower side, about a quarter mile off, Ryan could see what looked like a dried-out riverbed, snaking southward along the highway.

The air tasted bitter from the nearness of the storm. Ryan had considered going back to the homestead, but they were already too far along the road toward the Grandee.

Over the years he'd seen many bad chem storms. The nuke holocaust of more than a hundred years ago had done much more than just destroy human society—it had altered the face of the land forever and had changed the climate, giving it new extremes, new highs.

And new lows.

Doc was moving ahead at a slow canter, with Krysty riding second, her vermilion hair blowing

behind her like a mane of fire. J.B. was third, tow-
ing the mule, Mildred leaning over her mount's neck
just behind him. Jak was in fifth place, and Ryan ate
everyone's dust at the rear.

The albino turned in his saddle, glancing behind
him. For a moment Ryan thought that the boy was
looking at him, then he realized that the glowing
ruby eyes were focused far behind him, way back up
the winding blacktop.

"You could have stayed," Ryan called, pitching
his voice so that only Jak would be able to hear him.

The teenager heeled in his horse and waited for
Ryan to move up beside him.

"Yeah," he said. "Could've stayed. One day. Like
stop running. Killing. One day. Not now."

"And not there?" Ryan suggested, thinking about
the age difference between the snow-haired lad and
the rawboned woman.

Jak's answer was drowned out by the loudest crash
of thunder that there'd yet been.

And the first heavy spots of cool rain came pattering into the red dust.

Within thirty seconds the storm swallowed up the
group. Ryan immediately lost sight of the others, the
rain sheeting around him in a blinding, swirling pall.
He blinked as the water coursed over his face, running down his neck, under his shirt, chilling his
stomach. It was so powerful that it even trickled behind the patch over his destroyed left eye.

His horse pulled against the reins, then stopped
dead, lowering its own head, stubbornly resisting all

of his efforts to kick it along. Accepting the inevitable, Ryan leaned forward and waited. There'd been no cover anywhere around. There was nothing else to do.

And nowhere else to go.

Lightning pulverized an outcrop of sandstone boulders that had been about fifty paces to Ryan's right, making the earth shake and his hair stand on end. The air filled with the flat stench of released ozone, and the immediate roll of thunder was literally deafening.

"Fireblast!" Ryan shouted, trying to lift his voice against the maelstrom around him. He knew he'd shouted, but he couldn't hear himself.

Hanging on to the bridle, he slipped down off the back of the horse, pressing against its quivering flanks to try to give himself some minimal shelter. At one point he made the mistake of trying to look at the sky above him. The rain was so total that he had the momentary panic that he might drown.

Rain beat at his face, making the skin taut and painful, coursing into his nose and into his mouth as he gasped for breath. He coughed and choked, spitting into the thick mud that oozed around his boots. The horse stamped, and a red shower splattered his pants.

After another few minutes, Ryan felt himself becoming totally disoriented. It was like OD'ing on jolt. His head was rocking from the weight of water that streamed ceaselessly onto it, and his senses rolled at the overwhelming barrage of noise from the hissing lightning and endless thunder.

His back and head began to sting as the rain turned to hail, pebbles of ice rattling viciously on the stones around him. Ryan's mind turned to tales he'd heard around the campfires of the war wags, of hailstorms so cataclysmic that men had been killed, their bodies smashed to pulp.

This time it was unpleasant but mercifully brief, the hail turning back again to the torrential rain.

In the blinding storm Ryan was aware of something moving past him, catching a glimpse of a streaming neck and rolling eyes, hooves flailing at the slippery road, then vanishing into the murk. There hadn't been enough time for him to make out which of the horses it had been.

He was also aware of something else. Though he was soaked from top to toe, there was a tugging chill around his ankles that whispered problems. Peering down Ryan was able to make out a stream of bloodred mud flowing over his boots, already halfway up to his knees.

It prompted him to think about the topography they'd been riding through—steep slopes to the right and then falling away toward a riverbed on their left side. Classic territory for a flash flood.

He hung on to the reins, trying to stop his mount from spooking, only too aware that a lost horse in this harsh terrain would be more or less the same as a .45 round through the back of the neck.

Suddenly, like a faucet being turned off, the rain stopped and the wind eased. The lightning held its breath and the thunder was silenced. It was an eerie moment.

A moment that become almost supernatural.

In that great stillness Ryan distinctly heard a sound he'd only ever heard a few times in his life, on old vids, but a haunting noise that one could never forget or mistake.

Far-off, echoing, came the heart-chilling sound of a locomotive whistle.

But there was no time to try to think about that enigma as the eye of the hurricane passed over and the rain and wind came back with the same vicious force. Lightning again curtained the land in silver lace and the thunder beat at the stones.

The horse tugged at him, taking a few skittering steps forward, pulling Ryan remorselessly with it. His boots dug furrows through the muddy water, which was now only just below his knees.

He thought for a moment that he heard someone screaming, a man in desperation, or a woman calling for help. The others had been in front of him when the rains struck, but by now they could be anywhere. Certainly one of them had lost a horse. But the others weren't likely to be in much better straits.

The long gun strapped across Ryan's shoulders limited his movements and made him clumsy. He considered trying to swing himself back up into the saddle, but the risk of a fall was too great.

The horse jerked its head suddenly, heaving Ryan off his feet, trailing helplessly after the powerful animal.

Above the noise of the thunder he heard a pounding roar. Ryan knew what it meant, and there was nothing he could do about it. A moment later the horse was knocked off its feet and Ryan went with it, freezing water closing over his head.

CHAPTER NINE

"METHINKS WHAT PAIN it is to drown," Doc said in his usual sonorous, declamatory voice, the words ringing across the desert.

"Yeah. Fucking right," Jak agreed, running his bony fingers through the matted sandy tangle of once-white hair.

"Never was much of an expert at swimming," Mildred complained. "There's something about the way the fat's distributed through my body."

Krysty was emulating Jak, muttering as her nails snagged in her lank hair. "I really thought I was done for."

J.B. had laid his sodden hat to dry on a sunbaked boulder, rubbing at his shoulder where the force of the flash flood had ripped away his Heckler & Koch MP-7 SD-8 and carried it off. "Only just got that blaster," he said, shaking his head. "Nice rifle. Integral silencer. Laser-optic sight. Nice feel. Still, at least I took off my glasses and put them safe before that big red wave came down the pike and hit us."

Ryan looked around at his friends, realizing that it had been sheer luck that had brought all six through the disaster. The wave of water and mud had rushed across the old highway at lethal speed, carrying all the horses and the mule with it. At least everyone had been able to keep their heads above the flood, and they'd all managed to battle out of the rending current. As far as they knew, not one of their mounts had come through. Certainly the land was bare of life.

A hundred yards to the south he could see the limp carcass of a horse, which looked to be Doc's powerful black stallion. He'd been the biggest and strongest of the string, so if the black hadn't come through, it wasn't likely any of the other animals would have made it.

The storm had gone.

The deep purple clouds were now only a blur to the east, the occasional streaks of lightning barely visible, the thunder silent. But its passing had been disastrous for the six friends. It wasn't just the mounts that had gone—the pack mule and saddlebags had carried their supplies of food and water. Paradoxically the murderous flood of house-high water had nearly killed them, but it was gone, leaving the air humid and the sand a dark, damp orange. Within an hour or so, all traces of that torrential downpour would have completely vanished, and death by thirst was again a threatening reality.

Ryan coughed and spit, tasting grit in his teeth. He eased up the patch and ran a cautious finger around the puckered skin of the empty socket, still wincing at the delicacy of the sensation, twenty years after he'd lost it to his psychopathic older brother's hatred. He rubbed his hands together, cleaning them, and looked at what damage had been done. A nail had been ripped on his left thumb, and both hands were covered in grazes and small cuts. Most of the group had suffered in similar ways.

Jak had a deep cut across his upper arm, and Mildred had lost a tooth. Doc had lost a clump of hair, and blood still trickled from a gash beneath the lobe of his left ear. Krysty had a deep bruise across her ribs that made her wince when she tried to turn quickly. J.B. had dislocated his right thumb but had popped the joint back himself.

It had been a close call.

Night was still some way off and the sun was hot. There was no point in sitting around. The nearest hope of safety was probably the Ballinger spread. Jak Lauren pushed hard in their discussion for turning back.

"Go on, fucking chilled!"

Ryan couldn't find much of an argument to use against the teenager. To go on now, without any kind of provision or transport, was to invite a merciless death in the wilderness. But they'd taken the best of the horses from Christina Ballinger. To try to find enough mounts to move on again could take months—could take forever.

"We might find another ranch if we keep heading south," he suggested.

"And pigs might fly," Mildred snorted, shaking her head at him.

"And there's this Skullface person that Christina mentioned to us," Krysty said. "Could be we're moving into his territory."

Ryan batted a persistent fly away from his face. "Okay. Can't argue much with that." Everyone stood and began readying themselves for the long trudge back north.

It was Mildred, surprisingly, who raised her voice against the plan. "I know what I said about not finding a ranch in this dead land, but I surely would like to find another cryo-center. If we give up now it could be months before we can start south again. Six months in Deathlands is like an eternity."

"How typical," Doc commented. "Always changeable, are you not, ma'am? One moment there's flying pigs and the next—"

She interrupted him. "Button the flap, Doc. I'm just saying that on the far side of that dry creek there's a rise. Anything beyond it is in dead ground. It'd only take a half hour to get over there and take a look. Sure, there's probably damn all! But at least we'll know for certain."

"Why not?" Ryan said.

As they walked through the drying sand, Krysty fell back to join Ryan.

"In the storm," she began.

Ryan hesitated. "You heard something?"

"Yeah, in that quiet moment as the eye passed over us. You heard something, lover?"

"I think I mebbe heard something. Mebbe."

"Train whistle?"

"Mebbe."

She persisted. "But it *was* a train. Like the old locomotives before Deathlands got itself born. Is that what you heard, lover?"

Ryan stopped a moment, the buzzing flies becoming more insistent. He flapped at them irritably, looking ahead up the rise where Doc and Mildred were stalking along, side by side, obviously involved in a heated argument. J.B. was a few paces behind them, and Jak picked up his own path farther along to the left.

"Lover?" Krysty said.

"Sorry?"

"The sound."

"Trader used to say there's no point in talking about something that may happen tomorrow."

She smiled. "And Mother Sonja used to warn me never to get involved with a one-eyed man. She said they saw too little and thought too much."

Ryan tried to think of something witty to say in response, but a call from Doc, now at the top of the hill, put it from his mind.

"What is it, Doc?"

"Come and see for yourself, my dear friend," the old man replied.

His boots slipping in the soft sand, making three paces forward and two paces back, Ryan moved to join the others.

"Look," Mildred said, pointing across the featureless plain that stretched ahead of them.

"Where?"

"There."

Shading his eye with his right hand, Ryan peered into the heat-blurring brightness.

"Wags," he said doubtfully.

"Ox-drawn wags," Krysty clarified, her sight that much better.

"Dozen or so," Ryan offered.

"Fifteen. Can't count people. Too much dust getting kicked up."

"They're not heading south. Looks like it's a train moving west."

Krysty nodded. "You got it, lover. If we step out, we could be with them by evening. They can't make more than three, four miles an hour. Not over this kind of trail."

"Then let's go."

It's often the case in a vast wilderness that judging distances is difficult.

It was well past dark before the six friends finally closed in on the wag train. Their progress had been slowed by Mildred's suffering a violent headache. She'd complained of pain around her right eye. After an hour she had to take a rest, saying that the sun was surrounded by a great shimmering halo of light, and she thought she was going blind. While they stood helplessly around, she crouched in the dirt, doubled over, eventually throwing up in the sand. Gradually the attack subsided, and they were able to resume their journey toward the distant wagons. But by now the evening had come and gone and they could only trace the camp by the sparkling specks of red and orange that were the fires.

"Fifteen ox wags going west," Ryan mused. "Could mean something like your train, Krysty, when you was young."

"*Were* young, lover. Not was. But I guess you're right."

"How many in each wag?"

J.B. answered. "Just before I fell in with the Trader I had a job swatting flies away from an ox train like this one. Most had a family. Man and woman and anywhere up to six kids."

Ryan nodded, eye locked to the pinpoints of bright light a quarter mile off in the darkness. "Probably reckon on twenty to thirty men able to fight. Same number women and young women. And...and a shitload of kids."

"You thinking of taking them on, Ryan?" Mildred asked, sitting with her back against a large boulder.

"No. I'm thinking about this man Christina called Skullface. If he's around here with some chillers, then I just wonder how strong and prepared that train is down there."

"Best take care," J.B. suggested.

"Sure. They'll have guards out. Place like this, miles from anyplace, there could be Indians, muties, or—"

"Skullface," Jak said, finishing Ryan's sentence.

The loss of the Armorer's long gun was bad news for them. Now they had only Ryan's G-12 assault rifle for distance shooting. Everyone had a hand blaster, but there were times when a rifle was needed.

There was a sailing moon that sometimes peeked out from behind tattered shreds of high cloud, which provided enough light for them to see that the wag train had found a reasonable place for its campsite.

The trail dipped and there was a wide plateau, close to two hundred yards across that sloped toward the riverbed. Whether anything of the flash flood was now left was questionable. But at least it wasn't possible for anyone to come at the wags from cover. And whoever was in charge of the train had taken reasonable precautions.

"Four guards," Jak reported after he'd bellied forward to scout the camp. "Walk around. Two left and two right. Could get in easy."

Though he'd said nothing to any of the others, it had crossed Ryan's mind to get in by force of arms, take the travelers by surprise and then break out with a couple of the wagons. If they'd been horse-drawn, then the temptation would have been stronger. But oxen lumbered at their own tedious pace, and they would easily have been overtaken.

No. It had to be done straight. Straight and very careful.

He led them forward until they were within fifty yards of the nearest guard. Motioning for everyone to keep under cover, Ryan stood and cupped his hands to his mouth.

"Hello, the train!!" he shouted, then ducked under a fusillade of bullets.

CHAPTER TEN

"HOLD YOUR FIRE!" Ryan shouted.

The gunfire was spasmodic and mostly ill aimed, coming, Ryan guessed, from some hoarded M-16 carbines and a variety of self-mades and patch-ups, which was the usual kind of weaponry that was found in the frontier wilderness of Deathlands. A lot of the ammunition was poorly charged, and even at short range was barely reaching them.

"Hold your fire, you double-stupe brain-dead bastards! Think we're goin' to tell you we're coming if we want to chill you?"

The shooting slowed but didn't stop. It sounded like every man or woman with a blaster on the wag train had come rushing over to use it. Ryan considered that any intelligent attacker would have caused this kind of diversion and then marched in the far side of the defense perimeter and shot everyone in the back. Easy as taking jack from a dead mutie.

Suddenly they all heard a voice, rising above the noise of the firing.

"Hold your guns, men!! Hold your dad-blasted guns! Some of you get over the other side! Harry and

Buck. You get there. You're supposed to be on watch. Now stop that piss-ant useless shooting!''

One by one the guns ceased.

The angry voice bellowed again, this time without the biting edge. ''You people out there! You hear me?''

Ryan answered. ''Yeah, we hear you.''

''Name's Major Ward. This here's my train aiming for the west. Over the Sierras.''

''Not too much over the Highs except a lot of sea, Major,'' Ryan called, making sure he kept his head well below the level of the ridge.

''I heard that, son. Also heard there's Americans up there in space. Right now. Been there, circling and breeding for a hundred years. You heard that, son?''

''No.''

''How many of you boys out there, son?''

''Six of us. Name's Ryan Cawdor. Got three men and two women. We were heading for the Grandee when the flash flood took our horses and the pack mule after noon today.''

''You lost everything?''

''Kept our clothes. Most of the blasters. Not a lot beside.''

''We're good Christian folks here, Mr. Cawdor. If you and your friends would like to come in you're right welcome to share any vittles we got. Stand slow and easy and walk in the same way. Best you keep your hands out where the boys can see 'em. You'll have likely noticed some of them are real edgy.''

"Real poor shots, Major. Wouldn't back them to hit the door on a shithouse if they were sitting there on the hot seat."

He was rewarded with a cackle of laughter.

"Guess you got it right, son." They heard someone else's voice, but they couldn't catch the words. Major Ward continued. "Oh, yeah. Fella here says how we know you aren't with this Skullface and his chillers? What do you say, son?"

Ryan put an edge to his voice. "I say that's real stupid. I say we're tired and hungry and I'm not going to wait much longer. If we come in without your say, there'll be blood, Major."

"Guess if you was Skullface you wouldn't tell us." The invisible wagon master laughed.

Cautiously, keeping his arms out from his body, Ryan stood and took a few steps toward the circle of wagons. The others stayed hidden where they were, ready to give covering fire at the first sign of trouble.

"We see you, Mr. Cawdor! Don't see your friends yet."

"I come in and you see me. When I think it's safe I'll call them in."

So it was.

Major Seth Ward—Ryan never learned where he claimed the military title from—was in his early fifties, a grizzled man with a weather-beaten face and a neat silver mustache. He dressed like an old-fashioned cowboy with a pair of nearly matching Colt Peacemakers cross-strapped on his hip.

His wag train had started off from an area north of N'Orleans, a nuke-ravaged wasteland, rife with mutie diseases and infested with gangs of roving chillers. Nearly a hundred folk, half of them children under the age of fifteen, had met together and agreed to move west.

"Green grass, fresh water and a safe home" was how Major Ward put it.

They'd heard from traders of Ward and had sent word to him to help put together a train of fifteen ox wagons and lead them into their Promised Land.

Ryan had encountered such parties before, and Krysty herself had actually traveled on one. As was often the case, there was a strong—if primitive—religious feel to the group. Out of twenty-four men over the age of fifteen, no less than eight claimed to be self-ordained preachers.

They'd been readying themselves for the evening meal before the arrival of the six outlanders. Now, once the credentials of Ryan and his friends had been offered and accepted, the women went back to their preparing and serving of the food.

It was a stew of dried beef with small, bulletlike potatoes and good bread. From the scent in the air it was obvious that the settlers had brought their own oven with them. There were a half dozen milch cows with the group, but the milk was reserved for the younger children. Everyone else made do with warm, slightly brackish water.

The stew was ladled onto smooth wooden dishes and passed around, but before anyone lifted a morsel toward their lips, Major Ward rapped on the side of a wagon with the butt of one of his pistols. "Quiet for the Reverend!" he shouted.

A tall, frail man with a wispy white beard stood and pressed the palms of his hands together, closing his eyes and gazing heavenward with an expression of extraordinary beatitude. Ryan watched him through lowered lid, the thought crossing his mind that the preacher clearly considered that he was demeaning himself in speaking to the Almighty.

"We're here, Lord, another day along the golden journey. You didn't help much when the Chapman wagon threw a wheel at the start of the day, but I guess Your attention might have wandered. Anyways, we repaired her and we got moving again. But'd be good if you could watch and make sure nothing like that happens again, Lord."

Ryan hoped that God was paying attention and was looking suitably penitent for being so lax toward the wag train.

"We got us some strangers so keep an eye open for them, Lord. If they're false then cause them to fall screaming into the pit of eternal fire and damnation, where their skin will scald and their eyes burst and hiss in the flames."

Ryan was aware of a chorus of "Amens" all around them.

The old man, Elder Vare, hadn't quite finished. "Bless us all that deserve the blessing, Lord, and make this food taste better than the pile of hogwash the cooks gave us last night. Name Father, Son and Ghost. Amen.''

"Amen," the assembly echoed, and there was an immediate rattling of cutlery on platters.

Ryan caught Krysty's eye from across the narrow table and winked.

The coffee sub was brought around by some of the teenage girls, led by the daughter of Elder Vare. A startlingly pretty blond girl with eyes of cornflower-blue, Sharon Vare seemed to be paying a lot of attention to Jak. In turn, the boy seemed oblivious to her interest. Ryan and the others watched with some amusement, but her father gestured angrily for her to get on and serve the rest of the party.

"A girl who walks in beauty is a tinkling cymbal and a mote in the eye of decency,'' Elder Vare muttered piously.

"A pretentious old fart is a pain in the ass,'' Ryan whispered to Krysty.

Blankets were found for the six newcomers. After the rigors of the day and the disturbances of the previous night, all any of them wanted to do was to get some sleep. But Major Ward took Ryan by the arm after the meal was finished.

"I'd like a word, son,'' he said in a tone of voice that made it clear it was more than just a casual request.

"Sure. When?"

"Now."

"Where?"

"Yonder. Just outside the wag ring. Still be inside the sentries. There's a couple of things I'd like to touch on."

As they walked together past the outer wagons, the daughter of Elder Vare raced past them, her face flushed, patting at her mussed hair. A moment later, to their left, both Ryan and the wag master spotted a figure slipping between two of the canvas-topped rigs. There was enough light from the fires to see that it was a young boy, with hair like a Sierra winter.

"That's one of the things, Ryan," Ward said.

They stopped a few paces farther on. The night air was warm and soft, carrying the taste of sagebrush and mesquite. Ryan stretched and took a deep breath, facing the older man.

"Kids'll be kids, Ward."

"Not if one's the hot-thighs daughter of the leading elder."

"His problem."

The wag master shook his head. "No. If Elder Vare has a problem, then we all have a problem. Just try and keep the white-hair away from the girl, Ryan. That's all."

"I'll speak to him. Jak's not a child. He's probably chilled more people than any man on this train. You don't *tell* Jak. But I'll speak to him. What else was it you wanted?"

"I been around most places. Traveled these old blacktops most of my life. But I never been this close to the Grandee."

"Me neither."

"I heard about this Skullface. Seems he leads a bloody gang of coldhearts."

Ryan looked across the desert. His mind touched on the strange whistle that he and Krysty had heard, but he decided to keep quiet about that. "Folks mentioned Skullface to us. Sounds like a mean son of a bitch, but you got blasters and you go careful."

"Sure, Ryan. But that's not my big worry. I'm more taken by talk of muties."

Ryan laughed. "Come on, Ward. There's *always* talk of muties."

"Sure. But we passed a burned homestead five days back. Everyone was dead, and not a lot was left of most of 'em. Not after the muties, the coyotes and the buzzards finished with 'em."

"Sure it was muties?"

"Sure as I'm standing here. There were corpses of around a dozen of the bastards."

"What sort of mutie?"

"Stickies. Enough left of their hands to tell. And there was also some I never seen before. Real strange. What was left of the skins was like a lizard or a gator. You know?"

"Scalies, Ward. Yeah. I don't recall hearing of two tribes of different muties running together. Could be a real nasty mix."

The wag master stood in silence for a few moments. He pulled a worn briar from his pocket and stuffed some home-cure in it, got it burning and drew

contentedly on it. "Care for some, Ryan?" he asked.
"Got plenty in my rig."

"No, thanks."

"Reckon your arrival could be a matter of real
providence, son."

"How's that?"

"Another day or so without food or water and
you'd have been on your back looking at the sun."

Since the scout wasn't aware of the proximity of
Christina Ballinger's spread, Ryan decided not to
mention it. Privacy and safety in Deathlands often
came down to the same thing.

"Yeah. Could be."

"But the sword cuts both ways."

"What?"

"I heard your tale about being traders and losing
your animals and all. Bullshit, Ryan. Pardon me, but
it's bullshit. I seen mercies before."

"We're not mercenaries, Ward."

"You sure aren't traders, neither."

Ryan nodded slowly, allowing his hand to fall, very
naturally, toward the butt of the SIG-Sauer blaster
in its holster. Ward saw the movement.

"Have thirty guns here if you pull the trigger,
Ryan."

"Three hundred guns and you'd still be down and
gut-shot."

"That's a fact, son."

"We aren't hired chillers, and we aren't traders. If
you knew that, why d'you take us in?"

The older man sighed and tapped the pipe on the heel of his boot, the tiny ball of glowing ashes falling into the sand. "Been around, son. Like to think I know folks. I don't see you murdering us in our bed, but with blasters like you got, you could sure help out if we meet muties."

"Or Skullface. If he exists."

"Right, son. We feed you, and you stand at our shoulders if the muties come. That a deal?"

Ryan shook the wag master's gnarled hand. "Yeah, that's a deal. Mebbe you feed us and we never need to do any fighting. Long as that goes on, I'll be happy, Ward."

"Me, too, son."

Their happiness didn't even last twenty-four hours.

CHAPTER ELEVEN

THE NEXT DAY DAWNED bright and clear, with a fresh breeze from the southwest.

Ryan and the others watched, impressed, as the circle of wagons readied for the next part of their journey.

Everyone seemed to know their particular task. Men and women packed and stowed, young boys collected the patient, lumbering oxen from the makeshift corral and led them to the rigs to be yoked, and the young girls began to prepare breakfast.

The oven smoked and the camp was filled with the delicious aroma of fresh bread. Eggs were cooked in skillets over the embers of the night's fires, with slices of salted bacon.

As soon as everyone had eaten, the dishes were scoured in dry, clean sand and packed away in the wagons. The youngest children had the important chore of making sure all the fires were stamped out.

Within an hour of the dawn, they were ready to roll. Ryan spotted Major Ward and went along to join him.

"Congratulations," he said.

"How's that, son?" Ward asked, shifting a chew of tobacco from one cheek to the other.

"You got a hundred people woken, oxen watered and tied on and everyone fed. All of that in just under the hour. Good work. Now we get going."

"No."

"No? Then..."

The wag master simply pointed to the far side of the circle, where the skeletal figure of Elder Vare was stalking toward them, Bible firmly in his right hand, followed by his coterie of assorted preachers and women.

"Morning prayers, before we go," Ward said gloomily. "Lose us around three hours' good traveling time."

"Can't you tell him to go take..." began Ryan, but Ward shook his head.

"He's party leader. Elected. They pay my jack for this job, which means Elder Vare pays me the jack. So, if he wants to pray the sun away, I just stand back and let him do it."

"Me, I'd break his jaw," Ryan said. "Going across this part of Deathlands you can't waste time. Time's blood."

But Elder Vare had his way.

Since they were freeloading guests, Ryan and the others paid a token price by standing with the others as the preacher indulged himself. Ryan let his mind drift away, wondering about the mix of stickies and scalies that were reportedly in the area.

"Teach us to smite thy enemies, Lord, if any appear. But we hope you'll be taking care to stop 'em coming close to us. Because we warn you now that we're humble and obedient servants who cringe at the shadow of your passing. But we aren't into that turning the other cheek crap! Just so's you understand, Oh mighty and merciful Jehovah!"

And so it went on.

And on.

Apart from the drivers of the swaying wags and the very young children, everyone in the party walked. As long as the old prenuke blacktop held out, they could make good progress. But time and again an earth shift had broken the highway and the oxen were driven into the soft sand, slowing their pace to a bare crawl.

Ward was one of the few people in the group who owned a horse, and he rode it all morning, moving constantly from front to rear and back again, encouraging the stragglers and slowing the enthusiastic leaders. After an hour he reined in along Ryan and the others.

"Water!" he called.

"Short?" asked Ryan, who'd wound the long white silk scarf, with its lethal weighted ends, around his mouth to mask off the worst of the choking dust.

"You said it, son. Got us enough for another five, six days if we ration. Got me a map that shows water only a few miles ahead."

"You send someone to check it out?" J.B. asked.

Ward looked away, tipping his hat back and wiping sweat from his forehead. "Well, no. No, I haven't done that, Mr. Dix."

The Armorer's mouth dropped open in surprise. "You got some map that *mebbe* shows you where there's water, less than an hour's ride on horseback! And you haven't sent anyone. Dark night! Why not?"

"This Skullface guy and the muties. No point in sending a man alone, is there? And I can't send out an armed patrol and weaken the train."

"Fucking shit!" Jak exclaimed. "Man alone scouts good."

"You got no right to speak like that, kid! Not to—"

"Don't call 'kid,' you—"

Ryan laid a cautious hand on the teenager's arm. "Cool down, Jak. But he's right, Ward. You seriously telling me you don't have scouts out?"

"I lead this train my way, and if you outlanders don't like it then just walk on."

"Leave it," Mildred said. "A man has to do what a man has to do. That right, Major Ward?"

"Guess so, ma'am."

"So. Let's get on with the day."

They breasted a rise and looked down onto a region dotted with the rusted relics of ancient oil-derricks, resembling the frozen corpses of prehistoric birds. The road straightened and cut almost due west, vanishing between walls of red rock. Krysty, shading her eyes, thought she could see some trees beyond the narrow ravine. But the shimmer of the heat haze made it difficult to make out any details.

She told the wag master, who slapped his dusty hat against his thigh with a whoop of delight. "Well, if that ain't jug-drinking good news, little lady. Just where my map shows water!"

J.B. stood next to Ryan, and he nudged him gently with his elbow. "Figure his map shows what an ace-on-the-line place for an ambush that ravine is?"

Ryan didn't reply.

They'd come within a half mile of the opening of the steep-sided valley, its mouth yawning wider for every step closer.

Ward held up his hand, shouting at the top of his voice "Wagons, whoa!" But the dust and the problems of communication meant that everything piled up, nose to tail, before the last rig finally braked to a reluctant halt.

He heeled his horse to where Ryan and the others stood, to the leeward side, all looking at the highway ahead of them. They were joined by Elder Vare and his daughter, and several of the self-elected leaders of the party.

"That's all, folks," the wag master said, a comment that for some unknown reason made Mildred and Doc grin at each other.

The bewilderment grew as the black woman curled her lip, making her front teeth protrude, and said, "Eh, what's up, Doc?"

Both of them broke into infantile giggles, drawing angry stares from the preachers.

"Hold it down there," Ward said. "We figure there's water on t'other side of them there rocks, but we gotta make it through the pass to get there. The outlanders here been telling me they figure it could be a good place for a mutie ambush."

"I think it'd be best to send in a recce party," Ryan suggested. "I'll go with a couple of others. Muties don't have much tactical brain, so there's a good chance we'll either spot them or maybe even trigger any ambush they got hidden."

"Sounds good to me," Ward agreed. "By cracky, but it makes good sense. What d'you say, Elder Vare? Sound good?"

"No."

"No?"

The thin face of the leading preacher looked away from Major Ward, up into the untroubled bowl of azure sky. "No," he repeated.

Ryan opened his mouth, feeling one of the old surges of bloody anger dropping its crimson veil over his eye and over his mind. But with an enormous effort of will he didn't speak. He turned away, fists clenching in the struggle.

Vare spoke again, folding his hands sententiously and pasting a thin half smile onto his chapped lips. "Why should we fear the peril of the valley of the shadow, Major Ward? Oh ye of very small faith! We don't give a mule's pecker about evil. The Lord is going to give us a shield and a sword and arm us with his own righteousness. Sure he is.''

''I hope that the Good Lord also sees fit to provide you all with some effective blasters, or your wives and children are likely to have their faces removed by the sticky fingers of a legion of muties. Put that in your prayer book, Elder.'' Having delivered his broadside, Doc swung on his heel and stalked off, knee joints cracking noisily.

''An unbeliever,'' Vare said dryly. ''Let us go forward, Major Ward, if you please.''

Krysty stopped him. ''The way I see it, Elder, the outlanders and those who don't believe in your version of the Almighty aren't worth bothering about. Is that right?''

He looked down his nose at her. ''Guess that's so.''

''Then let three of us go on ahead and see if muties are there. Won't harm your beliefs. Might save lives from your flock.''

''Let them, Pa,'' Sharon Vare urged. ''I surely don't like the sound of them old muties, and I'm sure these folks know what's right.'' She favored Jak with a smile of glittering brilliance.

''Well, if you approve, little Rose O'Sharon, then I guess the Almighty could be using you as a vessel for his wisdom. Kind of stupid, it seems to me, but we shouldn't question that the ways of the Lord are often goshdarned strange.'' Elder Vare glanced around at his supporters, getting nods of approval. None of them now seemed that keen on encountering any murderous muties without warning.

"Very well, Major Ward. The responsibility lies with you. Let some of these strangers go forth and win my love."

"Rather go third and win a toaster," Mildred whispered.

Ryan went with Krysty and Jak, relying on them for eyesight and a speed of reaction above and beyond his own. He led the way, leaving his G-12 behind in the care of J.B., trusting to his hand blaster. Jak had his enormous .357 Magnum with its satin finish and gaping six-inch barrel. Krysty carried her smaller, 9 mm Heckler & Koch P7A 13.

Farewells had been short. Ryan and Krysty were becoming used to separations. A slow, lingering kiss and a smile was all it took, and a "See you soon, lover" from one or the other. This time it was good to be going out together, with just a handshake for Doc, J.B. and Mildred.

They covered the ground with a cautious speed, checking the pools of dark shadow within the canyon for any sign of movement.

"Could be other side. By water," Jak suggested.

"Yeah," Ryan agreed. "Could be. Knowing muties, they won't be that well hid. Doesn't look like they're either in the valley or on the tops, so you could be right."

Krysty stopped, wiping grit from the corner of her eye. "I got a bad feeling, lover. There's something about this. Maybe it's not muties."

"Skullface?"

"Don't know. I can't see enough. There's something around that— Gaia! I just don't know."

At the entrance to the pass the ground was covered with a lot of misshapen boulders and piles of earth of varying sizes. None of the three paid them much attention, concentrating on the caves of blackness in the depths of the cutting.

Which was a mistake. A dozen screeching figures leaped from their dusty hiding places.

CHAPTER TWELVE

IT HAD BEEN a trick common among some Indian tribes during the middle 1800s. Young warriors would lie hidden beneath heaps of sand, not moving for hours on end, totally invisible, suffering intense discomfort while they waited for their enemies to ride by.

The muties must have seen the great pillar of orange dust that the wag train sent soaring skyward, visible for miles in any direction. And it must also have been quickly obvious that the fifteen rigs were taking the old winding blacktop from east to west. Even for a mutie, the timing of an ambush wasn't that tough to figure. But what took Ryan completely by surprise was that the muties had actually pulled off their plan with so much cunning.

There was a fraction of a moment to recognize that these were all scalies, without a single stickie among them. They were almost naked, with just rags of cloth knotted about their genitals. It looked like they were all males, but with scalies it was hard to tell. Their leathery skin glistened in the sunlight, and all of them were armed with axes or long-bladed knives.

Odds were twelve to three, and the initial element of shock was on the side of the muties. But Ryan, Krysty and Jak all had blasters drawn and ready for action.

One of the creatures erupted from the dirt almost under Ryan's feet, making him stagger sideways, nearly losing his balance.

"Fireblast!" he gasped, finger tightening instinctively on the trigger of his SIG-Sauer blaster.

The high-velocity round hit the nearest of his attackers a glancing blow, burning across its ribs on the right side, making its scaley jaw drop in shock. A hideous screech of pain came from its open mouth, its fetid breath making Ryan gag. There was time for a second, better-aimed shot at the staggering mutie, the bullet hitting precisely where Ryan had hoped— between the eyes, knocking it on its back where it continued to scream for several anguished seconds.

Before he could get off a third shot, one of the scalies grabbed at him, its clawed fingers splitting the skin on his arm, blood coursing over his wrist and fingers. Ryan nearly dropped his blaster in the violence of the attack.

He heard the double boom of Jak getting off a couple of shells from his hand cannon and the lighter noise of Krysty's pistol. Then everything vanished around him in his own lethal struggle for survival against three determined scalies.

One of them had its hands locked around the SIG-Sauer, wrestling it away from him. His own blood-slick fingers were weakening, and the other two were going for his throat and face.

Seeing defeat lurching before him, Ryan suddenly let go of the gun and threw himself backward. The mutie in front of him toppled away, caught by surprise, landing on its back, the blaster dropping from its own hand. The other two scalies also fell away from Ryan, standing looking at him through their deep-set eyes.

On his other hip Ryan carried the heavy panga with the eighteen-inch blade. He'd taken the trouble last night to clean and oil the weapon, making sure the honed edge hadn't been damaged or dulled by the flood waters.

Now he drew it.

The three scalies that faced him had drawn their own weapons. One was a long-handled ax, a second held a heavy, short-hafted hammer and the third an ice pick.

"Come on, you bastards," Ryan snarled, beckoning them toward him. He heard two more shots from Krysty's blaster, and Jak's Magnum boomed once more. But he didn't dare take his eyes off the trio of scalies shuffling in closer, all making a soft mewing sound.

He snatched a second to wipe his bloody hands on his pants, taking a firmer grip on the hilt of the panga. He moved it slowly from side to side, hearing the steel hiss in the warm air.

The scalie with the ice pick kept looking behind at the fallen blaster. Finally it went for the weapon, dropping the pick and plucking the SIG-Sauer from the ground, fumbling with the firing mechanism. Ryan moved fast, dodging two clumsy blows from the ax and the hammer, the panga swinging shoulder high.

The scalie blinked at him, wincing from the threat of the cleaver.

Ryan's aim was true.

The steel sliced through the mutie's arm, halfway between wrist and elbow. The hand, still gripping the blaster, dropped to the earth. In a spasm of ruined tendons, the index finger tightened on the trigger and the severed limb fired one round into the sky.

Before the pistol hit the dirt, the panga was following through, up and across once more. The sticky, yellowish blood of the scalie was smeared along its length. Ryan felt the satisfying jar as his second blow reached its target.

Had he been fighting a normal man the steel would have passed clean through in a simple beheading stroke. But the mutie's skin was far tougher, deflecting some of the force of the blow. It still hacked the side of the throat apart, opening the artery beneath the creature's ear, sending it reeling, sickly ichor pumping from the wound.

Ryan was dimly aware that Krysty was yelling, and he caught a high-pitched string of vile curses from Jak. But his attention was focused elsewhere.

The Trader used to impress on any new members of the war wags' crews: "Save yourself first and always. Then, and only then, can you worry about trying to save a comrade.''

Two down, two still up and coming.

The one with a hammer made a grunting charge. Ryan considered cutting for its groin, but it was so stooped it was impossible. Instead he chose to ghost sideways out of the scalie's path, swinging the panga one-handed, inflicting a deep gash in the back of the mutie's left thigh. The hamstring was sliced apart, and the creature went down with a yelp of shock, the hammer clunking from its hand.

The last mutie stood for a moment, unable to force the reality through its brain that it now fought alone against the one-eyed murderous human.

The hesitation gave Ryan the opportunity to step in at the back of the crippled scalie and open its throat in a single deep slash.

''You and me,'' Ryan said grimly, coming in at the fourth scalie in a crabbed, shuffling walk, feinting with the panga at groin and then the throat.

The mutie lost its nerve and turned away from him.

Its movement was too slow to give it even a half chance against Ryan's electrifying reflexes.

The panga had a rough point, and Ryan thrust with it, feeling it find a path between the ribs at the back on the left.

The scalie threw its head back, so that its slit eyes stared into the sun, its voice giving a shriek of terror and shock. Ryan slid the panga out again, watching the mutie take a handful of stumbling paces and then crash face first onto the ground.

There was no time for hesitation.

He'd laid all four of his attackers in the warm sand.

But there'd been eight others.

A quick look told Ryan that they'd divided equally, with four going for Jak and the remaining four rushing Krysty.

The woman's blaster had put down three, two obviously chilled and one gut-shot and struggling to get up. Almost without thinking Ryan put a shot through its angular gatorlike skull.

Krysty had just kicked her last opponent smack in the loincloth, and it had fallen to its knees in front of her, jaw gaping, spittle and bile dribbling from its pendulous lip. She put a bullet between its eyes and turned to see how Jak was coping.

The white-haired youth's huge Magnum had blown away three out of the four scalies. One lay on the ground, virtually headless, half its left arm also missing. The second had been shot through the chest, not normally a terminal wound for a mutie. But the .357 round had angled sideways and exited beneath the right arm, taking half the ribs and lungs with it, blasting the heart to ruptured rags of torn tissue. The third one had been shot in the back of the head, removing anything that resembled a face and spreading it in shards of crimsoned bone over a twenty-yard radius.

The fourth scalie was standing a few paces in front of the albino teenager, making threatening gestures with an old hiltless hunting knife bound to a length of wood to make a crude spear. Jak was holding his blaster in both hands, struggling with it.

"Problem?" Ryan shouted.

"Fucker's jammed!"

"I'll take him out," Krysty called. "Move out of the way, Jak."

But it eventually penetrated through the clouded brain of the mutie that this wasn't a good place to hang around, that eleven of his comrades wouldn't be eating around their fire that night and that his own chances were slim. He spun on his heel and began to run with a clumsy speed toward the nearest wall of red rock.

Krysty leveled her pistol, but Jak waved her away. "Mine," he said, dropping the useless blaster in the dirt, plucking out one of his throwing knives. He gripped it by the taped hilt and snapped it toward the fleeing mutie.

Ryan watched the spinning steel, the light dancing off it like a tossed diamond. But the ground dipped suddenly and the running scalie stumbled and nearly fell. The knife hummed past his shoulder, clattering harmlessly among some jagged boulders ahead of him.

"Angry!" Jak yelled, his voice echoing from the valley ahead of them. His hand snaked down for one of his other knives, but Ryan was there first. The mutie was close to cover, and it was never a good idea to let an enemy escape if you could help it.

The SIG-Sauer coughed once and the scalie went over in a tangle of arms and legs, raising his own small cloud of dust, a cloud of dust that quickly evaporated, leaving nothing.

"Twelve up and twelve down," Ryan said.

"Would've chilled second knife," Jak moaned, running lightly toward the rocks to retrieve his blade, examining it carefully for any scratches or damage.

"Probably," Ryan agreed, reloading his blaster. "But if you'd been unlucky there wouldn't have been a chance for any of us."

"Funny they were all scalies," Krysty commented, looking at the corpses.

"Funny? Didn't hear a lot of laughing."

"Peculiar, if you prefer that, you pedantic son of a bitch, Ryan."

"Hey, keep gentle, lover."

She was still angered by his flippancy. "The ground opens and up jump a dozen scalies. It was a close call."

"Sure. I know that. Sorry. But why's it peculiar? The scalies?"

"Ward said stickies as well. No sign of them around here."

"Fucking good," said Jak, pulling a face. "Hate stickies more'n anything."

Ryan nodded. "Know what you mean, Jak." He looked toward the line of waiting wags up on the ridge, a half mile off. He knew that J.B. and the others would have heard the fusillade of shots and would be waiting anxiously for any news. He glanced at his wrist chron. Another few minutes and he knew that the Armorer would have been leading a charge after them.

Maybe a rescue charge.

Maybe for revenge.

Ward slapped Ryan on the shoulder, his face cracked into a huge smile.

"Jehosophat! You folks went and wiped out a round dozen of those limbs of Satan! I can't scarcely credit it, son. And one of you a woman, too," he said, marveling at the idea. Krysty dropped him a sarcastic curtsy.

Elder Vare was less impressed. "The Almighty did choose to help you outlanders, after all. It's obvious you'd all have been destroyed by the ungodly creatures from the blasphemous pit of nuke-warped entities if it hadn't been for divine aid. No credit to you for that."

He sniffed and turned away, his flock of preachers dutifully following at his heels like a crowd of sour-faced buzzards. Only Sharon Vare seemed pleased, and she blew Jak a kiss as she trooped after her father.

"How about the water?" Mildred asked. "While we've been waiting for these heroes to get back, the sun's been sliding down. How about if Doc and I rode ahead on a couple of your horses and recce the water hole?''

Ryan looked at J.B., raising a questioning eyebrow. "What d'you think? Should be safe. Still an hour or more to dusk."

"Guess so."

"What about the stickies?" Krysty asked. "Ward said they'd seen corpses of stickies as well as scalies, didn't he?"

"Yeah. Mebbe you—"

Doc held up a hand. "I realize that there are good reasons that you don't want the good lady and myself to entertain a venture with some degree of hazard to it, Ryan."

"What reasons?"

Mildred ticked them off on her fingers. "In my case it's sexism and racism. And in the case of the old fart there, it's plain ageism. That answer your question?"

"All right. Make sure your blasters are clean and loaded and keep your eyes peeled. We got ambushed by those bastards."

"And if I see my granny I'll speak to her about how to suck eggs," Mildred snapped.

Mildred rode a bay mare with a placid manner. A couple of dozen water bottles were strung across the saddle horn. Doc's gelding was similarly adorned. The old man looked down at the others, grinning at Jak's worried expression.

"Don't worry, my dear boy. We shall be back before you know it."

"Not worried."

"Then don't look it."

The boy shook his head. "That Sharon Vare. Keep on."

"She keeps on at you, Jak?" Ryan asked. "What about . . . or maybe I shouldn't ask you that?"

"Says likes me, but wishes was cleaner and taller. She said."

Jak stretched himself up to his full five feet and nearly four inches and tried to brush dust off his pants.

Doc grinned. "Tell her next time you'll be on stilts and carrying a tennis racket!"

As Doc and Mildred heeled their mounts toward the mouth of the steep valley, they disturbed forty or more buzzards that were gorging themselves on the feast of mutie flesh. The dozen bodies—or their ragged remains—lay where they'd dropped, now eyeless and missing all of the delicious soft tissue.

"You truly wish to trace this other cryo-center, Mildred?" Doc asked.

"Absolutely. You know what it's like to be stranded out of your own time, Doc." She shook her head. "Shit! Nobody knows it better. You gotta think now and again how good it would be to talk to someone from your own time."

He nodded. "I swear to you that not an hour of a day passes that I do not think about that."

For some minutes they rode on in silence.

The sun was sinking fast behind a low range of hills to the far west, throwing long blocks of shadow over the desert.

The sound of the horses' hooves clattered on the rocky trail. Other than the patient circling buzzards, there was no sign of life.

From the open jaws of the ravine to the clump of dusty trees around the water hole was only a quarter mile or so. It was just possible to catch the glint of reflected light from among the trees. Doc, leading, reined in and leaned his arm on his mount's neck, considering the prospect before them.

"See anything?" Mildred asked.

"No. Not a single capering Pathan to threaten our lives."

They moved on at a walk, in among the trees. The sun was well down, and the ground between the stunted trunks was impenetrable darkness.

They tethered the animals to a wind-blasted live oak and started to unsling the containers. The actual pool was in a natural rock basin, its surface covered in a sheen of dust and dead insects.

"Looks good," Mildred observed.

At that moment, the stickies came slobbering out of the shadows.

CHAPTER THIRTEEN

DOC GLIMPSED them first, emerging from the darkness, shuffling across the sand like the living dead.

"By the three Kennedys!" he roared.

Mildred swung around. "Oh, fuck," she said in a normal conversational voice.

There were five of the horrors—four males and one that was probably female, though technical details like gender weren't always that easy to determine with stickies.

They were all barefoot, wearing the usual assortment of cast-off rags. One of the men held an old sword with a tassel of maroon ribbon dangling from its hilt. A second, younger mutie, had a knife in each long-fingered, suckered hand. The other two men had short-hafted axes. The woman held a long-barreled remake musket, the muzzle pointing in the vague direction of Mildred and Doc.

The faces of the muties were a fugue to genetic malformation. The foreheads sloped sharply backward, giving them something of the look of a homicidal sheep; the ears were residual, like knobs of inflamed gristle jammed on each side of the skull; the hair was long and stringy, matted with grease and dirt; the upper bodies were generally muscular and wiry, tapering to narrow waists and spindly legs. Stickies weren't good walkers and were hopeless runners. Their eyes had a feline, split pupil, often bloodshot and encrusted with a yellow slime. Their noses were nonexistent, only raw holes between eyes and mouth that ceaselessly dripped gobbets of mucus.

Their mouths were almost lipless, peeling back to reveal the teeth, most of which were needle pointed, the remainder broken or missing and giving the appearance of a neglected arsenal. The fingers were exceedingly long and tapered, with small suckers across them—suckers that also covered the palms of the hands and often extended to the feet as well.

Stickies only really relished three things. They loved killing any weaker creature, using their mutie hands to tear skin and flesh off the living bones. They were also mystically attracted to loud explosions and to large fires.

The woman was nearest, shuffling toward Mildred, eyes lighted with a voracious fire of hatred. The black woman didn't hesitate. To fumble with her pistol would have meant death. She simply swung the half-dozen water bottles that she'd taken off her saddle, hanging on the leather straps, using them like a flail.

They hit the stickie across the shoulder and the side of the head with a satisfying clunk, sending her staggering sideways, dropping her blaster. She gave a high, thin mew of rage.

Doc had a couple of moments longer, and he used them well, dropping his water bottles and reaching for the Le Mat on his right hip, hefting the heavy pistol and thumbing back on the hammer.

Seeing the blaster, the stickies hesitated a moment, drawing closer together, around twelve feet away from the old man in the faded frock coat.

They made a perfect target for the scattergun barrel of the unique pistol. Because of the short barrel, the .63 round was useless at anything over twenty feet or so. At close range the effect was utterly devastating.

The gun gave a deafening roar, kicking so hard in Doc's hand that the barrel ended up pointing directly toward the flock of buzzards.

Mildred, already reaching for her own ZKR 551, was astounded by the explosion of the Le Mat. To her astonished eyes, Doc and the four male stickies that were threatening him had vanished behind a billowing cloud of powder smoke.

As it cleared away, Doc was stooped over his gun, his fingers nimbly changing the position of the firing hammer. There didn't seem to be too much pressure to hurry as all four of the stickies were down in a tangle of arms and legs and smeared blood.

The one with the sword was dying, his throat and most of his face ripped away by the starring cascade of lead.

One of the others had almost lost its left arm, only a few strings of sinew keeping the limb attached to the shoulder. The third mutie had taken a scattering of pellets in the chest, a few of them dotting his jaw and cheeks. He was trying to get up, spitting blood and broken splinters of teeth into the earth.

The fourth one looked like he'd hardly been hurt at all and was groping for his fallen knife.

Out of the corner of her eye Mildred saw that the female stickie was coming at her again, bare-handed, gibbering with a maniacal anger.

Mildred hadn't the lifetime of experience in Deathlands that Ryan and the others shared. All she knew was that a .38-caliber round from her pistol would be enough to put down any normal person. She aimed and fired, seeing the impact of the bullet, a neat dark hole drilled between the mutie's residual breasts. The creature staggered back several paces under the impact of the shot.

And kept on coming!

Meanwhile Doc had his own trouble. His Le Mat was proving stubborn. Despite all of the exhortations from J.B., he hadn't always been as scrupulous as he should about fieldstripping and cleaning his antique blaster.

Now he was paying the price. To adjust the gun from the sawed-off barrel to the revolver should only have been the work of a few seconds. It was *nearly* done.

Nearly.

Stickies weren't indestructible, but they took a lot of chilling. Just losing an arm might slow one down, but it would keep on at you. And a few scattergun pellets in the mouth would hardly hinder a murderous stickie at all. So Doc had three of them, in varying states of health, closing in on him again.

"Blast 'em, Doc!" Mildred yelled, unable to see what his problem was, aware only that the female stickie was moving toward her, fingers flexing.

"I'm trying, you lack-brain pavement-pounder!" Doc retorted, backing away and still desperately struggling with the recalcitrant weapon. His feet were on the brink of the pool.

Mildred squeezed the trigger of her customized target pistol twice more, taking careful aim for the stickie's head. Both bullets hit precisely the same spot, leaving a single entry wound. But they hit differing degrees of bone on the way through and started tumbling and distorting in different ways, exiting at the same microsecond four inches apart.

"Yeah," Mildred breathed.

It was about the most amazing thing that Mildred had ever seen—the simultaneous exit of the two rounds caused the stickie's head to explode.

For a moment the mutie's face remained in place, like a two-dimensional mask, but with nothing behind it. The whole rear part of the skull, from the ears back, had vanished in a mist of blood, brains and flying splinters of bone. A large watermelon hit simultaneously by both barrels of a 10-gauge might give some idea of what it looked like.

The female took two horrific, tottering steps toward Mildred, bringing up the short hairs at her nape in atavistic terror. Then the strings finally cut and the corpse dropped to the dirt.

The crack of the blaster and the extraordinary passing of their companion stopped the other three survivors dead in their tracks, goggling eyes turning toward Mildred.

Doc saw his chance and took it, backing away a few paces into the scummy pool until he was knee deep, all the while working on the Le Mat. He finally succeeded in shifting the stubborn hammer.

"Now, you demons from the deepest circle of purgatory..." He began to thumb back the hammer, and squeezed the trigger.

Each of the stickies collected three of the .36-caliber bullets. Doc wasn't the greatest marksman in the world, but at fifteen feet even he was capable of reasonable accuracy.

He'd also learned enough not to waste lead on the bodies of the stickies. All nine rounds hit their heads.

Mildred had holstered her own revolver, clapping her hands as the three stickies jerked and danced under the impact of the bullets.

"Good shooting, Doc!" she shouted. "Wins you a prize!"

They were back at the wag train with the containers of water before the sun had completely set.

CHAPTER FOURTEEN

RYAN JERKED AWAKE, his hand automatically closing on the butt of his blaster. Only when he had the gun firmly in his fingers did he start to think about what had awakened him.

He lay under a couple of blankets, head resting on his folded coat. The bed of one of the wags was over his head, his feet touching one of the large wooden wheels. Krysty was at his side, and Ryan sensed that she, too, was awake.

"You heard it?" he whispered.

She reached across the small space between them and squeezed his hand. "Yeah. Woke me. Think anyone else heard it?"

"Don't know. Probably it touches them and they come close to the surface, then sleep pulls them down again. Like a tiny muffled bell heard in a dusty back room of a huge house."

Krysty grinned. "Hey, that's real poetic, lover. Like some of those old books. I know what you mean. Think there really could still be a train running someplace, lover?"

"Why not? Barons out east are supposed to have whirly wags. We saw that flying wag a few months back. Why not a train?"

"Didn't they run electric? Can't be that sort of power left in Deathlands."

Ryan finally let go of the SIG-Sauer. "Some did. But some of the old ones ran on coal and wood. If there really is one still going we might see smoke as well as hearing the whistle in the middle of the night."

Before leaving the valley of death, where the carcasses of the muties were now stripped of all edible flesh, the wag train filled up their barrels, buckets and bottles with water, preparing for the trip farther west. Major Ward's map was a little vague on where the next water hole might be located, though it did show an old township, around two days' travel ahead of them.

"Called Salvation," the wag master told Ryan, showing him the inked name on the piece of paper.

"Be there around evening tomorrow," J.B. guessed.

As usual, the Armorer was right.

The next couple of days drifted by in a haze of dust and heat. From Ryan and his group, there was only one noteworthy incident.

During the evening of the first day, Jak had gone outside the circle of wags to relieve himself. He was gone for nearly a quarter of an hour and when he came back, it was obvious that something had happened.

He ignored his five friends and went straight to his own blanket, lying down with his back to the others.

Ryan exchanged glances with Krysty, J.B., Doc and Mildred, raising a questioning eyebrow. But all of them shrugged their own bewilderment.

Since they'd left the Ballinger spread, the teenager had been slightly more reticent than usual. But Jak was never a great one for idle chatter. Since they'd joined the wags, his only worry seemed to have been caused by the attention of Sharon Vare.

"Go ask him," Krysty urged.

"Okay," Ryan agreed. He stood and stretched, looking around as the train readied itself for the night. Guards were being set, and the last residue from supper was being tidied away. The young children were in their sleeping clothes, scampering around and trying to avert the evil hour when they'd be sent to their beds.

Ryan stood looking down at Jak for a moment, knowing the boy was aware of his presence. From behind, Jak looked even younger than his fifteen years, his slight frame and the cascade of pure white hair making him seem more like a little girl.

"Something wrong?" Ryan asked, hunkering down to lean against the metal-rimmed wheel of the rig.

"No."

"No?"

"Yeah."

Ryan half laughed. "That mean 'yeah' there's something wrong or 'yeah' there's nothing wrong?"

Jak muttered, "Yeah."

"Still no wiser."

The boy half turned, squinting up at the man. "Means something's fucking wrong. You know that, Ryan."

"Thought so. What is it?"

"My business."

"You said that about Christina Ballinger. Is this about her?"

"No."

"Sharon Vare?"

It was a fairly obvious guess, but Jak reacted as though someone had just pushed a branding iron halfway up his ass.

"Who told?" He threw the blanket to one side, jumping to his feet, his hand dropping to the massive blaster on his hip.

"Cool down," Ryan said, "and don't you ever move to draw down on me, Jak. Not now and not ever. You understand me?"

There was a lethal chill to the one-eyed man's voice, which Jak recognized. He nodded slowly, his body relaxing.

"Sit down."

"Don't want talk."

"The girl's pestering you, talking foolish and teasing. That sort of thing?"

"No."

"No?"

Jak looked directly at Ryan, licking his pale lips. "No. More."

"How d'you mean 'more,' Jak?" Ryan felt the first tug of worry.

"Was pissing. Nobody near. Sharon came. Talked fucking. Dropped pants. Lay down, legs open. Said fuck or would tell father."

Ryan had a flash of insight as to what had gone through the teenager's mind. Jak wasn't like other fifteen-year-olds and wouldn't be pressured by anybody to do anything he didn't want to do.

"Jak," he said, pitching his voice lower, "you didn't chill her? Didn't slit her throat, did you? Did you?"

The boy grinned, showing wolfish teeth. "No. Would have told you."

"You fuck the girl?"

Jak hesitated. Finally, "No."

Ryan sucked at his front teeth. "Let me just get this straight, Jak. Sharon Vare came outside the wags, while you were pissing, said she wanted you to fuck with her, and if you didn't she go tell her father that you'd done it anyway. Claim you'd raped her. That it?"

"Guess so."

"You didn't, and since I haven't heard anyone screaming about a lynching, it looks like she hasn't told her father anything."

"Yeah," Jak agreed. "But said she wouldn't."

"What?" Ryan dropped his head in disgust. "Fireblast! I'm getting really puzzled, Jak."

"Says loves me. Says won't cause trouble. But says will tell if I don't change mind. Fuck her. Marry her."

"Which, fuck or marry?"

"Both."

"Oh, great." Ryan looked around them, catching the scent of wood smoke from the guard fires. "You don't much want to do either, Jak. Is that about right? Neither?"

"Right. No fuck. No marry."

"We won't be with this train that long. Soon as we get someplace we can find some transport we'll leave. Horses. Wags. Anything. There's a town coming up tomorrow. Might be something there. Until then, be careful, Jak."

"Sure."

The trail became broader and easier to follow, and the wags made better time. J.B. announced that there were recent wheel marks on the dusty surface of the blacktop.

"Could be real close to that ville, Major," he said.

"Salvation?"

"That's it. And it looks as if there's some action around there. Must be the tracks of eight or ten different wags here."

Ward slapped his hat against his thigh. "By cracky! That's the best news I heard in a while."

"Unless the wags belong to Skullface," Ryan commented.

Elder Vare still refused to allow any scouting to go on.

"If the Lord wants us to plunge into the abyss, then that's his will. We'd just anger him by trying to guess what he's doing. We share our luck together."

"And get fucked together," Ryan whispered, angered by the tactical stupidity of the preacher.

It was close to sunset when the first of the wags breasted the hill that had slowed them throughout all the afternoon. The driver reined in, yelling for Ward to come forward. Almost everyone in the party came to see what the fuss was.

Ryan and his companions were among the leaders, trying to walk near the front and to one side of the wags, avoiding the dust thrown up from the big wheels. They stood together and stared out across a wide plain, which was cradled by some low hills about twenty miles to the west.

Ryan eased the G-12 caseless on his shoulder, where the strap was rubbing. Though the light was almost gone, it wasn't difficult to make out the remains of a town below them. From where they stood, there was no way of determining how badly it had been damaged by the nuking a hundred years ago.

But it wasn't the clutter of buildings straggling off a narrow main street that held everyone's attention—it was the rod-straight railroad lines running away from Salvation and the tiny object that moved along them toward the hills, trailing a plume of dark smoke.

Everyone saw a tiny thread of white steam, and heard the lonesome sound of the locomotive whistle.

CHAPTER FIFTEEN

DAWN BROKE from a dull, overcast sky, a light drizzle filtering through from the north.

Ward called a meeting, attended by Elder Vare and his cabal as well as Ryan and his friends. They'd eaten breakfast, and all of them now hugged metal mugs of coffee sub, steaming in the cool air. The major opened things up.

"That's Salvation. Map shows it right smack-dab where it should be."

"Water there?" Ryan asked.

The wag master shook his head. "Not so's I know it."

"Doesn't look like any signs of life there. No water. So why go there?"

Elder Vare answered Ryan's question. "I believe there will be food there. The Lord provides, even to those who do not believe."

"Oh, I believe, Elder Vare. I believe in a whole lot of things. But I don't believe in going blind into a ville that looks deserted. Not unless there's some real good reason."

"I wish to go," Vare said pompously. "That is reason enough."

"And you'll go in first?" The sting in Ryan's voice made the older man hesitate, eyes shifting nervously from side to side.

"Me?"

"You. First man in gets the first bullet from the shadows."

"What bullet? How do you know there will be a bullet from the shadows?"

Ryan smiled grimly. "I don't. Then again, neither do you."

"How about that train?" asked one of the other preachers, a stout man with a ready grin. "That means someone's around."

"Sure," J.B. agreed. "But do we all go in at once? Or do you want us outlanders to test the water for you?"

Ward looked from Vare to Ryan and back again, rubbing his chin worriedly. "I'm darnationed if I know what's best. Elder, you pay the piper. You get to call the tune."

Ryan watched, interested. He'd raised his questions partly to antagonize the preacher, who he'd come to greatly dislike. Krysty had spent ten minutes just after first light gazing down into the small ville, and she'd seen no sign of life. Nor did she "feel" any imminent danger. So as far as Ryan was concerned, Salvation was safe to visit.

"Perhaps," Vare began, swallowing hard. "The Lord's will must be served. We seek only the place of green grass and fresh spring water. Far to the west from here."

The wag master looked puzzled. "Yeah, I know that, Elder. But...but how's about this ville yonder? Do we go around or through? Or does Ryan here go take a look first?"

"Let 'em look," Vare snapped, spinning around and walking briskly to his own wag.

All six of the companions went. The drizzle had stopped, and the clouds were slowly clearing from the south. Ryan looked out in that direction, wondering if there truly was another cryo-center off toward the Grandee. He decided that they should leave the wag train in the next couple of days, steal horses, food and water and head out. The guards weren't fighting men, and they could get away easily enough.

The moral imperative was simple for Ryan Cawdor. He and the others couldn't get where they wanted to go without transport, and that meant horses, since there were no power wags anywhere. Unless you counted the mysterious locomotive.

"There doesn't seem much structural damage," Krysty announced. "Neutron bombs, I guess."

One of the few things that saved Deathlands from being even worse was the neutron bomb. Some of the nukes used in 2001 had been conventional "dirty" weapons, causing enormous devastation and 99.99 percent mortality from ground zero to eight miles out. And seeping rad leakage wiped out millions more over a larger radius, leaving the breeding genetic mutations to multiply until mankind became the inheritor of fleshly chaos.

A neutron bomb killed just the same as any other kind of nuke missile, but left buildings standing—as long as they weren't too close to the strike zone. That didn't help the general populace, but at least it was something for the next few enfeebled generations that came after.

Ryan knew places in Deathlands, mainly the once-great conurbations, that were totally and irreversibly destroyed. But there were also a lot of villes that had been hit by concentrations of neutron bombs. There, the people had gone but the walls remained.

And that was how Salvation, Texas, looked as they walked cautiously down the blacktop toward the main street.

Ryan's eye kept being drawn to the ruled metal lines that met at infinity. He knew from things that he'd read that the railroads had been all-powerful during the late 1800s and early 1900s. But by about the middle of the 1900s their authority had declined and lines were closing everywhere.

He'd seen rusting rails and worm-rotted sleepers at a lot of places out in the wilds, but he could see the way the watery sun was winking off the steel, telling of regular, recent use. But where did it go? To the distant hills? Then where? And who was running it?

In order to try to find answers, Ryan decided that they should split up, contrary to the Trader's usual rules about entering a strange ville.

"Stay close, keep quiet and have your finger loose on the trigger."

But Ryan had never known Krysty to be wrong. If she felt there was no imminent danger in Salvation, then that was good enough for him.

He and Krysty took the center of the main street of the township. Mildred and Doc formed an uneasy partnership going down the north side, taking the alleys and cross streets. J.B. went with Jak on the opposite side.

"The usual," Ryan told them. "Shot or a shout, come running. Meet the far end of the ville in, say, an hour or so from now."

Salvation was a typical one-street town, the civic equivalent of a shotgun shack—fire a blaster from one end of the main drag, and the bullet would go clean on through and out the other end.

Ryan and Krysty walked along the sidewalk, peering into the dusty interiors of the stores and houses. There were great clusters of weeds pushing through, but both of them noticed quickly that the ville wasn't an abandoned ghost town like some they'd visited.

"Plenty of boot marks," Krysty observed.

"Right. Must be the men riding that loco wag. Use this as a base, mebbe."

"This Skullface?"

"I don't know, lover. Why leave this ville empty? What do they use it for? Keep supplies? Sleep? Doesn't make sense."

The buildings, mainly adobe and crumbling stucco, were in fair shape. The wind and heat of West Texas had stripped every flake of paint from any exposed door or window, and the glass was dulled and crazed. But few roofs had caved in, and most walls were still vertical.

The corpses of the original inhabitants were long gone, mostly to the predators and carrion-jaws of the surrounding desert, but their ghosts still walked in the opalescent morning light.

The ville was heavy with the trivia of the last days before the sky grew dark, before the massive electromagnetic pulse circled the globe and wiped out every power source.

There was a row of small shops, covered from what had probably once been a livery stable and feed store. Ambitiously named The Salvation Shopping Mall, it held a dozen miniature stores. Ryan led the way into the shadowed alley, feeling that he was the first person to set foot there for nearly a century. But he almost immediately had to step quickly sideways to avoid treading into what looked like a decidedly human turd of recent vintage.

Barbie's Bootique had its window smashed in, and all of its stock was long gone. Footwear of any quality was always at a premium in Deathlands.

Ma's Apple pie and Fudge Emporium was next along the mall. There was a notice on the door, still legible—Due To Lease Renewal At An Exorbitant Increase, We Are Closing December 30th. Thanks To All Our Customers And Goodbye.

The lock was broken and Ryan pushed the door open, his feet disturbed a bunch of junk mail, dried out like fall leaves.

"Gaia!" Krysty said. "Every time we find a place like this I start feeling all excited. Mebbe we'll find some real treasure from before the long winters."

Ryan pulled the door closed again. "I know what you mean."

"Then you look around and there's always the same sensation. Dust and echoes and shadows. It brings a lump to my throat. You kind of glimpse people's hopes and ambitions, and you know they've all been dead. So long dead."

"Want to go out in the sun again?"

Krysty managed a smile. "No. Ghosts don't hurt you. Let's look on."

Saucy Lita. Ryan figured there was probably some kind of joke in the name, but he couldn't get it. He tried saying it several times, but it still didn't sound like anything he'd heard. Again, the lock was broken and he pushed the door open and walked inside, Krysty at his heels.

A printed notice on a curling card said "Over 16s Only. IDs May Be Requested. Another large one had fallen faceup on the floor—Warning. This Shop Contains Items Of An Adult Nature. If You Are Easily Offended, GET LOST!

Krysty stooped and picked up a piece of delicate rag off a broken table, holding it up against herself. It was made from black silk with some rotting ribbons and artificial lace. It looked as if it had once had elastic around the waist but that was long gone. There was about enough material to cover a man's hand.

"That what I think?" Ryan asked.

"Depends on what you think, lover." She grinned. "But I've only ever seen anything like this on that blue porno."

"Shame they've rotted. I'd have given good jack to see you in something like that."

"Look at this kid's doll," he went on, picking up the figure of an old man with white hair and beard, carrying a price sticker of $35.95 that read Naughty Uncle Fred The Flasher.

"What's a flasher?" Krysty asked, reaching for the unbuttoned overcoat on the doll and pulling it open. She immediately gave a shout of laughter at what was revealed. "Oh! So, *that's* what a flasher is!"

Most of the stock of the small, cramped store had vanished or rotted away over the past hundred years, but there were still a few remnants that gave Ryan and Krysty a better than good idea of what kind of place it had been.

"I just don't see how many people in a one-street ville like this, in the wastes of old Texas, would have bought anything like this," Ryan said, showing Krysty a massive artificial penis in purple plastic. It was at least fifteen inches from base to tip.

"Not getting jealous, are we, lover?" Krysty grinned.

A wooden torso modelled a white cotton T-shirt with the same slogan repeated hundreds of times, all over it—Tiny Tits. Tiny Tits. Another of the faded notes read We Have The Tiny T**s T-shirt In All Sizes Up To 50 Inches.

Ryan read it and smiled at Krysty's expression of disapproval. "Not getting jealous, are we, lover?" he asked.

"Salvation was sure big on muffler shops," Mildred said when they'd regrouped. "We saw five of them, with two launderettes."

"Only one of them fluff and fold," Doc added, wiping sweat from his forehead with his swallow's-eye kerchief.

"We checked a few houses. They've all been cleared out of anything worth taking." J.B. looked around the ville. "Funny though. Jak here spotted it. I hadn't noticed."

"What?" Ryan asked.

The teenager hesitated. "Not certain."

The Armorer grinned. "Sure he's sure. Tell 'em, Jak."

"Houses stripped recently."

"Recently?" Ryan glanced at the others. "Anyone else spot this?"

Krysty answered, "Now you mention it, yeah. Think about it, lover. Some of those places had the feel that they'd been untouched for a hundred years. Sure, there was some old damage. But a lot of it somehow felt...felt like it had been done yesterday."

"Fucking right!" the boy exclaimed, eyes glistening like a striking cobra. "Yesterday! Not enough dust around things broke."

Ryan sighed. "Sure. I saw it, too. But I didn't somehow register what it meant. Fireblast! Stupid of me. Getting old."

J.B. shook his head. "We're all getting old, Ryan. Been riding too many roads for too many years. The kid was... Sorry, Jak. Didn't mean anything by that. Just that you're young and you got young eyes. You see better and think sharper. You should get out of all this before you finish up like the rest of us. Seriously."

It was an unusually long speech for the normally taciturn Armorer.

The albino teenager nodded slowly. "Know that's true, J.B., and been thinking same thing. One day. Yeah, one fucking day."

There was a long silence among the group of friends.

They discussed whether it was worth bringing in a working party to go through the town more carefully, to see if there was anything tucked away in any of the houses that might be of some value. But they all eventually agreed that it was unlikely.

J.B. summed it up. "Seems that the ville's been turned over in the past few weeks. Could be the people who were running that loco wag. Either way, there's nothing here for the settlers."

Ryan agreed. "We'll go back and tell Major Ward and the smiling Elder Vare. Still be a good place to camp. There's that small creek for water and plenty of wood for fires."

"Good place for us to leave from?" Krysty suggested.

Ryan nodded. "Been reading my mind, lover."

Doc coughed. "Me and the lady found a poster tacked up inside a window. I confess it was more than a little faded, but still legible. Was it not, Mildred? Legible?"

"Course it was legible, you daft old goat! How the hell would we have known what it said if we couldn't read it?"

Doc shrugged, grinning in embarrassment.

"What did this notice say?" Ryan asked.

Doc answered. "It announced a grand reopening. Dated November of the year of Our Blessed Lord, 2000 annu domini. The Salvation to Silver Lode Railroad spur. Closed these one hundred and twenty years."

Mildred took over the account. "And the restoration of the engine house."

"Then let's go down and take us a look at this engine house," Ryan suggested.

"Must be that group of buildings to the west where the rails end," J.B. guessed.

That was where they found the first of the corpses.

CHAPTER SIXTEEN

"THE GOOD FOLK of Salvation," Ryan said quietly.

"Guess so," J.B. replied. "There were two or three of the old houses that looked like someone had been living in them. I figured it was probably pack rats, wanderers from the outlands. Could be they really lived in the ville."

The engine house stood alone. A cobbled yard was located at one end, with a huge turntable, carrying the rails where the loco wags could be turned around. There were a number of outbuildings, mostly in good shape. From the remnants of weathered signs it looked as though the idea had been to deck them out as ticket offices and museums of the old railroad. But sky-dark had obviously overtaken the project, and most of them contained very little.

Very little except for the corpses.

The longest dead was dried out and leathery, giving an approximate date of a month or so ago. The most recent was still covered in blowflies, the stench enough to make Doc gag. Death had been within forty-eight hours or so, not long before the locomotive had pulled out of Salvation's depot.

None of the townsfolk looked as if they'd been given an easy passing.

Something about the mangled bodies tugged at Ryan's memory. Deathlands wasn't a kindly place, filled with warmhearted, rosy-cheeked folk. But it normally wasn't a place of ice-heart brutality.

This wasn't a simple outburst of pesthole butchery, no bullets-in-the-neck execution.

These deaths had been slow and agonized, and a dreadful, racking pleasure had been taken by the killer. Expert hands had tied the knots and made the cuts; knowing fingers had pried out eyes and torn off genitals.

Ryan could almost hear the screams from the gaping jaws and the broken teeth, could catch the sound of hearty laughter at the tortured thrashings against the heated blades and the smoldering probes.

"By God!" Mildred breathed, shaking her head at the carnage in front of her. "There are some seriously sick bastards around this neighborhood, Ryan. Let's go."

"Just a minute, Mildred. We got to do some thinking about this."

"Well, you do your thinking in this charnel house, and I'll go and do mine outside in God's good, clean air."

"Thought you were a doctor, Mildred," Ryan called.

"Oh, thanks a million, buddy. Yeah, I was a doctor, and in all my life I never saw anything like this. I saw films of Belsen and Auschwitz and places like that. Man's inhumanity, Ryan! Sure I saw that. And I saw what the knights of the fucking invisible empire did to my own father. So, don't shit me about not handling violence. Right now, I've just seen enough for today!"

She walked away quickly, tears streaming unchecked down her cheeks. Krysty looked at Ryan and, without a word, followed the other woman into the bright sunlight.

Ryan bit his lip and stared at the most recent corpse.

It had probably been male, though it wasn't that easy to tell. Clotted blood, fly-coated, overlaid a scorched wound at the junction of the spread thighs. The victim had been strung up against the wall, hands chained and ankles also tied apart. The hair had gone, as had all the skin off the face, neck and shoulders. Ryan sniffed, catching the faint scent of gasoline. There were vicious whip marks across the chest, stomach and thighs. The deterioration of the body made it difficult to be sure, but there were what looked like a number of small-caliber bullet holes around elbows and knees. Most of the fingers were hacked away, and those that remained were bent and broken.

"Skullface," Doc muttered.

The other three looked at him, then back at the ragged, stinking corpses.

Ryan nodded. "Guess so. Muties wouldn't do this. Stickies might burn men, or women, but not this. This is someone else."

The thought of who that someone else might be continued to nag at him all the way through the ville and up the rise to the waiting wag train.

Ryan reported what they'd seen to only Major Ward and Elder Vare, refusing to talk about what they'd found in Salvation to any of the settlers. There were some delicate decisions to be made and it was best they weren't made by a mob.

He described the township, and told them that it seemed to have been raided recently. There was good water but no food supplies at all.

"Wood?" the wag master asked.

"Yeah. Enough to keep you going for weeks. Funny. Looked like a couple of old buildings, one of them a school, had already been pulled down. Plenty of wood with fresh edges to it."

"How about people?" the preacher asked. "Are there any of the Lord's anointed down there, Mr. Cawdor?"

"If they'd been anointed by the Lord, then they sure weren't talking about it."

"Dead, Ryan?" Major Ward took off his battered Stetson with a suitably mournful expression on his face.

"Dead as you can get."

"Those mutated sons of nukedom!" the preacher exclaimed.

"No."

"No?"

"Not muties. The way I read it, there were a few folks hanging on to some sort of life in what was left of Salvation. Along comes someone, likely this Skullface chiller they speak about, and he and his gang take over the ville."

"And they murdered the poor folks? Oh, that such wickedness should flourish! Are thine eyes closed to this, Almighty Savior?"

"Guess he can't be everywhere, Reverend," Ryan said.

"What do we do? Pass the place by, I guess. Or just stop for water and wood."

Vare wagged a bony forefinger in Ward's face. "If it be the place of blood, then we shall conquer it. Our women are tired and our babies weep for rest. That looked a likely and godly place down there. You saw no heathens, Mr. Cawdor?"

"None living."

The wag master looked to Ryan for help. "If this Skullface took the loco wag into the hills, then he might likely come back again. Anytime. We got no place to run. Ox wags don't get you away real fast. Ryan?"

"Not my business." He'd already made up his mind this train was bad news. Ward was right. Oxen meant death if the chillers returned. If they could butcher a dozen innocent folk, they weren't likely to draw the line at one hundred.

"It's my business, Major Ward," Vare's cold, grating voice continued. "Please see that my request is carried out. We will dwell in the remains of Salvation for three full days. Is that clear?''

Ward shook his head and clapped his Stetson back on. "Sure thing, Elder. Can't say I like it, but by golly I'll do it.''

Ryan left the one-sided meeting and rejoined the others.

The wag train wound its way along the blacktop until it reached Salvation. Ryan walked faster to snatch a word with the wag master, who was striding out, leading his pony.

"Be ready for trouble, Major. You'll see for yourself what's happened there. Could happen all over again.''

The older man grinned. "No way, son. You ever heard of lightning striking twice in the same place?''

"Yes," Ryan replied. "Yes, I have.''

CHAPTER SEVENTEEN

"A SHOPPING MALL?"

"That's right, son."

"Untouched?"

Ward nodded, pointing at his map. "Right smack on there. See."

Ryan sniffed. "I see a cross drawn, Major. I see the words Shopping Mall, Undamaged and Full-stocked. I see that."

"And you don't believe it?"

"Come on. You believe it, Major?"

"Man who sold me this here map said it was true. Said there was even some gas wags still sealed up ready to be driven away."

"Ah." That was maybe different. The idea of there being a shopping complex still unravaged any-where in Deathlands was so unlikely that Ryan barely gave it a second thought. But the story of there being some mint-fresh wags...

"Tempting, ain't it, son?" the wag master said, nudging him with a bony elbow.

"Sure. Course it is. But the chances of it being true..."

Ward grinned. "This here map ain't been wrong since I started using it. Water hole was where it said. And Salvation was just like it showed. Like manna for the chosen people."

"How far? Looks like a good day's ride from here. Northeast up into those hills."

"Day there, day back. Elder Vare wants a rest here. Don't need us, does he, son?"

Ryan considered that, looking away up the glittering metal rails, wondering where the locomotive had gone, with its crew of killers and torturers.

"Suppose Skullface comes back?" It was now somehow assumed by everyone that the railroad train had been taken by the mythical Skullface.

"We post a watch. Look out there. Anyone could see him coming the moment he leaves the foothills. Must be twenty or thirty miles off. Get a reception party for him."

"Don't know his firepower."

"Yeah, but we can hold the ville easy. Ring the railroad with blasters."

It made sense, and Ryan was occupied with the magical idea of an untouched mall, one with brand-new wags untouched for a hundred years.

"Okay. But I'll leave Jak, Doc and Mildred here. Me, Krysty and J.B.'ll come along."

"Just four of us," said Ward. "Be one hell of a scouting party. Start at dawn tomorrow. Just the four of us."

It turned out to be five. Jak flat refused to be left for two days among the settlers in Salvation. Particularly he refused to be left with the hungry daughter of Elder Vare.

The journey took the better part of the day. They kept their horses at a steady walk, occasionally heeling them into a canter. They stopped around noon for some jerky and a few mouthfuls of warm water, keeping on through the heat of the day.

The map showed the supposed shopping mall at the junction of two highways. They paralleled one of the blacktops that cut out from Salvation, angling away from the railroad, leading to a low range of hills, dull colored, like sand after a rainstorm. The junction was about eight miles beyond the point where the road reached those hills.

They'd seen the tumbling clouds, long miles ahead of them, that told of some heavy rain. Ryan thought back to the flash flood, but the terrain they were crossing was completely different—no deep draws to channel the bubbling, rushing water and mud.

As the sun sank and the light began to slither away toward dusk, Jak said he thought he'd seen something moving among the slopes ahead of them— something or someone.

But they saw no signs of life.

"We going to camp before we reach this place, Major?" Krysty asked.

"Safer out here than in among the arroyos, young lady. What does everyone else think?"

There was a general agreement with Major Ward's judgment.

With five of them they were able to split into ninety-minute watches.

With nothing to cook and no obvious threat from wildlife, there was no point in bothering with a fire. It wouldn't do anything to protect them, and it could lead any potential enemies toward them as easily as a billboard.

The night passed uneventfully. Ryan took the middle watch and was relieved by Jak. It was a virtually moonless night but the boy's parchment hair still glowed like a nuke halo.

"Nothing moving," Ryan said, readying himself to slide under his blanket, next to where Krysty lay asleep.

But Jak stopped him.

"Ryan?"

"What is it?"

"Can talk?"

"Sure." He squatted alongside the teenager, who sat cross-legged, cradling his huge Magnum blaster in his lap. Jak didn't say anything until Ryan prodded him. "You wanna talk, then let's do it."

"Yeah."

Another long silence. Far, far off they both heard the haunting sound of a hunting coyote.

"Come on, Jak," Ryan urged.

"Sharon Vare."

"What about her?"

"Likes me."

Ryan laughed quietly. "Like saying water's wet or red rad count chills. What about it? She hasn't been baring her...her soul to you again, has she?"

"No. But keeps talking. When nobody else hears. Every day."

"Talking? How d'you mean?"

Jak sighed and picked up a handful of fine sand, allowing it to trickle through his fingers.

"Says will fuck her. Will give kids. Will marry. Will fuck. Mostly will fuck."

"Why not? Oh, I know that her old man won't likely fall on his knees and thank his maker if he finds out, but I don't think he'll reach for his scattergun, either. So?"

"Don't want her."

"Hey, come on, Jak. Sharon's real pretty. Doesn't have the brains of a shithouse door...grant you that. But pretty."

"Wants marry."

"But you've been saying you wanted to leave us and this kind of life. Settle down." Ryan looked up as something fluttered overhead. From the erratic movement he guessed it was a bat. "And you know that we've all agreed with that. Fireblast, Jak! This isn't a real life for a young man."

"Like it. Like being with you, Krysty, Doc, even J.B. and now Mildred. Good. Friends. Not outcast. Like that."

"Sure, sure. But it's a today life and it's bastard short on tomorrows, Jak. One day we'll all get tickets on the last train to the coast, and what do we have to show for it? A lotta corpses, Jak. That's all we got to show."

The boy shook his head. "Not true, Ryan. You leave places an' people better."

"Well, that's a nice way of putting it, Jak. But that's not enough. You want to settle down and have kids with a good woman."

"Like you and Krysty?"

"Fuck you, Jak!" He raised his voice without realizing it. "Fuck you! What we do is—" He took a deep breath and calmed his flare of anger. "All right. Guess I got it coming. Don't preach if you don't do it yourself. But we will, Jak. One day we'll find the right place and the right time and we'll do it."

"Soon?"

"Sooner, not later."

Jak nodded. "Me same. Soon. But not Sharon Vare. Not her. Want to leave Salvation, Ryan. And leave wag train. Soon."

"Okay, Jak. If we can find this mall and its wags. Either way, we'll get out in the next two days. That fair?"

"Yeah, fair. Thanks talk. Go sleep, Ryan. Thanks talk."

Ryan lay down next to Krysty and pulled the blanket over him, checking automatically that both his hand blaster and the G-12 were within easy reach.

He closed his eyes and then heard Krysty's voice, barely a whisper. "Yeah, lover. Sooner and not later."

Eventually Ryan fell asleep.

CHAPTER EIGHTEEN

THE FOUR SAT on their mounts, reins slack, looking at the place that the map had marked. It was a good ten miles farther into the foothills, but it had certainly once been a major crossing of roads. The pass to the west was closed by a huge earth slip, looking like half of a mountain had come crashing down. But the shopping mall wasn't there anymore.

"Least it was here once," Major Ward said defensively, wiping sweat off his forehead. "Sign there says so, don't it?"

"It does," J.B. agreed.

Rubicon Pass Mall. Twenty store units under one roof. Air-conditioned throughout. Loads of parking. Open early, open late.

Ryan eased himself in the saddle. He wasn't particularly surprised or disappointed. It would have been a miracle if the myth had turned out to be true, and Deathlands was generally low on miracles.

It was impossible now to try and deduce the history of the Rubicon Pass Mall. The main outline of the walls was plain enough, so were the piles of rubble that had been the individual stores. Nothing else remained.

"Best be heading back to Salvation," Krysty suggested.

Ryan had known the woman long enough to be sensitive to shades of meaning in her voice. There was something there that *really* meant she thought they should head back to Salvation.

"Feeling?" he asked quietly.

Krysty nodded, looking tired. "Might be nothing to it," she said. "Just a feeling."

Their horses were tired, making it hard to move along as fast as they all wanted. The nearer they got to Salvation, the more Krysty became worried, constantly standing in her stirrups to try and look on ahead. Originally the plan had been to get to the mythical mall on the first day and then return easily the following day, back to Salvation before sunset on the second day.

Now that was shot.

The eastern sky was already darkening as the sun began to sink on the opposite horizon. The shadows had lengthened, and they were still a good fifteen miles from the ville, with the descent to the plateau to come and then the ride across the open desert to reach Salvation.

Krysty held up a hand, bringing them to a halt. "No good," she said, her face lined with tension, coated in sweat and dust, making her look like a carving of an Aztec goddess.

"Something wrong?" Major Ward asked, irritably waving flies away from his face.

"I've got a seriously bad feeling," Krysty replied. "The ville's under threat. I'm sure of it." She looked to Ryan for reassurance.

"Skullface?" he asked.

"I don't know. I can't see that kind of detail, lover. You know that."

The wag master stared at her. "You one of them doomies, I heard tell of, missy?"

"No, but I can sometimes feel danger. That's what I feel now."

Ward looked at the others. "Then I guess we best press on at the best speed we can make." He squinted up at the cloudless sky. "Looks like we could have us a good moon to travel by. That seem like a good plan to you, son?"

Ryan shook his head. "No. We could get caught in the jaws of a trap if we try that."

J.B. agreed. "If there's no moon, we can't risk riding on. If there is a moon, we'll stand out on that flat desert like cow chips on a girl's belly. Heads they win and tails we lose."

"Then what..." Ward began.

Jak interrupted him. "Fucking easy. Go round. Slower. Come in back."

The wag master looked at Ryan, who smiled. "Jak's right, Major. Only way. We circle to the left, and it'll lead us to cross the blacktop we came in on. That way there's cover all the way to the edge of the ville."

"But how long'll that take? If the little lady's right, then mebbe we should dig the spurs in."

Ryan looked at his wrist chron. "Be there around midnight. Best that way. Knife in the groin chills just as good as a sawed-off in the mouth, Major. We'll do it our way."

They moved on cautiously. During the detour they could just see the hazy shape of Salvation. Krysty thought she could just make out a speckle of lights that could be campfires being lighted for the evening meal. But that didn't mean a thing.

Ryan rode in silence, locked into his own thoughts, worrying about the mysterious Skullface and his band of killers. There had been something familiar about the way the inhabitants of Salvation had been mutilated and tortured before enjoying the mercy of death, something that yelped of a swift and evil nature.

It reminded Ryan of something from the past, but his mind wouldn't allow the memory to come forward and be recognized.

"Skullface?" he whispered to himself, shaking his head. "Skullface?"

Ward had been right about the sky. As the last crimson glow of the dying sun disappeared over the western rim of the world, a cold moon appeared, giving a sharp-edged reality to the landscape.

Ryan had been wrong about how long it would take them. The trail that cut up from the plateau toward the road was steeper and rougher than he'd hoped, and the animals were now pushed toward utter exhaustion. J.B.'s mount stumbled and fell, sliding fifty yards down the slope in a tangle of legs, sending rocks and pebbles cascading to the valley floor. The Armorer managed to kick his boots clear of the stirrups and step off as the horse went down, avoiding any kind of injury.

But it slowed them.

It was nearly midnight before they reached the blacktop, at a point less than three miles from the ville. An added complication was the sky clouding over, shrouding the moon, reducing visibility from a couple of miles down to barely a hundred paces.

Ryan called a halt. "These horses are totally done. Better we leave them here. Stops the risks of another fall, or one of them making a noise when it scents the other animals."

They all dismounted and tied the animals to a lone mesquite bush.

"If there'd been trouble, wouldn't we have heard something?" Krysty asked, rubbing the small of her back and trying to stretch the stiffness away.

"Not the way the wind's been blowing. Most of the time we were way too far off from the ville to hear anything short of a nuke gren going off."

As they left the horses, one of them started to nicker, tossing its head back, showing its teeth. For a moment Ryan thought he was going to have to put a bullet through its head, using the built-in baffle silencer in his hand blaster.

But Jak went and gentled the animal, standing in close and blowing into its nostrils. Ryan holstered the SIG-Sauer.

"Good trick, Jak."

"Christina told it."

"The Ballinger woman?" Krysty asked.

"Yeah."

They started walking toward Salvation.

Ryan was regretting the way he'd ridden off on this fool's errand without giving enough thought to the defence of the ville. Doc had the stoutest heart of any man Ryan had ever met, but that didn't mean that he was a great tactician in a firefight. Similarly everything Ryan had seen of Mildred made him trust both her intellect and her courage. But to have her trying to hold off this Skullface and his band was too much to hope. He should have stayed himself, or at least he should have asked J.B. to remain behind.

The Armorer was at his side. "Know what you're thinking, Ryan."

"What?"

"I should have stayed. Or you."

"Yeah. Damned right."

"Mebbe not. If they'd come at us in a big firefight, we could still have gone under. If Krysty's right and there's been real trouble, then it could be that you and me outside are a better bet."

It was true, and it reassured Ryan until they breasted the rise and looked down into Salvation. The moon had reappeared, and they could see the ville clearly, see everything—the armed men, the train standing quietly on the edge of town.

Then, the memory clicked. "Fireblast!" Ryan said. "Skullface! I know who he is!"

CHAPTER NINETEEN

THE FIRST DAY that Ryan and the others were away from Salvation was fairly uneventful. The liveliest moment had been a baptizing in the narrow creek that flowed past the edge of the ville. The oldest son of one of the coterie of preachers, named John Ridley, was in his early twenties and weighed in around three-twenty pounds. It had been obvious to everyone on the train that he lusted after Sharon Vare, following her like an overheated dog looking for a patch of shade.

During the morning he'd gone into convulsions and begun to speak in tongues. At least that's what his father claimed the garbled jabbering was.

Mildred, pointing out loudly that she was a qualified doctor, knelt by the thrashing, sweating hulk and slapped him across the face, sharply enough to snap his head to the side. Ridley immediately opened his eyes, flushing in anger at seeing who'd hit him.

"The bitch slapped me, Pa!" he moaned.

"Think the fit's over," she said dryly, standing up and walking calmly away.

But the settlers took it as a sign, and the young man was put down for an evening baptism.

It was all that Doc could do to persuade Elder Vare that they should still keep a watch out during the ceremony. One of the younger children had claimed to have seen a man standing on a ridge of rock behind the ville during the late afternoon. She said she'd seen the shine of the fading sun off something that glittered. Like field glasses, Doc thought.

Other than three reluctant sentries, every single member of the wag train, from youngest to oldest, lined the banks of the river. John Ridley was dressed in a long white shirt that came down almost as far as his knees. He was visibly embarrassed at being the center of attention, and his eyes kept turning toward Sharon Vare, who studiously ignored him.

Elder Vare stood by the side of the vast young man.

Mildred whispered to Doc, "Looks like that bit in Shakespeare, about the sow that hath o'erwhelmed all her litter but one."

By looking over toward the setting sun, Doc was able to maintain control over his face and not disfigure the religious occasion with a burst of raucous laughter.

"Dearly beloved," Vare began in his reedy voice, "we are gathered here in this wilderness ville to witness this young man, John Ridley, proclaiming his desire to join our Church."

He walked a few paces into the dark waters, which barely reached to his knees, holding the youth's hand in his. A battered Bible was gripped firmly in the Elder's left fist.

The creek was only fifteen feet across at its widest point, though it was flowing fast, with numerous eddies and swirling pools. But where Elder Vare was carrying out his baptism, it seemed calm and gentle.

The preacher led the congregation through a hurried version of the Lord's Prayer, then took two more steps into the river, bringing the water halfway between his knees and waist. Now the current was strong enough to make him stumble a little, hanging on to John Ridley's meaty hand to steady himself.

"Do you, John, refute the devil, Beelzebub and all of the minions and imps of Satan? Holding only to the true path of virtue and righteousness?"

"Yeah, I do!" the young man bellowed, closing his eyes and turning his sweating face toward the sky, where he imagined the Almighty resided.

"I will baptise you by immersion, as we did the apostles of old."

Vare, not looking behind him, took two more steps backward, leading John Ridley with him, the young man still staring blindly upward.

The watching settlers were transfixed by the ritual and its protagonists. Doc was staring at the surface of the water just behind the scrawny legs of the preacher.

He leaned down to whisper in Mildred's ear. "Truly doth it say that pride cometh before a fall."

"What?"

"Watch," he said, baring his gleaming, perfect teeth in an anticipatory grin.

"Prepare for the beauty and blessing, John Ridley, as I— Oh, fuck!"

There was a flurry of spray and both men completely disappeared.

"Told you," Doc said, as proud as if he'd arranged the vanishing act himself.

He'd spotted the slightly oily swirl and darker color of the river, indicating a deep, scoured hole in its bed, one that Elder Vare had stepped into, dragging the shocked young man with him.

Neither man could swim, and John Ridley's bulk had flopped on top of Vare, pinning him below the surface of the creek.

For several seconds, nobody moved. One of the women screamed out that Satan had plucked their leader away to Hades. At that moment the long goatlike head of Elder Vare broke the surface, mouth open in a strangled yelp for aid. Then an arm came out of the water, clad in white samite, and dragged him under again. Ridley's face appeared next, purple with terror, screaming for help. His voice so high and thin it sounded like a newborn baby's.

It took several minutes before the settlers got it together enough to rescue their leader and his overweight apostle from the creek. Vare was semiconscious, puking up a mix of water and bile, while John Ridley sat with his head in his hands, weeping copiously. The baptism was postponed indefinitely.

The next morning, the young woman who was on watch near the engine house reported that she thought she could see smoke. The word was carried to Elder Vare. Doc and Mildred heard the commotion and went to join the excited group of settlers.

"Smoke?" Mildred said. "Where?"

"Hills. Seems to be in line with the rails. Is it that locomotive coming back?"

There was so much fear in the air that you could taste it, slick and oily on the tongue, as bitter as a mouthful of aloes.

Knowing how touchy Elder Vare was about his leadership, Mildred and Doc waited for him to make his mind up about what they should do. But he stood there, mouth opening and closing slowly, like a landed fish, his eyes darting nervously from side to side.

"Tell us what to do, Elder," shouted an old man from the front of the jostling crowd.

"Yeah! Lead us, Elder. Guide us with your wisdom, Elder Vare!"

"We will... We will go and take a look at this smoke," he finally decided.

"Good plan," Mildred said sarcastically.

It was undoubtedly the locomotive, heading arrow-straight toward Salvation, trailing smoke behind it, moving at a bare walking pace and finally stopping, in a dip in the desert, about three miles off. The smoke faded away to nothing.

"What do you figure, Doc?" Mildred asked. "They waiting to attack us, or are we waiting for them to go away, or are they waiting for us to attack them? I don't get it."

"I confess that I am stricken with bewilderment myself," he replied. "If that is this legendary Skull-face, then I fear that his intentions are hardly likely to be at all benevolent toward us. Would you not agree with that?"

"Fuckin' ay, Doc. That's the way it looks to me, too."

Vare was like a rabbit squatting on its butt in front of a weaving rattler. He gave no orders, simply staring out across the sandy waste where the loco wag was hidden.

The day wore on and nothing happened. There was a single burst of dark smoke from the invisible engine, as though it were clearing its throat. Virtually the whole party was grouped on that side of the ville. Food was cooked and eaten around the middle of the day, but it was a skimped and hasty affair, with everyone wanting to get back to the old engine house and watch for the action.

It was only when Doc and Mildred created a fuss with the council of preachers that the menfolk of the wag train armed themselves.

"If that man is the coldheart that chilled those poor wretches you buried out yonder," Doc said, "I hope for all our sakes that you people are ready to defend this ville."

Reluctantly everyone carried a blaster, but there was no attempt at organizing any defence if the party aboard the locomotive should launch an attack on Salvation.

Toward the end of the afternoon, Doc came upon Mildred sitting alone on the shaded porch of one of the main-street houses. She was holding her head in her hands.

"Migraine plaguing you?"

She looked up, and the old man was taken aback at the look of worry on her face.

"Got a bit of a headache, but that's not it, Doc. I'm concerned."

"About the loco waiting out there?"

"No. Well, that's part of it. But not the main thing."

Knees cracking, Doc sat down by her. "Then share your concern, my dear Mildred. I am all ears."

"That's likely Skullface out there?"

"I would have thought that it was a touch more than just conceivable."

She nodded. "We heard about what a danger he was. A force for evil. And we saw what's probably the remains of his sport with those bodies."

"Indeed. But I confess I don't quite see where all this is leading?"

"Look, the train appears and then sits and waits. So every mother's son is out that side watching it. Doesn't anything occur to you, Doc?"

"Not really. Am I being very dense?"

"As thick as a pair of house bricks, Doc. You've ridden with Ryan for a long while. Hasn't anything rubbed off on you?"

"A little. I don't believe that I'm quite such a nice person as I once was."

They both looked up at the sound of the locomotive whistle, three long blasts, followed by three short.

"There," Mildred said.

"Signal?"

"If you were Skullface, and you knew that we could probably defend against a straight-on attack from the railroad, what might you do, Doc?"

"I might— Ah..." His eyes widened. "I might well bring the locomotive in to draw everyone's attention and then...then send some of my men in a wide loop to the south and come in along the same blacktop that we did. And take everyone by surprise."

"Right. Let's go talk to Elder Vare."

She stood and brushed dust off her dark blue pants, then realized that Doc's attention had been caught by something behind her, farther up the street toward the blacktop.

"Turn slow and easy," Doc urged. "Too late, I'm afraid."

There were at least a dozen men in camouflage jackets and pants coming toward them, all carrying blasters.

CHAPTER TWENTY

THERE WASN'T a single shot fired. The surprise attack, following precisely the pattern that Doc had imagined, took the settlers by surprise. Most of them were still gazing vacantly out across the flat land toward the locomotive. There were eighteen men and three women in the assault group, nearly all of them armed with M-16s, and they appeared from the hills behind the ville. A shouted command from a tall, slant-eyed man with a tiny mustache warned Elder Vare and his traveling congregation that they were prisoners. Blasters clattered in the dirt and hands were raised.

Doc and Mildred had been able to hide their own weapons under the porch of the house where they'd been sitting before the attackers reached them and swallowed them up. It was a poor consolation in the face of such an overwhelming defeat. Doc was more worried about what Ryan would say.

"He'll be so disappointed that I've let him down so badly," he whispered to Mildred.

"Not sure 'disappointed' quite covers it," she replied.

One of the gang was carrying a beat-up signal pistol, but it worked efficiently, discharging a star-burst of green and scarlet that hung for a few moments over the concealed train before vanishing.

There was an answering toot from the loco wag whistle.

Under armed guards the settlers were walked away and made to stand in silent rows on the cobbled stones in front of the engine house. From where they stood, they could quickly hear the noise of the engine and see the dark smoke that plumed from its stack. Less than five minutes later there was the hiss and metallic screech of brakes being applied, and the locomotive eased to a halt just a few yards short of the turntable in front of them.

Doc strained to his full height to see how many were on the train, and to try to catch a glimpse of the legendary Skullface. But a woman guard, with a barely healed scar that ran from her left eye to the right side of her mouth, jabbed at him with the muzzle of her blaster. "Stand still, you old bastard, or you don't get to be no fucking older."

"I really am most awfully sorry," he said, managing a half bow.

Mildred had noticed that most of their captors had a swarthy complexion, as if they came from close to the Grandee, and they wore a sort of uniform, like sec men.

Elder Vare stood a little to their left, his arm protectively around the shoulder of his blond daughter. Though he was trembling, the preacher was struggling to keep control of himself. He'd made one brief attempt to lead the others in a prayer, but the man with the mustache had stepped in close to him and touched him lightly on the cheek. Vare had recoiled as though it had been an adder's bite and since then had kept very quiet.

The sun was almost gone, and the attackers had gone around the campsite, lighting the fires that lay there ready. Apart from a small boy who kept whimpering that he was hungry, there was little noise.

Doc could feel growing pressure on his bladder, but he decided that it would be as well to keep quiet about it. The scar-faced woman didn't look as though a request to be excused would be well received.

"Sec force, shun!" The command came from the apparent leader of the initial assault group, bringing everyone to attention. Doc glanced around, seeing that a group of men—and one woman—had appeared, presumably from the train.

One of them was probably Skullface, but Doc couldn't make them out very clearly. The flickering light from the numerous fires competed with the rushing darkness of evening, throwing darting shadows across the buildings of the ville.

For a moment the old man was reminded of a painting he'd seen when he and the world had been young. He couldn't recall where he'd seen it—perhaps in one of the great European museums and galleries that he and Emily had visited on their honeymoon—but he could remember that it had been medieval. A scene from hell, with imps and demons capering around their helpless victims, tormenting them with forks and spears. It had been firelit, and there had been a half-hidden figure at the back of the picture who had seemed like the ruler of this infernal principality of pain and blackness.

"Must be Skullface," Mildred whispered. "Sweet Jesus, what a dreadful-looking man." One of their guards turned his brutish head toward her and she fell silent.

The leader was standing directly behind one of the blazing fires, making it impossible for Doc to see him. Mildred, a little farther to the side, could see him clearly.

During her childhood in the 1960s and 1970s, the black woman had seen more brutality than most people can imagine in their nightmares. But it had mostly been the animal cruelty of ignorance, overlaid with the unmistakable taint of fear, a fear that was sometimes hidden behind white hoods and sheets and was smothered in the safety of being part of a baying mob.

Skullface didn't look like anyone she'd ever seen in her life.

He was several inches over six feet tall, and she guessed his weight around two ten, a lean, gaunt figure, dressed entirely in black leather—tight pants and a loose jacket over a white shirt with ruffles at the neck. His high black boots were polished to a brilliant sheen that reflected the red glow of the fires.

But it was the face!

Thin.

That was the word.

A mouth like a steel trap; narrow eyes that didn't move yet saw everything; a carved nose that split the scoured cheekbones like an ax blade; a bald head, with a fringe of dark hair around the back, and a strip of black mustache that leaked down over both corners of his cruel mouth.

Mildred's doctor's eyes picked up on two other things about Skullface. The mustache didn't quite conceal the twisted lip that looked as though it had once been hit a crushing blow, and the little finger on his right hand was missing.

There was a blaster at his belt, and a rifle slung across his shoulders. Mildred recognized the pistol as a 9 mm Stechkin, but she couldn't make the long gun.

If J.B. or Ryan had been there, they'd have immediately recognized the unusual weapon as a Russian sniper's rifle, the SVD PSO-1 with a sophisticated scope sight. It was a gun so rare that there were probably no more than two in all of Deathlands.

The man moved to one side, hands on hips, a small whip dangling from his right wrist. And Doc Tanner saw his face.

"God save us all," he said. "Cort Strasser."

CHAPTER TWENTY-ONE

"STRASSER," said Ryan. Once he'd made the connections, he saw the skeletal figure, shining in its black leather carapace like an elegant and lethal beetle.

Skullface because of the gaunt, bony face, leading a gang of cold-stone chillers.

Ward was puzzled. "Who in tarnation's this Strasser feller?" he asked.

As quickly as he could, Ryan outlined the bloody history of the man called Cort Strasser, now known as Skullface.

A while back, Jordon Teague had been the baron of Mocsin, one of the worst pestholes on the entire gaudy-ridden frontier. But the ville had really been run by Teague's sec boss, Cort Strasser. Both Krysty and Doc had fallen into Strasser's hands, as had Ryan himself. His escape had been helped by smashing a pistol into the sec boss's mouth, crushing lips and teeth and leaving him permanently scarred.

Then, months later, they'd crossed paths again with Strasser. He'd recruited a gang of killers and was masquerading as the reincarnation of General

George Armstrong Custer. Jak had been a victim of the man's evil and perverted lusts and had barely escaped, snapping one of the ex-sec man's fingers as he did so. Strasser had managed to escape the final massacre on that occasion, and vanished into Deathlands.

But now he was back, holding the lives of nearly a hundred men, women and children in the crook'd palm of his hand. Including Doc Tanner and Mildred Wyeth.

"What'll we do?" the wag master asked. "I mean to say that even a real ice-heart bastard can't butcher a hundred folks. Can he?" Nobody said anything as he looked from face to face.

Doc felt as though someone had filled his veins with Sierra meltwater. Seeing Strasser brought back the shuddering, mindless fear that the man had instilled during the time Doc had been in Mocsin, his heart broken, no willpower or hope. He hadn't even known who he was or where he was. And for much of the time, Doc's befuddled brain hadn't even known "when" he was.

Mildred was only aware that the old man at her side had begun to shake as if he'd been stricken by the most virulent fever. She'd heard the name "Strasser." She thought she recognized the name from some fireside reminiscences with Ryan and the others. But she couldn't link it to any particular adventure. However, she had no doubt at all of the dreadful effect the sight of Skullface had induced in Doc.

"Cool it," she said, not moving her lips, taking care not to look in the old man's direction.

"Strasser." The word hovered in the dark air around them.

"So?"

"Death incarnate. Cort Strasser. If he recognizes me then..." Doc ran out of breath in his panic, and the sentence faded into stillness.

"You know him, Doc?" Unconsciously, in surprise, Mildred had raised her voice, earning a warning glare from the nearest guard.

"Long, bad story. Oh, bad, bad."

If she'd been able to see Doc's face, Mildred would have been very concerned. His eyes were glazed, like mirrors sprayed in a dull oil, showing no sign of life or intelligence. His lower lip drooped and a thread of saliva looped down across his unshaven chin.

The attackers had made no attempt to secure a perimeter once they'd taken the ville. There wasn't any need. As far as they knew, everyone from Salvation was already a prisoner. The departure of Ryan, Krysty, Jak, J.B. and Major Ward had gone completely unnoticed by them.

From such a distance, Ryan and the others couldn't make out what was happening. It was comparatively easy and safe to move quickly down the slope, keeping parallel to the blacktop, picking their way to less than two hundred yards from the edge of the ville. There was no guarantee that Strasser hadn't by now thought to put a couple of his men to patrol the outskirts of Salvation. To get caught now, or chilled by a lucky bullet from a nervous guard, would be utterly stupid.

"What's going on?" Ward hissed, squinting toward the circle of fires. The bulk of the ox wags were on their side of the township, and it was hard to make out what was happening.

"Looks like Strasser's strutting around telling everyone how clever he is," Krysty said. "Gaia! But he freezes my heart."

Ryan had unslung his G-12 and resisted the momentary temptation to put it to his shoulder and peer through the laser scope, center it on the lean throat beneath the white ruffles of Strasser's shirt and pull the trigger, stop that evil heart forever. At that range it would be difficult to miss. But the cost in human life could be terrible. They only had a single long blaster between them, and there were almost thirty in the attacking party, all heavily armed. If their leader went down, neck-shot and fountaining blood, there would likely be a dreadful massacre.

"What do we do, son?" Ward asked.

"Wait, Major. Watch and wait."

"Wait, Doc. Maybe he won't recognize you."

"He knows me, Mildred." To her horror she caught the glitter of tears coursing down his lined cheeks. "Strasser made me...made me do things for him. Did things to me, made his sec men… Laughed at … laughed.''

"It's dark and there's a hundred folk here, Doc. He probably won't bother to—''

"Shut your fucking mouth, bitch,'' one of the guards snarled, ramming the muzzle of his rifle so hard into her stomach that she gasped in pain and nearly threw up.

Strasser paused in the center of the open space, looking around him with a proprietorial smile, the whip tapping gently against the side of the mirrored boots.

"Very good. Stand at ease. Good.''

Mildred watched, trying to put into operation the things that she'd learned from Ryan and the others. Look for weakness, exploit it.

She sighed. It was impossible. The surprise had been total, and she knew that there was nobody traveling with the wags who could lead a rising against their captors. Though Skullface's gang was outnumbered by roughly three to one, they still had complete control. They held all the blasters and with them went the initiative.

A woman stood next to Strasser, and Mildred focused on her. She was dark skinned, looking Mex rather than Yanqui, and her long black hair was tied back in a ponytail with a bow of red velvet ribbon. She was only average height, dressed in a white blouse and a black, divided riding skirt, over knee-length boots, polished as highly as Strasser's own. She had a pistol at her hip and also carried a silver-tipped quirt. She was beautiful in a strangely blank way.

"My name is Cort Strasser. You might know me by the name that the foolish and the superstitious use. Skullface."

Nobody moved or spoke. Mildred was wondering whether Doc was slipping into a catatonic trance. And where was Ryan Cawdor?

Strasser went on. "My friends and I have taken over this ville as our base. We have made the locomotive work and it carries us to another, smaller ville, in the hills. You people may help us."

He began to move around as he spoke, heels clicking on the cobbles, gazing incuriously at the settlers as he passed them. Strasser had started on the far side from where Mildred and Doc were standing. Just a little past stood Elder Vare, his arm around Sharon's shoulders.

"We can always use workers. Women to cook. Men to fetch and carry. Children to—" There was a burst of cruel laughter from one of the bandits and Strasser slowly turned his long, narrow head, eyes seeking the man who'd made the sound. "Take care, Hernandez," he said quietly. "Children will be cherished. We aren't men and women of blood. Those who obey will live and live well. Those who don't will perish and perish hard. It's as simple as that."

He'd walked slowly past half of the settlers. Mildred noticed that nobody had actually looked Strasser in the face. She resolved that she would try hard to avoid staring at him. To remain anonymous must be the least worst option.

The lean, black-clad figure halted, looking hard at one of the settlers, a frail man named Caunter, one of the gray anonymous figures distinguished only by the fact that he wore a black patch over his left eye. With a thrill of realization, Mildred was suddenly aware of why Strasser had stopped.

"Your name, One-Eye?" Strasser called.

"Caunter. Robert Caunter, sir," he replied in a trembling voice.

Strasser stepped in very close to the man, lifted the metal tip of his riding crop and touched him gently on the face, beneath the patch. He nodded slowly and then moved on.

Ryan glanced at J.B. "What d'you reckon? Move out, or try to find us a place to hole up inside the ville?"

"Like that better," the Armorer replied. "Won't be that long before Strasser finds out about us. One way or another he'll learn it, then he'll put up guards or come hunt us. Best place could be inside."

Krysty tugged at Ryan's sleeve. "That row of stores. There were rooms above. How about that?"

Jak answered. "No. Trapped. Better gardens big houses west ville. Not trapped."

She nodded. "Sure, Jak. Guess that makes more sense. Wouldn't fancy getting trapped by Cort Strasser. No way."

Ryan began to edge away. "Can't do anything here. Probably nothing much'll happen now. Let's go and find ourselves a good place to hole up."

Strasser reached Elder Vare.

"You in charge, old man?"

"I have the honor of being appointed by the Lord as the shepherd in charge of this humble flock of poor sheep who wander—"

Strasser held up a hand. "Asked you if you were in charge. Didn't want a sermon, preacher."

"I am so sorry, Mr. Strasser. Yes, I am Vare, Elder Vare."

"And this?" The tip of the short whip nearly touched the breast of the man's daughter.

"Sharon, my daughter, Mr. Strasser. She is—"

"I can see that for myself, Elder. Indeed I can see that. We all can. Can't we, Rafe?"

The slit-eyed man with the mustache smiled. "Sure can, boss."

He was absently twirling a pair of rosewood nunchaku sticks, linked by eight inches of steel chain, the fighting instrument making a whirring, clicking noise in his hands.

Strasser beckoned to the girl to step forward, but her father stopped her with his hand on her arm. The skull-faced man never stopped smiling for a moment.

"We have a problem, Elder Vare?"

"She's my daughter and I won't have her harmed by someone like you."

Mildred heard Doc drawing several long slow breaths, as though he were fighting for his life, and heard him whisper, "Uh-oh," at the preacher's protest.

"Brave," she whispered to him.

"No. Stupid."

Cort Strasser ignored the whispering from along the line, his attention concentrated on Elder Vare and the pretty little blond girl. "Someone like me?" he repeated.

"I meant that—"

"What?" Strasser was smiling, rocking gently back and forth on his heels. He transferred the whip to his left hand, leaving his right hand free.

"Nothing."

"You mean nothing?"

"Yes."

"Your daughter's nothing to you, Elder Vare. Well, I think she can be something to me."

The tip of the whip darted in under the girl's skirt, thrusting up hard into her groin. She gasped in shock, her face reddening. Her father grabbed at Strasser's left arm, trying to push him away.

"Stupid," Doc whispered.

There was a narrow-bladed knife with an ivory hilt sheathed on Strasser's belt, just to the left of a large brass buckle. He drew it in a whisper of movement and pulled it once across the front of the preacher's neck, so fast and so delicate that for a fraction of a moment nobody in the crowd could be sure what had happened.

Not even Elder Vare knew.

His shock at the assault on his daughter had prompted him to snatch at the tall man's leather-coated arm. He caught a glimpse of firelight off steel in front of his face, and felt a sharp pain across his throat, as though a wasp had stung him.

He heard someone cry out and wondered who it was, though the voice sounded familiar. There was rain falling around his feet, pattering on his shoulders, soaking him in its warmth.

"Warm?" he said, as dizziness overwhelmed him and he slumped to the bloodied dirt, his hand loosing its grip on Strasser's arm.

There was a long, muted sigh from the watching settlers as they saw their leader die, blood pumping across the sand and cobbles. Sharon Vare turned away, burying her face in the arms of the woman on her left.

Strasser stooped with an angular grace and wiped his blade on the dying man's coat, sheathed it and straightened again.

Doc took a half pace forward, shrugging off Mildred's attempt to stop him.

His voice was hoarse with anger. "Nothing changes, does it, you murderous dog?"

Strasser turned, face puzzled. He stepped toward the old man and then halted. "Well, well, well. Journeys end in old friends meeting, Dr. Tanner. This *is* a surprise!"

CHAPTER TWENTY-TWO

JAK FOUND the perfect house for them to use as a hiding place. It was constructed from concrete blocks and stood in about a third of an acre of totally over-grown garden. A dusty yew hedge, dotted with towering spikes of yucca, made the house itself almost invisible from the side road that jutted from the back of the main street. The white-painted walls had flaked and peeled long ago, and the glass in the windows was crazed by the long scouring winds of the desert.

The back door had been kicked off its hinges many years ago, and anything that had ever been worth taking had gone. The main furniture remained, most of it only shells, ruined by insect predators.

"Fine," Ryan said, peering through the moonlit shadows.

Ward leaned his hand against the wall by a long picture window. "By cracky, son, but I don't see what in thunder you and me and three other good folks can do against that ruffian out there."

"Me, neither, Major. But Strasser's now holding two friends, and I don't see how we can just walk away from that."

Despite his heroic words, Ryan was essentially a realist. Living close to middle age in Deathlands had imposed that on him. He liked Doc very much, and he'd come to respect Mildred. But there was no way that he'd simply throw his life away for them.

"What do you think Strasser'll do, lover?" Krysty asked.

"Soon as he finds out what he's caught he'll probably try and hunt us down. If that fails, he'll look for some way of trading."

"Trading?" Ward asked, puzzled.

J.B. answered. "Strasser would like Ryan best, and young Jak here as well. They both hurt him. Ryan mashed in his mouth and Jak broke a finger for him. Man like Strasser savors revenge better than any other meal. Won't mind waiting for it. He'll likely offer Doc and Mildred for Ryan and Jak. Fair, straight trade."

The wag master shook his head. From the moment the gang took over Salvation, he'd been out of his depth, floundering helplessly. "So, what will you do? Don't seem likely that Skullface would keep his word in a trade."

Ryan couldn't control a grim smile at the idea that Cort Strasser might ever keep his word about anything.

Krysty sat on the floor, leaning against the wall. She sighed and rubbed her eyes. "Gaia! This is a bad one."

"Best all try and get some rest." Ryan looked around the room, his eyes caught by a painting of a woman with a blue face that hung crookedly on the wall by the door. "Didn't know they had muties before the long winters," he said. "Have to keep watch."

J.B. nodded. "Five of us. Have two on and three off. Split the breaks."

Ryan and Krysty took the first spell on guard, one at the front and one at the back. With an odd number, the normal way of arranging the rotation was for them to alternate. After an hour Krysty was replaced by Jak. An hour later Ryan was replaced by J.B., and an hour after that Major Ward was awakened to take Jak's place. It meant everyone had a chance for a reasonable period of sleep and kept the watchers fresh.

Ryan took the rear door, squatting on the floor in what would once have been the kitchen. The moon came and went, giving periods of good light followed by long minutes of total darkness. When you were on watch at night, you didn't use your eyes all that much. Should call it being on listen, Ryan thought.

As he waited, hearing the Texas wind sighing through the undergrowth, he wondered how Strasser would play this one. Most of the cards were already in his clawed fist.

Less than a half mile away, Cort Strasser was talking to Doc. The rest of the settlers, including Mildred, had been taken away and locked into the engine house. The corpse of Elder Vare had been

dragged by the ankles and heaved out into a dry ir-
rigation ditch alongside the railroad.

The only scintilla of brightness in Doc's heart was
the knowledge that nobody had yet told Strasser of
his connection with Mildred. But if the ex-sec boss
started interrogating any of the settlers it would only
be a matter of time before someone blurted out the
link, and told Strasser all about where Ryan and the
others had gone. The interrogations of the skull-
faced man had that effect on people. Doc knew that
from personal experience.

Doc had been taken onto the waiting train, finding himself aboard a coach of amazing luxury. It had
obviously been lovingly restored just before nuke-
day, bringing it back to its glory days. It was a bizarre experience for Doc, pushing his toppling mind
nearer still to the fingernail edge of madness. It was
precisely the kind of railroad coach that he'd traveled on with his young wife, Emily. Past and future
blurred.

Strasser followed him, sitting on a luxurious pad-
ded seat, resting his feet on the brocade material. The
woman came with him and sat in a corner, worrying
at a ragged edge to her skirt. Two of the armed
guards stood silently in the doorway, holding their
M-16s at the ready.

Strasser was almost hugging himself with delight.
"Dr. Theophilus Algernon Tanner. So good to meet
you again after so many months. You're looking
well, my dear Doctor."

With a considerable effort of will, the old man succeeded in jerking himself from the warm memories of the past into the bleak reality of the hideous present.

"You'll kill me, Strasser. I'm not the foolish, frightened old imbecile that you used to sport with. So I'd appreciate it if we could abbreviate this conversation and then you can get on with the killing. If you don't mind."

He felt absurdly proud of himself that he hadn't allowed his deep, round voice to tremble, even though he was as terrified as he'd ever been in his entire life. Sweat was running down the small of his back, and his mouth was sand dry.

Strasser nodded approvingly. "That's very good, Dr. Tanner. I'm genuinely impressed." He turned to the woman. "Bring us some liquor, Rosa." She was slow to respond. "I want it tonight and not sometime tomorrow."

The voice had the remembered softness, overlaying homicidal violence. Like a straight razor in a velvet box. The woman jumped to her feet and walked quickly out of the door toward the rear of the train.

Strasser watched her go and smiled. "Rosa has great strengths, Doctor. She will share any sexual experiment, no matter how...unusual it may be. And she also shares my own curiosity about inflicting pain." He sighed and laid his quirt on a walnut veneer table. "But set against that is the fact that Rosa is overwhelmingly, utterly stupid."

"Which goes to prove that even you can't have everything, Strasser," Doc said, rather proud of his continuing control.

"True. But let's talk about you. How've you been since our last meeting?"

"Well enough. Most kind of you to ask. And yourself? You haven't traveled far?"

Strasser grinned. "Life hasn't been unkind. I was lucky enough to fall in with a raggle-taggle band of mercies eager to work for whoever could provide them with the most jack. Give me a few good guns and I could rule all Deathlands."

Doc nodded. The more time that slipped by, the better were the chances of Ryan and the others escaping. He had no illusions about his own fate. Strasser would chill him. When the moment came, Doc had already decided he would try to snatch a blaster and ensure himself a swift passing.

"But what about you, Doctor? And what of my dear, dear friends?"

"Friends, Strasser? I confess that I was not aware any living creature would number you among its friends. Who are they?"

The vanity of the lean man was one of his areas of weakness. And Doc was prepared to try to buy what time he could by playing on that.

"Ah, Doctor. Friends. People that I'd like to see again. That's friends, isn't it?"

Doc glanced out of the window, past the tasseled draperies. But that side of the carriage faced over the desert and the distant hills.

"Most of my friends are dead."

"And mine, Doctor. And mine. But there are two that I would seriously like to see again." He leaned forward, swinging his feet off the couch. "And you know where they are."

"A clue, Strasser?"

The crooked mouth came close to a smile. "Don't do this, Doctor."

"What?"

The smile disappeared like a smoldering ember doused in water.

"Ryan Cawdor and the white-haired boy! Jak Lauren! Where are they?"

"I know that you and Ryan were never particularly close companions, Strasser, but why do you want to see Jak again?"

Strasser held up his right hand, showing him the missing finger. "Because of this, Doctor. The boy did this."

"Cut your finger off? I believed that he had only broken it."

Strasser rose to his feet and made a move toward the old man, who winced in anticipation of the blow. But Rosa came back into the carriage, carrying a plastic bottle that contained an amber liquid, and two small shot glasses.

"Ah, my dear little cock biter! You just saved this old fool a little pain. Pour out a measure of the rot-gut."

She did as she was told, handing one of the thick glasses to Doc, who took it, schooling himself not to tremble. He also fought the temptation to drain the liquor at a single gulp, sipping at it and then holding it in his hand.

Waiting, aware of an invisible clock that was ticking away time. Time for Ryan and the others to make good their escape.

"The rat-faced little bastard didn't just snap the bone, Doctor," Strasser growled, draining his glass in one gulp.

"I would like to relieve the pressure on my bladder, if I may," Doc said, trying to divert the black-clad man opposite him.

"You want what?"

"A piss." Doc glanced at the blank-faced woman. "If you will pardon me for the language, my dear young lady."

"No, and don't interrupt me again, you horse-toothed old fucker."

Doc nodded. He'd spent enough time around Cort Strasser to know that the man could only be pushed so far without a serious risk to life and limb.

"After he broke my finger and you all ran away from me, it got gangrened."

Deathlands was low on any kind of medical knowledge, and antiseptics were almost unknown. Doc wasn't surprised to hear the damaged digit had become infected.

"So I cut it off," Strasser said, baring his teeth again in a mirthless grin.

"You did?"

"I took this knife—" he flourished it in Doc's face "—and I laid my hand across the bole of a tree and I hacked the finger off. It took three attempts, Doctor, but it was useless to me and so it went."

Doc took another sip at his fiery drink, finding to his surprise that he'd somehow managed to empty the glass.

Strasser nodded grimly at him and sat down again, sheathing his knife and showing the gnarled stump of the missing finger.

"Now, Doctor, the night is passing. You may tell me what lies you wish. I don't give a flying fuck about you. Either you tell me the truth about Ryan, Jak and the redhead, or I find out."

Doc shook his head, knowing the futility of the gesture.

Strasser smiled at the gesture. "Oh no, Doctor Tanner, not you. I'll send Rafe out and bring in the youngest child and its mother. I shall press my thumb in behind each of the babe's eyes and pop them from their cute little sockets."

"They're gone," Doc said blankly.

"Ah."

"Ryan's here with me. Jak Lauren. Krysty. The four of us."

Strasser pointed at him, hands still together. "No, Doctor. I know more than that. The Armorer is here, isn't he? Dix?"

"Yes."

"And that's all?"

Doc reached over to put his glass on the table, buying a moment before answering. Did Cort Strasser know about Mildred Wyeth? Probably not. But if there was an interrogation then he'd find out almost immediately, and he'd be angry with Doc.

"That's all," he said. "Nobody else traveling with us."

"Truth, Dr. Tanner, my friend."

"Oh, yes. There's the wag master with them, an elderly man called Major Seth Ward. Sorry, Strasser. I forgot."

"Good. Five marks out of five, Doc." He held out the glass and the woman silently refilled it. Doc shook his head to refuse more liquor, wanting to keep a tight hold on himself. "Want to go for ten from ten, Doc? Try."

"I'm listening, Strasser."

He jumped as the bald man slapped himself noisily on the thigh. "Fuck'n blood! You've changed, old man! Be pleasurable to break you all the way back down again, wouldn't it?" Doc didn't reply. "But for now you just tell me where One-Eye and the others are, and when they're due back."

Once again Doc knew that Strasser could easily torture the information from any poor innocent off the wag train, so there was no point in lying.

"Scouting. Due back after dawn."

Strasser rose and stretched, eyes locked to Doc Tanner's face. "Sounds possible. Course, I'll ask around to make sure. But that probably means

Ryan's already here in the ville. Come first light we'll have us a hunt. Thanks, Dr. Tanner. Ten out of ten." He turned to the guards. "Put him with the rest and keep him real careful. Old fucker's priceless."

CHAPTER TWENTY-THREE

RYAN HAD SPENT some of his waking hours trying to look ahead and guess how Cort Strasser might react. The former sec boss would have Doc by now. He might have chilled the old man, but Ryan didn't see that as a likely possibility. Doc alive was far more valuable than Doc dead, and Strasser had always been strong on values.

Mildred was a different matter. There was still a chance that the black woman remained safe, hidden by the sheer numbers of the settlers on the wag train—until someone saw the value of betraying her. Ryan's choice for that role was Elder Vare.

By now it was more than a possibility that Strasser was aware that Ryan and the others were somewhere out there. Skullface's mind worked in simple ways: I have Doc Tanner, he'll know where Ryan Cawdor is, I'll torture him to find out. Or rather: I'll torture someone else in front of kindhearted Doc Tanner and *then* he'll tell me where Ryan Cawdor is.

So, Strasser would try to take them. That was one area where there wasn't any doubt at all. Forgiving and forgetting didn't feature in Cort Strasser's mind.

Stay or run?

To run was a tempting option. With the horses tethered back up the hill, they could put a lot of distance between themselves and Salvation, loop around south toward the Grandee and carry on like before.

"Like nothing happened," Ryan whispered to himself, sitting by the back door of the ruined house, watching the first tendrils of light from the false dawn creeping across the sky.

He shook his head. No. At least not yet. Despite what his tactical brain told him, there was no way he could just walk away from Doc and Mildred. Not until all the other options had totally disappeared.

If they were dead he'd probably try to pick off Strasser with the G-12 and then run. As long as he knew they were both alive he'd do what he could.

J.B. appeared out of the dim half-light at his shoulder, wiping smears of condensation from his glasses. The night had been cool.

"We staying, Ryan?" he asked.

"Yeah. For a while. That okay with you?"

The slight figure nodded. "Sure. Hell, I knew that all along, Ryan."

None of the prisoners were fed that morning. Strasser and his force were too busy for that kind of consideration.

A caldron of creek water was carried in, and the settlers straggled up to dip their cupped hands in it and drink.

When Doc had been returned to the others, he'd made a deliberate attempt to keep away from Mildred, knowing that Strasser was wily enough to watch him and see if he had any special friends among the group.

The black woman had caught his warning signal and had stayed away, waiting until Doc joined the line for water. Then she managed to push in alongside him in the gloomy confines of the engine shed, glancing around to make sure none of the armed guards were paying them any special attention.

"You all right?" she whispered.

"Thank you, ma'am, the agony has somewhat abated now."

"What?" Mildred wondered if Doc had really slithered back over the edge.

"A small jest. They know about Ryan and the others."

"How? You tell them, Doc?" She was unable to keep the reproach from her voice.

"Oh, there was a choice, Dr. Wyeth," he hissed. "I could have simply sat in that luxurious coach and watched as Strasser popped children's eyes from their sockets."

"Oh, shit. I'm sorry, Doc. Truly."

"He knows Ryan and the others are somewhere out there, but he doesn't know where. He'll try to hunt them down this morning."

The old man received a slap across the upper arm from a guard who'd stepped in close. "Shut youse fuckin' mouth, dog's prick!"

Doc kept quiet.

Krysty had found an old photograph, its glass cracked, fallen behind the shell of one of the beds. It showed three children, two boys and a girl, squinting at the camera in a placid, sun-drenched afternoon, before sky-dark and the mega-cull. Someone had written the names of the three children very neatly beneath the picture. Though it had faded, it was still legible: Cathy, Feroze And Randall—The Three Immortals.

Ryan read the inscription and laid the photo back on the floor, in a corner.

"Immortals," he said sadly.

Jak broke into his thoughts, calling in a low urgent voice from by the rotted screen of the front door.

"Company."

Ryan and J.B. had talked through their plans, though it was totally flexible, depending on what Strasser did.

With about thirty men and women under his control, the ex-Mocsin sec boss wasn't likely to commit them all to a dangerous chase. He also had about a hundred prisoners, which would require at least a dozen guards. Salvation was a small ville, but the buildings were well spread and largely overgrown.

"What if chance chill fuckers?" Jak asked, coming into the living room.

"Good question."

Ryan glanced at J.B. "We stay hid and Strasser might figure we're long gone. Could relax."

The Armorer bit his lip. "You figure that, Ryan?"

"No. Guess not. Too much iron and blood between us. He'll know we'll come back. So, if you get a safe chance to take one of them out, do it."

Major Ward stood to one side, hands hooked in his belt. "I was never that good at close-in fighting."

"That's fair," Ryan agreed. "Man says he can do what he can't can screw up everything. Just keep with us, and keep quiet. That's the main thing. Quiet. And keep watching for any signal. Worst comes to it and you have to start shooting, make all the bullets count. All right?"

The wag master tugged at his neat silver mustache. "Sure, sure." He had a clear note of hesitation and doubt in his voice.

"What?" Ryan probed.

"Never shot a man before."

"Good time to think about starting," Krysty told him.

Strasser did it the way that Ryan would **hav**e done it—two men each side of the township, covering any possible break from the buildings, the rest in a skirmish line, moving through the ville and trying to check out every house, store and garage.

But the derelict home that Ryan and the others had chosen was off the main drag, near the edge of the ville, some way off from the railroad terminal.

And searching for armed killers is a very slow and nerve-racking business. There could be a blaster behind every door and window, in every loft and cellar, under every shrub and clump of mesquite.

Strasser's gang were ice-heart killers, but they weren't a disciplined sec force. Within an hour there were complaints, and the line was beginning to straggle and break up.

Jak sneaked out, Magnum in his belt and one of his lethal throwing knives clenched in his teeth. He reappeared in a half hour, a feral grin showing his teeth, eyes glittering like bright rubies.

"Lost it," he said, glancing back over his shoulders, toward the enveloping yew hedge.

"They still coming?" J.B. asked.

"Sure. Some given up. Some one house, some others. Hot. Tired. Fuck-useless."

Ryan glanced out of the back window. There was a fresh temptation to leave the house and head for the dry creek bed, try to work around beyond the deteriorating line of hunters. But he resisted, knowing that the best cards would still lie in his hand if they all kept together and waited.

Their own water supply was shrinking fast, but the afternoon was well on, and once dark came it would be relatively simple to creep around to the river.

The house also protected Ryan and the others from the worst of the day's heat. It was very warm and sultry, with insects humming busily through the low-ceilinged rooms. But the pitiless power of the brazen sun was kept outside.

Each of them took a quadrant, waiting below the level of the windows, every now and again risking a quick glance. Ryan kept moving around, pausing and listening by the front and rear doors.

Every now and then he could hear sounds from the advancing searchers, an odd yell or the shrill blast of a whistle. Once there was a shot and a lot of shouting, but that had been over an hour ago.

Jak offered to go out again for a recce, and after some thought Ryan agreed. The more they knew about Strasser's plans against them, the better they might combat them. This time the albino boy was back in less than ten minutes.

"Close. Got three now on hill, far side creek, watching. Some gone back. All split up. Not alert. Strasser's far side street."

"How many houses away, Jak?" J.B. asked, drawing his Tekna knife with its distinctive, serrated back edge.

"Three."

"Time to get ourselves ready, friends," Ryan announced, drawing his own heavy-bladed panga and spitting lightly on the steel.

Rather than bunch together it had been agreed that they would split up and hide themselves separately amongst the lush vegetation of the garden.

Ryan picked a huge clump of brilliantly flowering hedgehog cactus, sliding in behind it, his back against the impenetrable wall of yew.

Outside in the later afternoon sunshine he could now hear Strasser's hunters drawing closer. He slowed his breath and waited.

CHAPTER TWENTY-FOUR

STRASSER HAD TAKEN UP a position on the western side of the main street, keeping himself in the spreading pools of shade as much as possible. As the abortive search dragged on, he was beginning to regret his decision to scour the ville.

His men were tiring, and it had been necessary to flog one of them into bloody unconsciousness to prevent a direct challenge to his authority. He tried to put himself into Ryan's mind, struggling to guess what the one-eyed man might be planning. All he could hold to was the certainty that Ryan wouldn't have left the ville while the old cretin Tanner was still in his hands. But where? They'd already combed through nearly three-quarters of Salvation, and there hadn't been the least sign of them.

He saw his lieutenant go across one of the side streets, still twirling the nunchaku sticks.

"Rafe?"

"Yeah, boss?"

"Keep 'em at it."

"Sure."

"The one who finds them gets the pick of any five of the prisoners. For anything they want. Tell them that."

Rafe held up his right hand, bringing finger and thumb together. As he half turned away again, Strasser called again to him.

"Tell 'em to watch out."

Peering around the spikes of the cactus, Ryan was able to see the corner of the house and part of the wall near the broken front door, watching as Strasser's patrol finally reached them.

"Tired and careless," Ryan breathed.

There were four—three men, and a woman in torn pants. All carried M-16s, and all looked as if they came from somewhere close to the Grandee.

They were only going through the motions, and if Ryan and the others had been hiding inside the house, all four would have died almost immediately. Two waited outside, either side of the door, while the other pair ran halfheartedly inside.

After a muffled shout, the four were inside and Ryan could glimpse them through the dulled glass of the side window, moving around the rooms.

Using the baffle silencer on the SIG-Sauer, Ryan was tempted to ghost in after the four thugs and chill them. But he figured that Strasser would probably have ordered some sort of backup patrol following to check any attempt to slip out the back door from the searchers.

The four came out again, barely bothering to take even a cursory glance around the wilderness that had once been a trig and trim garden. Three of them lighted cigarettes and stood together talking quietly. One of the men, short and plump, had allowed his right hand to creep around the back of the woman, fondling her buttocks, slipping his fingers through one of the ragged tears in her pants and caressing her high between the thighs. She, in turn, pressed her hip against his, turning to smile at him.

Ryan felt a trickle of sweat running down his chest, across the flat, muscular wall of his stomach. Moving with infinite slowness he switched the panga into his other hand, wiping sweat from his fingers on the thigh of his breeches.

Waiting.

There they were. The backup that he'd predicted Strasser would have ordered. But he guessed that Jordan Teague's old sec boss wouldn't have been pleased to see the languid way his men were now operating, late in the tedious, sweltering day.

They had their rifles slung across their backs, and they sauntered into the garden, hands in pockets. Both were smoking and greeted the other four with a negligent shout.

They all hung around, chatting, and Ryan realized that these six must be the lingering rearguard, with nobody else following behind. If they were going to deplete Strasser's forces, this could be the time to think about it. But it had to be done quietly.

One yell and they could have another fifteen or more armed killers surrounding them.

Two of the original four started to move off, leaving behind the pair of newcomers and their own comrades. The man and the woman.

It was the woman who said something to the tailgaters, getting a muted guffaw of bawdy laughter. It became obvious to Ryan what she'd been saying as she turned and slid down the zipper on the plump man's pants, inserting her hand in an utterly unmistakable gesture.

The two of them started to pick their way through the garden toward Ryan's hiding place, making him draw his hand blaster. But they veered to the right, behind one of the yuccas, and he could hear them pushing through some long, dry grass.

The last two of Strasser's men lay back in the door of the house, dozing in the late-afternoon sunshine. Away toward the street side of the garden, Ryan thought he heard the faint sound of a scuffle, but he strained and heard nothing more.

The only sound now in the garden was a woman giggling and then the sound of a slap, followed by laughter. One of the men by the house pushed his cap back off his eyes and joined in the laughter, calling out some words of encouragement to his comrade in what Ryan guessed was Mexican.

Bringing more laughter.

Now the noises that Ryan could hear from his right were unmistakable—a rhythmic, thrusting sound, the dry grass crackling as it was crushed down. The voice of the woman reached him, muttering in a guttural monotone, the words keeping time with the movements.

Ryan squinted again past the cactus, noticing that the pair of Strasser's men by the house's faded walls were both dozing, eyes closed. To his right was a clump of heavily scented mountain laurel, covered with violet flowers. Behind it was a narrow gap to the thick hedge of dark green yew.

Cautiously, and totally without any sound, Ryan eased himself from behind the cactus, along past the glossy leaves of the laurel, hearing the panting of the couple growing louder and more insistent.

The smooth hilt of the panga was snug in his right hand, and he'd slowed his breathing, maintaining full control over himself, knowing that the next minute or so could alter the lives of everyone in the garden.

Eduardo Mengele was drawing close to the gates of paradise. Maria Holt had been Rafe's woman. Then, when the lieutenant of Skullface became tired of her incessant demands, she had shifted to Raul. On to Iago Compostella and then...then Eduardo couldn't remember. But he'd begun to think that Maria would never look in his direction at all.

The news they were to hunt the township for a man with one eye, a woman with hair like living fire and a boy whose hair was like the cold snow on the high peaks beyond the Grandee had been painful at first. Then he had found himself allocated to a foursome with Maria—Thunderthighs as she was known around the campfires.

She'd smiled at him, taken the cigarettes he'd offered her and laughed at his joke about the mutie and the two handfuls of buffalo chips even though he'd gotten the ending a little wrong. As the day and the heat wore on, Eduardo had felt his need for her growing as he watched the chubby segments of dusty thigh that peeked through her ripped pants.

Now Boss Strasser had called them in, said they'd start again in the morning. Eventually they'd catch these enemies. Then there'd been pleasure in watching how the boss dealt with them. Eduardo Mengele knew about pain, and he'd never seen anyone so skilled as the black-clothed man in administering it.

Now, he was thrusting his way toward the gates of paradise.

Ryan was conscious of the strong smell of old dry dust as he pushed his way quietly past the sharp leaves of the yew hedge, moving with an infinity of caution until he could see the interlocked figures ahead of him.

The man was on his back in the small, trampled clearing, pants hoicked down to his plump ankles. The woman's torn trousers were in the grass and she squatted on top of the man, bracing herself with hands on his hairy chest, head thrown back. The guttural panting was jerked from between her clenched teeth as she neared her own climax.

Ryan edged around until he was directly behind her, out of sight of the moaning man, whose boots were now pushing hard against the sandy soil, pressing himself onward and upward.

It was a scene frozen in a wilderness. Apart from the thrashing couple and their silent watcher, nothing else existed. They could all have been a thousand miles away from another human being.

Ryan, crouching, stepped from cover, the panga in his hand.

Eduardo was locked tight in a living daydream. His eyes were squeezed shut and his nails gouged into the yellow earth beneath him. All that had been said about Maria was true. She was truly giving him two downs for every up, her hips sucking him deep into the warm, moist core of her body. Her nails were raking at his chest, but the pain was a tiny and insignificant thing.

"Oh, yes... Yes..."

Eduardo was coming, feeling the wonderful, draining, pumping orgasm overwhelm him.

Maria was sharing it, he could tell. A bubbling sigh of pleasure erupted from her lips and her body went slack, slumping down across him, hot sweat flooding the side of his neck and shoulders. His nostrils twitched as he caught an acrid, unpleasant smell.

Ryan leaned over the woman's corpse, trying to avoid the arterial blood that still gushed from her severed throat, and thrust the point of his panga into the man's gaping mouth. It splintered teeth and sliced his tongue down the center. Ryan put his weight and strength behind the long blade, driving it out the back of the helpless man's neck and a foot deep into the earth behind his skull.

Eduardo wriggled, trying to push the body of the woman off his chest, but her slumped mass kept him trapped. He tried to yell, but blood filled his mouth and flooded his lungs. His last sight as his eyes misted and life departed was the deathly smile on the face of the lean one-eyed man above him.

Ryan set his boot across the dying man's forehead and braced himself to draw out the panga, wiping it hastily on the woman's pants.

It was now important to move fast, before the two dozing members of Strasser's killer band woke up. If they could also be chilled without raising any alarm, then Skullface would take it hard. And it wouldn't do his people's morale a lot of good.

But there was no need to hurry. Both men still lay where they'd been, unmoving, M-16s resting across their thighs.

All it would take was two quick, carefully aimed shots from the silenced pistol.

Ryan leveled the SIG-Sauer, sighting along the slide, picking the man on the left first. For safety it would have to be a brain shot, between the eyes. The range was less than twenty paces.

His index finger whitened on the trigger, and he braced his wrist against the impact. The silencer was one of the best he'd ever come across, muffling the crack of the explosion to a quiet cough. He saw the man's skull jerk as the bullet hit home and a small neat hole appeared smack between the eyes.

Ryan's mind registered the odd fact that there wasn't even a residual twitch from the man's arms or legs. He lined up the second shot.

Again came the muted kick of the pistol. The other man's head knocked back, and the hole drilled through the center of the temple. And, again there wasn't the slightest movement from the body.

Looking around, Ryan parted the undergrowth and stepped out, the muzzle of the blaster probing at the warm air. But nothing stirred. Several houses away he could dimly hear the sound of voices calling out orders, and once there was the sharp shrilling of the whistle.

Like a child's puppet springing from a box, Krysty appeared in the doorway to the left of the bodies, smiling broadly at him.

"Made you jump, lover?"

"Stupid bitch! Could've put a couple of rounds through you!"

"Be like you to waste a couple of rounds, Ryan," J.B. said, easing himself around the corner of the wall to the right of the corpses.

"What d'you mean, man?" Ryan asked, thrown slightly off balance by what was obviously a private joke between J.B. and the woman.

"Look at the stiffs."

Ryan stared down and sucked at his teeth, grinning at his friends. "Fireblast! Couldn't see from over there. Both had their necks and chests in shadow. Nice ones."

The men had already been killed, which answered the question about why they had been so still when he shot them. Both had their throats neatly opened, the blood soaking quickly into the thirsty earth.

Major Ward appeared then, at the edge of the garden, beckoning to them with the barrel of one of his Peacemakers.

"The kid says he figures we best get moving as soon as possible. Thinks that Skullface and his men could be coming back real soon."

The wag master was pale, and he looked away from the two corpses by the house. The flies were already gathering, attracted by the fresh sweet blood.

Ryan, Krysty and J.B. followed him into the bushes, spotting Jak squatting on his heels by the rotted remains of the old front gate.

"You see the other two leaving, Jak?" Ryan asked. "We chilled the other four."

The teenager jerked his thumb behind him. Lying against the hedge were two corpses.

"Killed 'em both with thrown knives," Major Ward said wonderingly. "Damnedest thing I ever did see."

Ryan nodded approvingly. "Good, Jak. Real good. Now let's go find some other place to hide. Cort Strasser's going to be well pissed at us."

CHAPTER TWENTY-FIVE

"Six. Eduardo Mengele, Maria Holt, Jésus Martinez, Diego—"

Cort Strasser held up his hand and shook his head. "That's enough, Rafe. Names don't mean shit. But to lose six of our fighters, just like that..."

His voice was calm and gentle, which worried his lieutenant more than one of the boss's blinding crimson rages.

"The two by the house had their throats opened up and *then* they were shot."

Strasser looked up. The fine oval mirror, with its brass cherub supports, reflected his puzzled expression. "After they were dead?"

Rafe nodded. "Seems that way. Bullet wounds hadn't bled none."

"And two were butchered in mid-fuck," Strasser mused with a sardonic smile. "Ryan Cawdor is developing himself a fine sense of humor."

"Kind of end of fuck rather than the middle, by what we found," added the lieutenant, relieved now that it looked like Strasser wasn't going to chill him on the spot.

"And two with stab wounds. Perhaps the snow-headed little fellow with his throwing knives? Six dead. I think it is time to operate Plan B, Rafe."

"What's Plan B, boss?"

"Hunting failed. I blame myself for that. Should have figured Ryan would chill the shit out of some of the offal we got here. Now we'll enter the trade mode."

He glanced across the carriage to where the woman, Rosa, sat at the walnut table, playing a complicated game of solitaire. As Strasser looked at her she came to the end, blocked by a red ten. He smiled as she tore the card in half and dropped it on the carpet, continuing with her game.

"Yes," he said. "Change the rules of the game, Rafe. That's our next step. But we'll wait awhile. Keep Ryan in suspense. Keep the prisoners carefully and give them some food and water. A little."

"Supplies are kind of low, boss," Rafe said, shifting his feet uneasily, making the chain of the nunchaku sticks jingle.

"Yeah. First light I want a work party cutting wood. We'll head off into the hills day after tomorrow. Take what's left."

"What about trading?" Rosa asked, completing her game. Five torn cards were on the floor by her polished boots.

"Tomorrow. Ryan's not going anywhere, nor is Dr. Tanner. Tomorrow morning we'll have us a small lottery."

"Lottery, boss?"

Strasser stood up, locking his hands so that the knuckles cracked like pistol shots. "Folks like a gamble. Tomorrow morning we'll have us a lottery."

Ryan had been surprised by the reaction of the skull-faced former sec boss—or rather by his lack of reaction.

"We chill about a fifth of his bastard army and he don't do nothing."

"Doesn't do anything," Krysty corrected.

For once he ignored her.

"They found bodies. Watched." Jak was eating some peaches he'd found growing wild along the banks of the dry creek.

"Strasser even withdrew patrols," J.B. commented, busy in his nightly ritual of fieldstripping and cleaning his Steyr AUG 5.6 mm pistol.

Major Ward had been out into the brush behind the house they'd moved to, which was at the opposite end of town from their previous hiding place. Since evening he'd been taken short four or five times and left with a muttered explanation.

"Something I ate," he mumbled.

Ryan looked up at him. "More likely something you didn't eat."

"Could be, son. Belly's emptier than a hot spot crater."

"Too risky to go in tonight." Ryan glanced at the moonlit sky. "Strasser'll look for that. Just have to eat some of Jak's peaches and put up with the gut rot."

"Least we got water off that roof tank," J.B. said, holstering his blaster. "Flash flood did us some good in the end."

"Same guards as last night?" Krysty asked.

This time they'd been careful to pick somewhere unlike their last hideout. Most of the house had fallen down, food for giant termites, but an end wall and the rectangular garage remained. Ryan had chosen it because it was in such a poor state that no patrol would give it a second glance. And if they did, there was an alley out back that gave them access to another four buildings. It would do.

Mildred couldn't believe what she was seeing. In the opalescent light of early morning, the cobbled yard was bustling with people, and the feeling was like everyone was involved in an old-fashioned barn raising or a church picnic.

Yet Strasser couldn't have made it plainer what his intentions were.

Word had gotten around fast that six of the gang had been murdered by Ryan Cawdor the previous afternoon. Someone had seen the corpses being carried in on a flatbed wagon.

Food had been issued before Strasser made his speech to everyone, and it had lifted folks' spirits. Mildred found it hard to credit the overweening optimism that ran through the settlers. The surviving preachers circulated, openly telling anyone who'd listen that things weren't going to be too bad, that Mr. Strasser wanted some workers for a while and then they'd all be allowed to go on their way.

Mildred was so outraged that she grabbed one of them, Jeremiah Moorbane. "How can you all believe this of Strasser? Have you forgotten those tortured corpses we saw? Or what that skinny son of a murdering bitch did to Vare when he tried to defend his own daughter from him?"

The man smiled at her with a patient, saintly shake of the head, making Mildred want to punch his lights out. "That was yesterday, sister. And this is a new today."

"You brainless, worthless piece of shit! Can't you—"

But she saw the futility of it. Even before Strasser made his speech, the woman realized that no help would come from the settlers.

"A lottery, ladies, gentlemen and children." The skinny, black-clothed man had assumed the role of a tout, soliciting for trade outside a center-ville gaudy house.

Mildred hadn't been able to snatch even the briefest word with Doc. The old man was being kept apart from the others, ever since the word came in of the multiple slayings.

"Six of my people have been cruelly sent to buy the farm. But I know who's done this. One-eyed Cawdor and his filthy companions! It's their fault that we will have this lottery, and it's Cawdor who can save lives."

All around Mildred there were mutters of agreement, and several of the settlers turned to glare at her, as though it was her fault that Strasser's men had been killed.

"This bucket is filled with white stones. There are six black stones, one for each of my people. Everyone draws, and the six black stones get to pay the blood price for what the butcher Cawdor did." There was a murmur of consternation all around the yard as everyone came to realize the truth that lay veiled behind Skullface's words. But he held up a hand for silence and carried on. "But I shall make sure that Cawdor hears of this. All he has to do is surrender himself and the white-haired mutie freak, and not a drop of innocent blood will be spilled."

To Mildred's amazement there was a ragged cheer from the men and women standing near her, as though Strasser had just promised each of them a hatful of jack, along with forty acres and a mule.

"How about children?" a voice called out.

"Child dies just as well as a grown man," Strasser replied. "Every family with young ones has the father draw for them. Let's go."

For several long heartbeats nobody made a move.

Strasser slapped his whip against his leg, the noise as loud as pistol shot. "I'll not wait!"

A stout lady, breathing heavily, took a cautious half step forward, catching the eye of the skeletal man in black.

"Ah, a volunteer. May you be lucky. What's your name?"

She blushed at finding herself so much the center of attraction. "Name's Jackson, sir. Shirley Jackson. Come from the ville of Castle House, back east."

"Then you can come draw first."

There was a big oil drum cut into half and filled with small stones. It was placed on a trestle table, high enough so nobody could actually see into it. As an extra precaution a cloth had been draped over the top.

Watched in silence, the large woman came to the table, the light morning wind tugging at her sprigged cotton dress. It threatened her bonnet, and she raised a hand to hold it in place.

Mildred stared at Strasser. He wasn't paying much attention to the proceedings, his slit eyes roving around the crowd as if he was watching for some special reaction. Mildred dropped her gaze to avoid looking him in the face.

Rafe was standing next to the large bucket to check on what people drew. Shirley Jackson reached up and in, holding her stone in her right hand, closing her eyes for a moment before looking at what she'd drawn.

"White!" the lieutenant called. "Lady draws a white pebble."

There was a cheer, and everyone started chattering excitedly.

The lottery took well over an hour. Until all six black pebbles had been drawn.

Three hundred yards away, using J.B.'s glass, Ryan watched it all.

CHAPTER TWENTY-SIX

"WHAT'S LOTTERY?" Jak asked.

"A sort of a gamble," Krysty replied. "There's a prize and everyone does what's called 'drawing lots.' Means like there's lots of bits of paper and one has a red cross on it, or something like that. One who draws it out gets to win the prize."

"Oh, yeah. So what's prizes fucking Strasser's giving?"

"That I don't know," she replied. "You got any ideas, lover?"

Ryan had led the others down before dawn, wanting to get in close to the railroad, having a gut feeling that his old enemy might try something during the day. They'd picked their way through the stark blocks of ruined houses, crossing the main street one at a time, watching for guards. But there wasn't that much light, and few people saw as well in semidarkness as the albino teenager. He took over from Ryan at the dangerous points in their journey, holding up a pale hand to halt them as a patrol went by. Ryan was again tempted to make a further hit on Strasser's forces, but decided the risk was too great. The six they'd already chilled was a fair enough start.

Now they were safely hidden in the first floor of what had been Salvation's firehouse, a wooden frame building that now seemed held together only by a handful of nails and a lot of memories.

They were able to look out across the glittering tracks to the engine house and the open yard in front of it. The locomotive had got steam up, a white pillar of smoke spiraling into the cool morning air.

"Ryan?"

"Sorry. Thoughts were miles away."

"What do you think Strasser's prizes are in his lottery?"

"Easy."

"Thunderation! I don't see no dad-blasted way you could know, son."

Ryan glanced sideways at the wag master. "Think about it, Major."

"I did."

"I know," J.B. said quietly, taking the spyglass from Ryan and peering through it, adjusting the milled knob to alter the focus. "Reckon I'm certain."

Krysty, Jak and Ward still looked puzzled. Ryan shook his head. "Just do some counting. How many look like they got the different bits of paper or stones or whatever they are?"

"Five," the wag master said.

"No, six," Krysty disagreed. "It was six, wasn't it?"

"Yeah, it was six."

"Oh, Gaia! I get it. Don't like it, but I think I get it."

"Six?" Ward said. "But why six?"

Jak spit on the chipped boards beneath his feet. "Got it! Fucking dirty bastard!"

"How many of Strasser's guns did we send off on the last flight out, Major?" Ryan asked.

"Man and woman you chilled. Two by the house and two by the... Oh, yeah. Six."

Strasser switched on the big blue loudspeaker and blew into it, testing for sound.

"One, two, three... Checking for sound... Checking for sound."

The amplified voice, flat and toneless, filled the ville, flooding out into the surrounding desert, easily reaching the ears of Ryan and the others.

Strasser waved the speaker in the air. "All right, all right. Let's get to the meat and potatoes."

In front of him, heads bowed, stood the six members of the wag train who'd drawn the black pebbles in the lottery—two women, three men and one young child, who every now and again would look around for his mother and then turn away, gobbets of tears falling from his chin.

"This message is for my dear old friend, Ryan Cawdor, One-Eye himself, and for the people with him. I'm not that certain how many or who they are, but I'm not interested in all of them. Just Ryan and the mutie child, Jak Lauren."

"Fucker," Jak gritted. "Not mutie and not fucking child. Chill him, Ryan."

With the G-12 it would have been a ridiculously simple shot, and Strasser must also have been aware of that. But he still stood up there, tempting Ryan, confident that his enemy wouldn't waste him with the knowledge that the result would be a total massacre of the innocents.

"If Ryan and Jak come in here and meet up and talk some with me, then not a single drop of blood gets spilled."

An automatic valve on the locomotive opened and there was a sudden noisy jetting of white steam. Strasser looked around at the interruption, then carried on with his speech.

"I know they can hear me. I know they're in the ville. And I don't want to waste time on waiting for them. We have to get back into the hills tomorrow or we run short of supplies. So, here's the sharp end of it, Ryan." He paused for dramatic effect.

"Deadline time," Ryan said, taking back the spyglass from the Armorer, centering it on the gleaming black figure, easing it sideways a little to take in the trio of guards who were covering Doc Tanner. The old man had probably never received so much close attention in his recent life.

The amplified voice boomed out once more, the volume turned to maximum.

"Come in, Ryan. And the boy. Take your chances here. If you don't, these six good people will go down, one after the other. Every ten minutes by my trusty old chron. Nothing'll save 'em, Ryan. Just like the blood of my six good people, the blood of this six will lie on your heart.'' He paused again, then carried on. ''And after these six we'll have another lottery, One-Eye. And another. Until this square is waist deep in corpses and ankle deep in their innocent blood.''

Mildred knew instantly in the core of her soul that Strasser was totally, clinically, homicidally insane. She didn't doubt that he spoke the truth, nor that he'd carry through his promise until not one of the settlers remained alive. She also knew that if Ryan and Jak were to surrender themselves to Skullface, their passing would be both long and hard.

''You got ten minutes before number one goes down, Cawdor! Ten minutes!''

Five minutes later, in the sun-bleached bones of the old firehouse, Ryan stared blankly out across the baked land, his eye unfocused, his mind racing furiously. Krysty joined him, touching him gently on the arm, stirring him from his reverie. He looked around at her, seeing the question in her eyes, answering it.

''I don't know, lover. I truly don't know.''

CHAPTER TWENTY-SEVEN

THE DISTORTED, echoing voice boomed, "Nine minutes and counting, Cawdor! I know you're out there, listening, probably watching. So, watch this."

Mildred had eased herself back in the crowd, toward the half-open door of one of the smaller buildings linked to the main engine house. Her eyes roamed around, looking at the nearest guards, trying to find out what they were watching, how alert they were.

Ryan had twice brought his G-12 rifle to his shoulder, peering through the sights at Strasser, finger hovering on the trigger. Then he put the long gun aside, knowing that this wasn't the time.

"Too late this time around, Cawdor!" Strasser laid the speaker aside and gestured to Rafe to bring the first lucky winner of the black-stone lottery to the front.

"It's Frank Wells, boss."

Mildred recognized him. He was the brother of one of Elder Vare's cabal of preachers, a quiet man, who was married to a deaf-mute woman, who stood near Mildred, silently tearing a handkerchief to bits.

Strasser put the machine pistol onto single-fire. "Any last words, Mr. Wells?"

"This ain't right," Wells said so softly that his words barely carried.

Cort Strasser nodded approvingly. "That's the truth, Mr. Wells. Just step here and open up your mouth a moment. I promise you this won't hurt you hardly at all."

The settler did as he was told, looking up at the immensely tall man and dutifully parting his lips for the muzzle of the Stechkin.

To the crowd looking on, the sound of the shot was muted. The bullet tore through and smashed away the back of Frank Wells's skull, sending a chunk of bone as big as a saucer to land spinning in the dirt only a foot or so away from his wife, who promptly dropped in a dead faint.

Mildred didn't blink at the execution. The sight reminded her oddly of the home movie of the assassination of John F. Kennedy, with a mist of blood and brains hazing from the exit wound.

The same memory struck Doc Tanner. "By the three Kennedys," he muttered, drawing a warning glance from one of his trio of guards.

Of the group of watchers across the desert, only Jak said anything, and that was a single, harsh expletive.

Major Seth Ward turned his head and threw up on the dusty planks of the firehouse floor.

Strasser picked up the speaker again. "See that, Cawdor? That's one. Sure you don't want to save lives? Number two comes up in—'' he consulted his wrist chron again ''—in nine minutes and eleven seconds.''

The minutes ticked by, and this time it was one of the women, an elderly matriarch with a squint who tried to swing a roundhouse punch at Strasser and was eventually held by two of the guards. The bullet was administered, classically, in the back of the neck and she went down like a sack of rags, life flowing from her as the crowd looked on in silence.

''Soon be three, Cawdor!''

The discussion was urgent and intense. It was obviously out of the question for Ryan and Jak to even think of giving themselves up to Strasser. It would have been simpler to kiss their own blasters.

''Just chill Strasser,'' was J.B.'s suggestion, ''then put as much lead as we all can into the guards. Let everyone take their chances.''

''Doc and Mildred could go down, but we can't hold off until that ice-bellied son of a bitch shoots everyone.'' Krysty fought to control her anger at what was happening, anger at their helplessness in the face of Strasser's malevolent cunning.

''I know that! Fireblast! You think I'm some fucking triple stupe?'' Ryan was losing control of his own temper, unable to see a better option than that offered by J.B., yet knowing that the inevitable result would be a charnel house with dozens left looking blank-eyed at the sky.

''Let me creepy-crawl. Knife Skullface.''

Ryan shook his head. "No, Jak. That's no better than any other idea. Worse, because it'll probably mean you getting chilled as well."

Krysty punched her right hand hard into her left fist. "We have to do *something!*"

"Three!"

The child, a little boy, had seen the two executions, but clearly hadn't made the connection with his own presence out in front of the crowd. Now, as one of the women guards took him by the hand to lead him to the waiting Strasser, he began to weep, pulling back, red-eyed and bawling.

"Let him go!" a man shouted.

"You come and take his place? Then come on down, sir!"

"I will! Oh, Sweet Savior on the Cross! Spare him and take me instead!"

Mildred was now against the half-open door, hands brushing the flakes of sunbaked paint, testing it gently and feeling the hint of movement. She had no idea what was inside, but she knew that it had to be better than what was happening out there. She pushed a bit harder, wincing as hinges squeaked, unoiled for a hundred years. But nobody looked around. Everyone was glued to the drama at the center of the square.

"You the mother?" Strasser called, pointing the riding crop at the crying woman.

"Yes, sir. Yes, I am." She was in her thirties, with lank blond hair and pendulous breasts. Tears coursed over her cheeks and dripped down the front of her dimity dress.

"Then call out to Ryan Cawdor and mebbe he'll hear you. Mebbe the cries of a mother will soften that stone heart."

Strasser smiled contentedly as the mother of the little boy ran a few hesitant steps forward, cupping her hands to her mouth and looking all around her, as if Ryan were going to appear in front of her. The former sec boss gestured for her to start calling out.

"Mr. Cawdor! Come in, please do. And my Gavin'll be saved. He's only a little lad, Mr. Cawdor, and you're a man, full grown. It's not fair for him to suffer for you!" Her voice was so loud that it seemed as if her throat would tear apart.

Strasser picked a gap between her screams. "Fuck this, lady. It's a waste of time. Bust the kid, Rafe. Don't squander a bullet on it."

The hardwood sticks whirred like a plunging falcon and one of them cracked across the side of the child's head, splitting the skull like a soft egg.

The mother stared, unbelievingly for a moment, then ran clumsily toward the twitching corpse, hands outstretched. Strasser leveled the Stechkin and shot her once between the breasts, the impact knocking her flat on her back, hands flailing for balance. She fell in the dirt, still crying out. At a movement from Strasser the woman guard knelt and efficiently opened up the artery in her throat.

The speaker came up again to the thin, stenciled lips. "See that, Cawdor? Three and four go down together. Soon be five and six. Best give yourself up now!''

Ryan had the G-12 again at his shoulder, looking stone-eyed along the barrel, whispering to the others out of the corner of his mouth. ''That's it. Get ready and we'll try to—''

J.B., who'd been using the spyglass, stopped him.

''Hold it.''

''What?''

''It's Mildred. She's gone.''

CHAPTER TWENTY-EIGHT

MILDRED WAS AS MAD as hell, and she wasn't going to take any more. What she'd seen had pushed her back in time, to when she was a little girl in the South and witnessed the strange fruit that dangled from the trees, blackened and mutilated. Ever since then she'd been possessed of a virulent hatred of injustice and bloody oppression. Her only wish now was to find the house where she and Doc had hidden their blasters and their ammo and return to the stone yard.

"Chill as many as I can before they chill me," she muttered to herself, moving quickly through the shadowed depths of the building, passing relics of the railroad, including torn posters, signal lamps and, tucked away in a corner, a peculiar trolley with flanged wheels and a center-mounted pumping handle.

But none of that interested the woman. Knowing that all Strasser's forces were gathered by the engine house, she was able to take chances. She exited a side door, blinking in the bright morning sunlight, and cut across by the row of small shops and down an alley between a video rental store and a thrift shop.

She hesitated a moment as she emerged into a wider street, looking left and then right, finally recognizing where she was.

Mildred could see the house where the weapons were hidden, and she was already slowing from a jog when she heard the unmistakable crack of the Stechkin being fired again.

"Four," she whispered, four of the original six that the lottery had selected.

She stooped and fumbled under the porch, feeling the chill as her hands only encountered rubbish—old cans, amorphous paper, and cardboard and plastic. Mildred felt further, ignoring the booming voice of Cort Strasser through the speaker, warning Ryan that the deaths would continue.

"Ah, thank you Jesus," she said, fingers touching the smooth heaviness of gunmetal. She pulled out her ZKR 551, tucking it into the back of her navy pants, finding the handful of ammo and slipping it into her pocket. She grabbed Doc's massive Le Mat, filling her other pocket with his spare ammunition.

"Now," she breathed.

"Think Skullface'll really take the lives of all them good folk?" Major Ward asked. "Don't seem right to me."

"Doesn't seem right to me, either," Krysty agreed, "but that's what he'll do."

"Won't be long before he realizes that you're not going to come out," J.B. said. "Then what, Ryan?"

"Then he'll use Doc. That'll be the next step along."

There were still two of the doomed hostages, standing together. One was visibly weeping, but the other was managing an outward display of bravery.

"Mildred?" Jak asked.

"She'll be looking for us, I guess. Mebbe we should move to try to link up with her."

They all heard Strasser again. "I'm getting tired of this, One-Eye! Let's take out five and six together. Then I figure it's time for our mutual friend, Theophilus Tanner, to do his stuff. Maybe he'll be more persuasive than me."

J.B. had the glass to his eye, his spectacles pushed up on his forehead, in the shade of the fedora's brim.

"Making them kneel," he reported. "Doc's still got three blasters around him. They're watching the killings. Everyone is."

Ryan reached a decision. "That's enough. I'm going to chill Strasser now. We'll go in and take out who we can. Rest'll have to look to their luck. It's gone on long enough." He brought the smooth shape of the G-12 to his shoulder.

"Strasser's come down off his box."

"I can still hit him. A head shot."

J.B. was scanning the crowd. "They look like they're all in shock. Don't know how... Dark night!"

Ryan took his finger off the trigger. "What is it?"

The Armorer turned to him. "It's Mildred. She just came back."

Mildred had heard Strasser's booming voice, promising the double execution, and she hurried to rejoin the crowd of settlers. She'd hidden Doc's old pistol in the top of her pants, pulling out her white blouse to cover it. Her own pistol was resting snugly in the small of her back.

The door she'd escaped through still stood a few inches ajar. Mildred slowed to a cautious walk, aware that there could easily be armed men waiting for her behind that door.

"If there are, then there are," she said, drawing the Czech target revolver and feeling its reassuring weight in her hand. There would be real compensation if only she could take some of them with her, leave things a little cleaner.

Through the gap, she could see the backs of some of the settlers, none of them looking in her direction. Every one of them was staring fixedly toward the center of the square.

Mildred eased herself through the doorway, blinking as her eyes adjusted again to the bright morning sunlight. The corpses lay where they'd fallen, the pools of blood thick with gorging flies. Two men knelt before Strasser, one of them with his hands clasped together in prayer. The leader of the gang stood towering over them, the Stechkin held loosely in his right hand. Over to the right, near the entrance to one of the engine-house buildings, Doc Tanner stood with three armed men around him. The rest of the twenty or so guards stood in a loose circle, three or four of them near the locomotive.

The settlers were like a flock of patient sheep, their faces showing emotions that ran from anger to blank disbelief. But the threat of the overwhelming firepower kept them cowed.

"Very well, Cawdor! Here goes with the next two! And then we'll take us a break and have us another lottery."

Mildred was about forty yards from Cort Strasser, barely half that distance away from Doc Tanner. She eased the ZKR 551 from its hiding place.

J.B. dropped the glass. "Rad-blast it!"

"What?"

"Get ready. I just spotted Mildred pull out that target blaster of hers."

In the square Mildred steadied her breathing, making a conscious effort to slow her heart. She used the Zen techniques that she'd been taught when she'd taken up pistol shooting, techniques that had brought her an Olympic silver medal.

Strasser was leveling the machine pistol, his reptilian tongue darting out to brush his bloodless lips.

"Listen to death, Ryan Cawdor!" the leather-clad figure screeched.

"Spare me, Jesus!" one of the kneeling men yelled.

"Die slow, you bastard," said the other, face turned stubbornly up to Strasser.

"Die fast, fucker," the ex-sec boss replied, squeezing the trigger twice.

The first bullet drilled between the man's eyes, knocking him on his back in the dirt, all life immediately gone.

The noise of the gun made the praying man start sideways, so that Strasser's second shot, even at point-blank range, nearly missed. It ripped off his ear, creasing his skull, bringing a fountain of blood, the spent round burying itself in the man's right shoulder.

He slapped at Strasser in his agonized shock, struggling to get to his feet. The Stechkin snapped a third time and he went down alongside the other corpses, one hand opening and closing convulsively.

The cobbled yard was totally silent, and every single pair of eyes was focused on the scene of the brutal executions.

Every pair of eyes but one.

Mildred's.

As calmly as if she stood in the target butts of her old hometown of Lincoln, Nebraska, she leveled the revolver and began to shoot, careful, spaced shots, picking her targets with care.

"Let's go," Ryan ordered.

CHAPTER TWENTY-NINE

Doc was the only person out in the yard who'd spotted the disappearance of the stocky black woman, and it had been a great relief to him to see her make her safe getaway. If Strasser hadn't been blinded by his own quest for vengeance against Ryan and Jak, he'd probably have followed a slower course of careful interrogation, which would have meant speedy betrayal for Mildred.

Now she was gone.

Doc had taken a private wager with himself, trying to figure out what Ryan would be doing. He guessed that the first deaths would do nothing to stir him from hiding, and that Ryan's fighting brain would tell him that Strasser would go through with his threat, would massacre every man, woman and child on the wag train just to ease his own lust for blood.

The only question was, when would Ryan make some sort of move and how would he do it?

Doc knew his own fate was sealed. The odds were too high for any rescue bid, but there was the hope that Ryan might be able to use his rifle to take the life of Cort Strasser, even though it wouldn't save most of the hostages.

"Might be joining you shortly, Emily, my dear," the old man whispered.

Then Mildred came back again. Doc blinked, wondering whether his brain had slipped sideways into the darkness once more.

"Why?" he said, wincing at the triple echo of the last execution shots. Then he saw the gleam of sunlight off blued steel and he knew.

"Save a last bullet for the woman." The words rolled around Mildred's mind, even though she couldn't recall what old flick she'd heard them in. It sounded like big John Wayne should have said them. Maybe he did.

The Zbrojovka revolver had been chambered to use the common Smith & Wesson .38-caliber rounds, six of them. Mildred had thought through what she was going to do with all six, and she moved her hand steadily from target to target.

For someone who had a party trick of putting a bullet clean through the center pip of the five of hearts at thirty long paces, killing men at less than that range wasn't hard. Not once you'd set your mind to doing it.

Doc winced at the hot slicing sound of the bullet that killed the guard on his immediate left, striking him smack between the eyes with a noise like a whiplash.

One and a half seconds later, before anyone had time to react and move, there was the same hissing sound, followed by the venomous crack of high-velocity lead impacting on human skin and bone.

The third of Doc's personal guards had begun to turn, eyes raking the rows of startled faces, where heads were beginning to seek the source of the shots. But he was way too slow.

Doc, still ducking, noticed a different note as the third of the .38s struck home. Instead of the flat slap, there was a more muffled, pulpy noise. He glanced at the lean man as he fell, seeing that Mildred had shot him clean through the left eye, the bullet exploding the aqueous jelly from the socket, leaving a dark hole that leaked a little clear fluid.

"Black bitch!" Cort Strasser roared.

He jumped off to one side, diving full length in the bloodied sand, behind the two most recent bodies. Around him, the men and women of his gang were reacting with varying degrees of speed.

Mildred shifted her aim from Strasser at the last fraction of a second, putting her fourth bullet through the side of the head, just above the left ear, of the nearest guard. The bearded man spun to the cobbles.

Out of the corner of her eye she noticed another man in a camouflage jacket drop his rifle, hands flying to his throat, where blood was gushing from a gaping wound.

"Ryan," she breathed.

By one of the broken windows of the firehouse, Ryan cursed. "Fireblast! Missed the dog. He got down fast. Took out one of his curs."

The woman with the barely healed scar that disfigured her face was close to Mildred's left. "Bitch!" she yelped, the word mutilated by her badly broken nose. She spun and opened fire with her M-16, nearly cutting in half the man next to Mildred, whose flesh saved the black woman from instant death.

"Bitch yourself," Mildred spit, putting a fifth bullet through the shattered bridge of her nose.

"Doc! Run for it!" Mildred had backed again into the half-open doorway, wincing as a burst of fire tore splinters from the frame near her head. She wasn't sure, but the blaster sounded like Strasser's Russian Stechkin pistol.

But now it was the lords of chaos who leaped grinning into the arena of death.

Ryan had gunned down two more of the attacking band with his Heckler & Koch, cutting Strasser's force still further. The original thirty was now barely half.

The survivors had begun to open fire, shooting indiscriminately, spraying the huddled masses of the settlers, killing twenty of them in the first few seconds.

Doc saw his chance and took it, knees cracking like cherry bombs as he hurdled a dying woman and dodged around a crimson-masked man who tried to tear him into his embrace. Mildred was beckoning frantically to him, waving his own beloved Le Mat pistol in her free left hand.

A blaster kicked sand around his feet and something plucked at the sleeve of his old-fashioned frock coat, but he ignored it.

Mildred moved farther into the doorway, holding her revolver with its vital, last bullet set under the hammer. She saw Doc closing fast, then she spotted one of Strasser's thugs with his rifle at his shoulder, drawing a bead on the old man.

She didn't hesitate, aiming and firing in one sinuous movement. The big .38 round struck the stock of the M-16, took off the top joint of the shootist's thumb, then ripped into his right cheek. Splinters of wood and lead peeled away the flesh like a surgeon's scalpel, shredding the sighting right eye.

J.B., Krysty, Jak and the major watched the killing ground. Only a little group of women, clutching children, remained upright. Everyone else was either lying down taking cover, or they were chilled. Ryan had taken out six of Strasser's butchers, accidentally killing one of the settlers when he darted for cover across the line of fire.

"Chill the old man!" Strasser shouted, keeping himself safely behind cover, not realizing that Mildred's blaster held only six rounds.

A stunted man in a camouflage jacket, and pants cut off at the knees, suddenly erupted from the ground in front of Doc, holding his carbine at the hip. His face was twisted with anger and hatred, and a thread of spittle hung from his lip.

Ryan saw him and fired a shot, but he was too quick and the bullet missed by a clear couple of feet.

Doc skidded to a halt, looking past the venomous dwarf to Mildred, appealing for her to shoot. Like Strasser, he hadn't been counting rounds.

The woman shoved the empty revolver in her belt and tugged out the massive Le Mat. Its scattergun barrel wouldn't do the job at anything over a few feet. It might wound the killer or distract him, but it wouldn't save Doc's life. Holding the gun by its polished walnut grips, Mildred lobbed it high in the air.

"Catch it!"

There was a brief cessation in the fusillade, and her voice rang out like a warning bell, making Strasser's man half turn toward her, a nervous tic pulling at the corner of his mouth.

Ryan saw something flying through the air, reflecting the sun. It hung for a long moment at the zenith of its flight, then began to fall earthward, toward the waiting hands of Doc.

"Catch it," Ryan said quietly.

Doc realized that the Le Mat was going to drop short and he began to move, powering himself forward and to his right. Fingers straining, he brushed the metal, dropped it, fumbling again and plucking it from the air, inches from the dirt. He nearly let it fall as he landed, rolling clumsily on one shoulder and coming up, miraculously, with the blaster cocked and ready in his fist.

Strasser's man stood gaping, less than a yard away, his finger numb on the trigger of his M-16, half second away from buying the farm.

Doc pulled back on the Le Mat's trigger, feeling the powerful jolt from the .63-caliber shotgun round.

There was the boom of the charge and a burst of black powder smoke. Standing behind the diminutive killer, Mildred had a ringside view of the effect of the big Le Mat blaster.

Sharon Vare was cowering in the dirt just behind, and the shock of the Le Mat lifted the small man's body clear on top of her. The scattered round had starred into his throat and ripped it apart. The artery fountained with bright blood, and chips of shattered vertebrae peppered the wall near Mildred. His lower jaw vanished in a welter of crimson, speckled with fragments of ivory.

"Come on, Doc!" Mildred yelled, seeing the old man frozen on his knees, a rictus of delight on his face at his own agility and the success of the shot.

He rose and lumbered toward her, sliding through the door moments before Strasser emptied his machine pistol at him.

"Thank you, my dear Mildred," Doc panted. "I am considerably in your debt."

She squeezed his arm, fighting to control her own incipient shock. "Yeah. Now let's haul ass out of here."

Cort Strasser shared her sentiments. It had to be Ryan Cawdor who was picking off his forces from cover somewhere on the edge of the ville, and using a long gun with lethal accuracy. At a quick count, Strasser could only see about a dozen of his original strength still moving.

"We got them cold," Ryan said, squinting out of the firehouse. "Mildred and Doc are safe away. Bastard Strasser's lost his cards. We circle around him and we could hit the ones left."

"How many of the good folks are still living?" Ward asked, voice trembling.

J.B. answered him. "Could be half of 'em chilled, Major. Still means a lot more living than if we'd held off."

Krysty was leaning against a rotting window-frame, shading her emerald eyes as she stared toward Salvation. "They're breaking for it," she said. "Strasser's hiding behind a group of the women, going for the loco wag."

Ryan managed to shoot two more of the gang as they moved toward the waiting locomotive. They didn't bother to use the turntable to move the train the right way. As soon as Strasser was aboard, encouraged from a carriage window by his woman, smoke began to gush from the stack. The wheels spun around as the reverse gear was engaged too quickly, but the train eventually began to move slowly toward the mountains.

The last that Ryan saw of Strasser was a fist shaken from the driver's cab of the vanishing train.

When Sharon Vare saw Jak she ran to him, throwing her arms around his neck, crying in great sobbing gulps. She was covered in dappled patches of drying blood.

The scene was one of total confusion. The cobbled yard was slippery with pools of scarlet, and the dead and dying were everywhere. By the time Ryan led his group back into the ville, every one of Strasser's gang within Salvation was dead. Most had died quick and clean, taken out by Mildred or Ryan himself. Two had been wounded, and they'd been butchered by the women of the wag train, who'd used scissors and knives.

Major Ward took a swift count of the losses of the settlers, reporting back to Ryan with a grim face. "Hell, son, it's bad. More'n half gone to meet their maker, another dozen with bullet wounds. Elder Vare was first to go, it seems."

"Yeah. Doc and Mildred told us that already."

The wag master had aged ten years in a single morning, and he shook his head in bewilderment. "Over seventy dead right here."

"Strasser would have slaughtered every one," Mildred told him. "You have to believe that."

"I guess so, ma'am. But what happens now?"

The twin steel rails arrowed away from the township. A black dot topped with a smudge of gray showed that Strasser was nearly in the hills.

"Shame there isn't another of those loco wags," Ryan said. "The odds are way down now, and I'd like to go after Strasser. Try to end it."

Mildred managed a smile. "Not exactly a loco wag, Ryan. But it'll do."

CHAPTER THIRTY

THERE WERE FAREWELLS.

From most of the settlers there was a bitterness that verged on outright hatred and violence. Several of the older women survivors spit at Ryan and the others. Sharon Vare wouldn't be separated from Jak, throwing herself at him even when she was forcibly removed.

"Let him be, child," urged a white-haired matriarch. "Him and the one-eyed man and the rest just brought us trouble and a mess of dying. We got to leave this place of blood as quick as we can. Set him by, girl."

"I won't, y'old witch, Carrie Reece! He come back and saved us. Jakkie loves me true and wants to come with us and be with me forever and ever. Don't you, lover?"

"Jakkie!" exclaimed J.B., who stood with the others, watching the touching scene.

"Fuck you," the teenager said very quietly. Despite his pallid complexion, Ryan could almost have sworn that the albino was blushing.

"He wants to stay, don't you, honeybunch?" the girl protested.

"Do you, Jak?" Ryan asked. "Often said you wanted to drop out when you meet the right woman. You met her?"

"Yeah."

"Yeah?" Krysty said, her eyes wide in surprise.

"Want drop out one day."

"But you also said something about wishing to make the acquaintance of a suitable young person of the opposite gender, did you not, Jak?" Doc asked.

"Yeah. Find woman."

Sharon Vare clutched at his hand, pressing it to her lips. "And now you've found me, dear heart, haven't you?"

"No."

"Oh, my breaking heart! You said you'd met the right woman." She stood, hands on hips, glaring at him accusingly.

"Yeah."

"Me!"

"No."

Everyone was now thoroughly confused. Ryan was the only one who saw the gleam of light in what Jak had been saying.

"You mean that Sharon here isn't the lady you've found. But you have, somewhere, found yourself a lady. And you want to leave us now to go and be with her. That it?"

"Two out three, Ryan." The albino grinned, eyes glittering like tiny chips of living fire.

"Now *I* don't know what the dark night's going on."

Jak sighed. "One. Not her." He pointed a long, slender figure at Sharon Vare. "Two, woman someplace. Yeah." He smiled at Ryan. "Three, not leave you now. One day. Mebbe close, Ryan. Not yet."

"Want to tell us who the lucky young woman is?" Mildred asked.

"No."

Everyone drifted away from the outlanders, leaving only Major Ward to watch them as they got the pump trolley out of the cobwebbed building, heaving it up onto the rails.

"Wish I could come with you, folks," he said, tugging at his mustache. "Like to see that Strasser down in his own blood."

"It'll happen," Ryan promised. "You got these people to get on the way to their own promised land. Won't be easy."

The wag master smiled. "Just between you and me, son, I'm not heartbroken that Elder Vare ain't with us no more."

Ryan grinned. "Know what you mean. But we gotta go."

"Man's got to do what a man's got to do," Krysty said, shaking the gnarled hand of the wag master. "Know what I mean?"

"Indeed I do, little lady. You go after Strasser to make him pay the price for his evil."

Ryan also shook Ward's hand. "Partly that. But we're heading that direction, anyway. See you, Major. Take care now."

With a little food and some fresh water, the six friends climbed aboard their flatbed wag.

Only Major Seth Ward waved goodbye. The others were busy burying their dead.

It was a little before noon when Ryan and the others began to move along the rails, pumping on the double handle that propelled the trolley. The sun beat down directly overhead with a ferocious intent. It didn't take long to establish a good rhythm.

The handles would accommodate two people on each side, leaning into them and riding the rise and fall. Ryan and J.B. took one side while Jak and Krysty started on the other.

The speed began to pick up, and the wind tugged at their clothes. Mildred and Doc sat perched on the front of the trolley, enjoying the movement and the breeze.

"Washes away the smell of blood, Doc," she commented.

"I fear that nothing ever quite removes that oppressive stench," he replied.

Pale pink soapberry bushes flashed by, lining the banks of the winding creek. Ahead of them the locomotive had vanished in among the hills, though they could still catch a glimpse of its pillaring smoke now and again.

"This is going to get one hell of a lot harder if we have to start pumping away up a grade," J.B. said, his fedora pushed to the back of his head. Sweat trickled down his narrow cheeks.

"Major's map shows it near another river," Ryan panted, timing his words in short rushes to fit in with the pumping of the driving handles.

"Heading which way?" Krysty asked, her flaming red hair streaming out behind her like a crimson veil.

"South. Lands shifted since before the long winters. Cuts toward where we want to go, toward Big Bend and the Grandee."

Jak had been working with a grim intent, the snowy wraith of his hair flowing around his lean shoulders. "Chill Strasser then south," he grunted.

"Couldn't have put it better myself," Ryan agreed.

J.B.'s concern soon became fact. As they neared the far side of the open plateau, Salvation only a vague smudge on the distant horizon, it became obvious that the rails were already beginning to climb into the foothills. They crossed the narrow creek over a crumbling trestle bridge that sang and hummed beneath the clattering wheels. The relic of a spur line wound away to the north, the wooden sleepers rotted into the dry earth. It occurred to Ryan that the speed they were moving at, on a brakeless vehicle, could leave them vulnerable to any kind of sabotage of the mainline track.

Very faintly, at the edge of hearing, they caught the sound of the loco wag's whistle, echoing from peak to peak, like the lonesome wailing of a lost soul.

"Could mean he's reached the ville up there," Krysty suggested.

"Sounded high," Jak said.

Ryan eased off a moment, wiping sweat from his eyes, viewing the contours ahead of them, seeing that the rails were climbing and twisting.

"Let's try three a side," he said. "Get as far as we can."

The going became harder and harder, the handles seeming to move slower and slower.

"He won't expect us to be trying to follow him, will he?" Mildred asked. "This trolley was partly hidden, and there wouldn't be any other way we could get close."

Ryan didn't waste any breath on words, contenting himself with simply nodding. It was something that had featured large in his tactical planning. If Strasser had suspected he was being pursued, then he could simply have reversed the direction of the locomotive again and turned hunters into hunted.

By the time they reached the crown of the first shallow bend, their speed had fallen away from near thirty miles an hour to something less than ten miles an hour. And it was taking all of the energy of all six of them to even maintain that.

"Can't go much farther," Krysty said. "Soon be quicker to walk."

Once the ascent became even steeper, Ryan called a halt. Krysty was right, and they all hopped off the trolley. Nobody bothered to try to hold it, and it rattled ponderously away from them, gathering speed as it vanished round the bend.

"Should make it halfway back to Salvation," J.B. grinned.

Doc slumped down against a moss-crusted pile of railroad ballast. "Upon my soul!" he gasped. "When I was filled with the warm sap of youth, I would hike many a mile across the wilderness trails. Now in my sere days, I confess to feeling more than somewhat...somewhat buggered!"

"You fit to go on?" Ryan asked. "Want to get after Strasser as quick as we can."

"I shall not let the side down, Ryan. I hope you can rely upon me for that."

The one-eyed man patted Doc on the shoulder. "Course I know it."

Jak was eager to go, leading the party along the side of the iron road, his eyes raking the hills ahead and above for any sign of a potential ambush.

The cliffs closed in on either side of the tracks, dotted with sparse clumps of pine trees. A couple of times in the next half hour they spotted small groups of goats, picking their way along invisible trails.

J.B. moved alongside Ryan, walking step for step. "What happens when we get up there? We going to go for Strasser, no matter what?"

"Depends. Don't know if he'll stay in this ville. Knowing Strasser, he'll likely run and keep running. Bastard's not stupid. He knows he's lost so many that he can't guarantee to take us out."

The Armorer shook his head. "Mebbe right, Ryan. But you never know when a rabid dog'll turn and snap at you."

The middle of the afternoon drew near, the sun vanishing behind banks of dark purple cloud that threatened a chem storm come evening.

The long bends had become steeper and sharper, finally leveling out between tree-covered slopes. Ahead, Ryan could make out the shallow notch where the lines ran toward Strasser's hiding place. Once they'd startled a group of marmots, gamboling together in a sunny clearing, and they could hear the thunderous sound of fast-running water.

"Bridge," Jak said, pointing a quarter mile ahead of them.

It was immensely high, made from weathered timber and cross-laced with steel and wire. There was no handrail and only a narrow walkway on the right-hand side, less than a yard away. Beyond the gorge they could see the scattered buildings of the ville, with the train standing there, smoke trickling from the gleaming stack.

"There the villain hides," Doc announced.

CHAPTER THIRTY-ONE

"THAT IS TRULY a perilous drop," Doc said, peering down over the rickety rail.

"Five, maybe six hundred feet," Mildred agreed.

"I'm amazed that heavy loco wag and all the coaches made it across. You can feel it shaking under your boots," J.B. Dix stamped his feet to prove his point.

The river tumbled and pounded its way over sawtoothed rocks, throwing up a shimmering rainbow veil of spray. Far below, on the western bank, they could just make out a narrow road, worming its way toward the south.

"If that was navigable, we could take it down toward the Grandee," Krysty said.

"White water rafting was popular among some of the thin-lipped fellows who worked on Overproject Whisper. Said it made their blood race. I admit that it never occurred to me that anything other than ice coursed through their veins."

Doc's words made everyone lean, cautiously, on the rail and stare into the sounding deeps of the gorge. To Ryan the idea of taking any sort of water wag over those foaming rocks smacked of total and utter insanity.

"What next?" Jak asked, turning away and looking toward the distant ville. "Fuck!"

"What?"

"Light off glass. Some bastards watching."

Ryan looked around at the darkening sky. "It'll be Strasser. He'll be surprised if he sees us."

"How do we get in at him?" J.B. asked.

Ryan turned from the hypnotic attraction of the distant river and looked along the narrowing rails that arrowed deep into the heart of the township. His guess put it at around two and a half miles, with the valley close in on either side. The trees would give them plenty of cover if they wanted to try to attack Strasser in his headquarters.

The wind rose in a whistling gust, and he felt the movement of the high wooden trestles trembling beneath his feet.

And an idea came to him.

"What d'you see, Rafe?"

The lieutenant laid down his nunchakus and took the high-power glasses from his boss's hand. He focused them where Strasser pointed, beyond the locomotive, toward the distant, shimmering skeleton of the bridge. The clouds were sailing lower, and the light wasn't as good as it had been.

"Mebbe people."

"Mebbe?"

Rafe sniffed, then tried to bring the image to greater clarity. "Yeah. People. Four. Six. Eight. No more'n eight, boss."

"You make any of them?"

"Hell, no! Not at this distance."

Strasser snatched the glass back. "By dog guts and stinking death! It must be Cawdor. But how did he get this far this fast? Horse wouldn't have done it for him."

"Maybe he's a witch," said Rosa, who sat in a broken chair on the porch of the old house.

"Sure, Rosa, sure. They're witches, and they flew up here on white rats." Strasser turned toward her, his face working in one of his frequent rages. The tip of the quirt slashed down on the arm of the chair, missing her wrist by a scant inch. The metal tip tearing a furrow in the wood.

"Sorry, Cort, sorry. Please, don't—"

"Still more of us than them, boss," Rafe interrupted, saving the woman from a whipping.

"That's true. But we lost us twenty or more to One-Eye. We chilled some of those peasants, but not any of them."

"They're just coming in straight along the rails," Rafe told him. "They got a lot of nerve, no?"

Strasser watched for a few minutes, biting his twisted lip. "No good trail off either side, is there? So, if we took them by surprise we could hunt them down before they even got back to the bridge."

"Be close, boss."

"Sure, sure. What's the odds? This side of the bridge or that side. Don't matter which it is. We can split them up. Maybe chill some."

Rafe picked up the glass and looked through it once more. A shaft of sunlight darted through the chem clouds and illuminated the valley, turning the dull metal of the rails to glittering silver and giving him a better view of the attacking group.

"One's got red hair, boss. And one...one's got white hair. Or some kind of white hat with—"

"Triple-stupe son of a poxed gaudy slut! That's the snow-head kid, Jak."

"Six in all. Shit." The sun went in again, and it was no longer possible to see with any clarity.

Strasser picked up his Russian sniper's rifle from the three-legged table. "Doesn't matter. We'll go for them. Here's how we do it."

Strasser couldn't resist the bait that was dangled ahead of him. The idea that he could take Ryan Cawdor out in the open, helpless, was too attractive. To take power over the helpless was Cort Strasser's ideal of paradise. But he was too careful to risk his own neck out there.

With Rafe, Rosa and one of his gunmen, named Mendoza, Strasser retreated deeper into what had once been a trendy little tourist town. One of its attractions had been a military museum, and Strasser had been delighted to find a small arma wag from World War Two that he'd been able to put into running order. It was now fueled up and ready to go.

Just in case something went wrong.

All the remaining survivors of his gang were aboard the train—four in the driving cab and the rest scattered along the coaches, the barrels of their M-16s protruding through the windows. Strasser had ordered them to raise steam and not engage the forward gear until the needle on the gauge was teetering into the red.

It was a matter of fine judgment for the black-clad former sec boss of Mocsin to wait until Ryan and the others were fully committed, out in the open, yet not let them close enough for the one-eyed man to use his lethal long gun.

The distance from the bridge to the ville was about two and a half miles. From a standing start, the locomotive would reach the bridge in somewhere near four minutes and thirty seconds.

Ryan and his companions couldn't hope to cover a half mile of rough ground in less than five minutes, which made the sum fairly easy for Strasser to calculate.

"About a half mile, boss," Rafe said, watching carefully through the glass.

"Give them the signal."

The sallow-faced man leaned out of the window and fired off the stubby Very pistol. A maroon star shell floated into the dark sky. The loco wag gave a piercing whistle and began to move into shuddering life.

From their high observation point, Strasser and the other three watched and waited, seeing the tiny dots halt and then begin to move quickly back along the tracks.

"We'll take them." Strasser sighed. "What's in that hut by the bridge? Not a place they can hole up in, is it?"

Mendoza replied, "No chance, boss. Just full of junk. Railroad stuff. Bits of wood and rail, rags and grease and stuff."

Strasser turned slowly, his eyes blazing.

Mendoza backed away, seeing death in the etched lines of uncontrollable rage.

"What? What's that?"

"Just the stuff in—" He stopped as the whip tore across his face, opening the flesh of his cheek with the silky ease of a razor. Blood gushed over the man's shirt as he lifted his hand to the deep gash. "Boss! Why?"

"You said *grease*, idiot!"

"Yeah."

Strasser looked away, watching his train as it gathered momentum across the floor of the valley, the smoke streaming behind it. His nails clenched into the palms of his hands with impotent anger as his tactical brain saw the threat.

Ryan's plan was simple. Even with a good glass he knew they couldn't identify everyone at such range, or even count them accurately if they kept moving. He also knew that when it came to the sprint, Doc and Mildred wouldn't keep up. So, they'd talked it through.

As soon as they saw the jetting of smoke that told them the loco was on the move, they all began to run back toward the bridge. But once they'd covered a hundred and fifty yards, Doc and Mildred cut away along a narrow deer trail to the left, vanishing among the trees, leaving J.B., Krysty and Jak to run on alone.

"Rafe!"

"Boss?"

"Go and get the arma wag ready."

He turned to Mendoza. "And stop that fucking blood will you? Rosa, wipe his face."

The woman stood and walked languidly across the floor, touched the stream of crimson with her finger, raised it to her lips and sucked at it, eyes half-closed.

Rafe hesitated in the doorway. "Why aren't we waiting, boss?"

Strasser's eyes gleamed in the pits of wind-scoured bone. "Because I think Ryan Cawdor's thought up an ace on the line for us."

"How?"

Strasser didn't reply, and his lieutenant walked quickly from the building.

"How?" Rosa asked through red-smeared lips.

"Watch."

CHAPTER THIRTY-TWO

As HE RAN, Ryan was conscious of the sticky, slippery grease that coated his hands. He'd tried to wipe some of it off on the tufts of dry grass near the end of the bridge, but there hadn't been that much time.

A risky glance over his right shoulder told him that the train was gaining fast. Its brightly painted cowcatcher ate up the yards as it thundered closer to them. Even in that one stolen look he saw the white puff of smoke from a rifle, fired by someone leaning from the window of the cab, but he wasn't aware of the bullet coming anywhere near.

"Gonna be close!" Krysty yelled, sprinting lightly at Ryan's elbow, hair like streaks of living fire.

Jak tried to look behind at the train and tripped over some loose ballast, recovering his balance with miraculous agility.

Ryan wished that he'd hidden the G-12 caseless before setting out on the dangerous scheme. The strap was loose, and the butt kept jolting him in the small of his back. But there was no time now for second thoughts or hesitation.

They were less than four hundred yards from the end of the bridge, but the locomotive was huffing and puffing at their heels. Ryan didn't hear the sound of the shot above the noise of the pounding engine, but he saw the flick of dust at the edge of the track, where it was overgrown with twining weeds. From the rattling, jerking cab of the loco wag, it was good enough shooting.

Now he saw J.B., kneeling in the undergrowth among some laden thimbleberry bushes, holding his Steyr pistol in his right hand, waiting patiently for the moment.

The runners were twenty yards from their mark. A strip of ragged cloth tied to the lower branch of one of the adjacent piñon pines.

There had once been a U-shaped drainage ditch, but over the years it had been partly filled with leaf mold and blown earth. But it was still a deep hollow, more than six feet across.

"Watch your feet on the rails!" Ryan yelled, seeing that the steel at their feet was now dulled with a thick layer of smeared grease, grease that ran all the way onto the towering trestle bridge over the gorge.

A bullet hit the oiled metal by Ryan's feet and sang, sparking off into the shadowed gloom beneath the trees.

They'd reached the mark and all three dived together into the soft dirt of the hole. The lumbering bulk of the loco wag was above them, the sudden screaming of brakes almost deafening.

Normally, at the speed that it was traveling, the train would have had no problems in grinding swiftly to a halt, giving the surviving members of Strasser's gang a good chance of pursuing and chilling Ryan and his companions.

But the thick layer of age-old grease and oil that had smothered the rails gave the braking system no chance.

From the cover, Ryan crouched to watch the last carriage roll past them. He glimpsed a swarthy face, peering at him, boggle-eyed, from the observation car at the back.

The wheels were no longer revolving, skidding along the rails, drawing ever closer to the high bridge, where J. B. Dix was waiting.

Back at the ville, Cort Strasser stared back, stone-faced, seeing events unfold precisely as he'd feared.

"Go, baby, go," Krysty breathed, craning her neck to watch the sliding locomotive.

"They'll jump," Jak predicted.

"Doubt it." Ryan shook his head. "They'll be angered, but they won't guess."

The cowcatcher on the front of the loco wag was now moving onto the bridge, the ponderous weight making the entire structure quiver and shake.

To the side, J.B. narrowed his eyes behind the glinting lenses of his spectacles, finger curling over the trigger of the 5.6 mm blaster. He'd be aiming for the chunk of plas-ex that was jammed between two of the main bracing timbers. J.B. always tried to keep up his supply of armaments whenever he could, but he'd run perilously low on the high-impact explosive.

In another half minute he'd know whether he'd had enough.

Now the train had reached the end of the greased strips of steel, its wheels finally beginning to bite and slow its impetus. The front of the locomotive was virtually in the middle of the bridge, the wheels spinning again as the driver slammed the engine into reverse.

"Now," Ryan whispered.

The crack of the pistol was muffled by the pounding of the loco wag. J.B. winced instinctively, ready for the expected explosion, but nothing happened. He peered through the branches and hissed between his teeth with exasperation. There was a gouged splinter of white wood about a half inch below the dark shape of the plas-ex. The Armorer took careful aim and fired again, conscious that the ornate train was already beginning to crawl backward from the bridge.

The detonation was surprisingly quiet, overlaid by the raging rapids far below and the shrieking of the loco wag's whistle. But J.B. had carried out the placement of the plas-ex with the greatest care, picking a spot where main timbers would be torn apart, ripping away supporting cables and iron bars.

Ryan climbed onto the track, staring at the drama beginning to slowly unfold before him. Krysty and Jak were at his side, and Doc and Mildred were jogging down behind them, stepping from sleeper to sleeper.

The bridge began to unfold itself, like a child's tower of twigs. Wires twanged and parted, and metal twisted and sheared. Wood splintered, sending showers of dust into the gorge. Hundreds of century-old nails and screws were projected from the collapsing bridge, pattering hundreds of feet into the air, falling all around the stunned watchers.

Slowly, like a dignified spinster giving way to alcohol, the train began to tilt to the right, the whistle still screeching in a spear of white steam.

"Gaia!" Krysty sighed. "That's such a sad and sorry shame."

"They'd have chilled us if they'd gotten the chance," Ryan replied.

"Not them. That lovely old loco wag."

"Yeah," Jak agreed.

The locomotive was going, tipping away from them, dragging the carriages along with it. Two men jumped from the rearmost car, slithering onto the falling bridge, scrabbling for a hold on the rocking timbers. Ryan took careful aim with the Heckler & Koch G-12 and shot them both through the chest, sending them screaming soundlessly into the maelstrom.

J.B. moved out from the pines, staring with an awed fascination at the carnage that he'd wrought.

The whole bridge was going, pulling itself apart, the crashing beams dislodging other struts until the air was filled with debris. The loco wag's whistle was shrieking, someone's hand locked to it in a frozen paroxysm of dying.

Ryan ran to join the Armorer, and the two friends watched together. The noise of the river was swamped by the cracking of wood and the high-pitched twanging of snapping wires. Ryan thought he glimpsed a face pressed against the glass of the last car, and there were certainly two men leaping to their deaths from the cab.

By the time that Krysty, Jak, Doc and Mildred had reached the jagged timber that marked the edge of the bridge, it was over.

All that was left were a few dangling lengths of wood, festooned with a twisted nest of rusting wire. On the far side of the gulf the twin rails protruded for a few feet. On the near side, they'd snapped off clean, level with the chiseled brink of raw stone. Far, far below them, nothing could be seen through the impenetrable wall of misty spray thrown up by the racing river.

"That it?" Krysty asked.

"Looks like it, lover."

"Was Strasser on the train?" Mildred asked. "Couldn't see him."

"Me neither. I somehow have the feeling that the bastard's too triple smart to put his own cock on the block." Ryan looked at J.B. "You didn't see nothing, did you?"

"Anything," Krysty corrected. "Anything, lover. Not nothing."

J.B. gave her one of his rare, thin smiles. "I tell you, Ryan, that I didn't see either anything or nothing. My guess is that the ice-heart's back in that ville. Or he's off and running someplace.''

"Then I venture to suggest that our conversation here is somewhat superfluous. Should we not be considering pursuit of that swift and evil fellow?"

"Doc," Ryan said, "you never said a truer word. Yeah, let's go. Fast and careful."

CHAPTER THIRTY-THREE

"YOU GOT just one more minute, Mendoza. Then I cut off your pecker and jam it down your useless throat."

"You're making Gil real nervous, boss," Rafe warned.

"I'm making him nervous? That what you said, amigo?"

"Yeah, but—"

"But fucking nothing, my man. You saw the way that witch, Cawdor—that Rosa here says can do magic—pulled the best disappearing trick in history."

"You mean the train, boss?" Rafe asked, trying for a confident laugh and ending up with a thin, nervous giggle.

Strasser glanced out of one of the wired windows of the arma wag, seeing the afternoon light already fading. "Yeah, Rafe, you could say that I mean the fucking train. Bang! There it goes. Bridge and all."

In the driver's seat, shaking like an aspen branch in a hurricane, sat Gil Mendoza, panting and sweating as he tried to get the engine to fire. The blood still seeped from the gash on his cheek, but he ignored it

as he turned the starter knob for the twentieth time.
He heard the sullen cough from the antique engine,
and a splutter that raised his hopes for a moment.
But it still didn't start.

"I'd say thirty seconds is all you got left to make
this place stink, Mendoza. Thirty seconds is tops."

"It's real near, boss," he stammered.

Once again the starter motor whirred and mumbled to itself, failing to kick the engine into life.
Mendoza, rank with the sweat of fear, licked his lips
and tried it again.

"You're goin' to flood it, Gil," Rafe warned unnecessarily.

"Into the last ten seconds, Mendoza. Then there'll
be more bleeding."

"It's coming, boss, coming."

Rosa laid a hand on Strasser's thigh and smiled at
him through sleepy eyes. "I bet he says that to all the
girls."

The engine of the arma wag finally dragged itself
protestingly into rattling action, the cab filling with
light blue fumes.

Strasser coughed and waved his hand to try to clear
the air. "Get moving."

"Where we going?"

"South."

"Across the river?"

"Sure."

"Down that winding road?"

Strasser gritted his teeth so hard that everyone in
the wag heard the sound. "One more question and I

cut your fucking throat. We're going south toward the Grandee. Heard of a hidden redoubt down that way, along with some other secret places. That's where we're going.''

For one unbelievable moment it seemed as if Mendoza were going to ignore the furious warning from Cort Strasser and ask yet another question. But he finally shrugged his shoulders and crashed the small, cramped wag into forward motion.

Once they were clear of the gorge the sound of the river faded away behind them to a gentle murmur. The wind whispered through the trees, carrying the refreshing scent of the piñon pines. Above them the sky was darkening with the promise of a sullen, clouded evening.

"Don't forget Strasser's got that Russkie sniping rifle," J.B. said.

"Poor light for shooting," Ryan replied, "but we can come in closer through the forest, circle in around."

"How many left?" Jak asked.

"What, Strasser's shootists?"

"Yeah. Lot on loco wag."

Mildred interrupted. "I watched as carefully as I could and I'm sure that there were at least eight or nine of them. There can't be very many left alive now."

"How do you know that the leader of that monstrous regiment wasn't with them in their descent into the river?" Doc asked.

"I don't," Ryan said. "Just got a feeling. I reckon he's still up there in the ville, or on the run out of it."

Krysty held up a hand. "Quiet."

They all stopped, Jak shuffling his feet in the shingle, which earned him a glare from the woman.

"What is it, lover?" Ryan strained his own hearing to try to catch what it was that had snatched her attention.

"Wag."

"In the ville? Coming this way?"

"Yes. No."

Ryan understood. "Big one?"

"No. Small, with a real rough engine, coughing and choking. Sounds like it's heading in...in that direction." She pointed a stabbing finger toward the southwest.

They were still nearly two miles from the nearest buildings of the small township, and Ryan knew that it would be pure foolishness to go rushing blindly in.

"Take us a good hour to get there," he said. "If that's Strasser, he could easily be twenty miles away by the time we get there, and I doubt the son of a bitch'll have left us any transport around the place. Not likely."

"With the bridge down, how are we going to get back to move south?" Krysty asked.

Ryan grinned. "We'll cross that bridge when we come to it, lover."

With the gathering clouds, the dusk came creeping across the hills at uncanny speed. The road that

Strasser had picked to take them away from their
unrelentless pursuers was an old tourist trail that
snaked across the face of the cliffs, down toward the
misty crystal glitter of the spray. Over the years it had
suffered badly from earth slips and rainwash. Now
its surface varied from barely adequate to razor-edge
dangerous. Gil Mendoza, barely recovered from his
flirtation with death, gripped the small steering
wheel, his foot permanently on the brake, peering
out through the ob-slit at the narrow track.

"Can't you go any faster?"

"No, boss. Not without turning us over the side of
the trail."

"All right, all right. Once we get to the bottom we
should make better time."

"But, boss, there's—"

Strasser leaned forward and gripped the driver by
the back of his scrawny neck, fingers biting in like
steel claws. "Just drive."

"Soon be full dark."

"No lights showing anyplace," Jak said. "Can't
see nobody."

Ryan glanced automatically across to Krysty who
half smiled, but held her peace.

Once they'd come to within the mile, they'd all
filtered off to the right, keeping close to the fringe of
trees in case Strasser's narrow eyes were squinting at
them along the barrel of his SVD PSO-1 with its
telescopic sight.

Now the ville was less than a quarter mile away from them.

"You hear the wag?" Ryan asked Krysty.

"No. Not for a half hour or more. Must be long gone by now."

Strasser looked out the side ob-slit, seeing that they'd finally descended to within a couple hundred feet of the river. Below lay the gorge with the tumbled ruins of the beautiful train, its inlaid walnut paneling and Waterford mirrors in splintered fragments.

"It's near dark," he said.

"Doing my best, boss, but you see what the trail's like."

"Yeah, yeah, yeah." Strasser nibbled at the ragged corner of a nail. "Will Cawdor come after us? And how close can he get?"

"No other serviceable wags in that shit ville," Rafe replied.

"True, comrade, true." The skull-faced man sighed deeply. "But I just got a feeling that he's going to come anyway. Like a shadow you can't shake off your shoulder. Like seeds in a melon. Like warm blood on your hand when you gut some bastard. You can't get away from it." There was a long silence, and the wag lurched slowly onward. Strasser suddenly leaned in his seat and clipped Mendoza hard across the back of the head. "Put your fucking foot to the metal, you triple-stupe bastard!"

The town was deserted. The sickle moon peered over the surrounding mountains as the six friends walked slowly among the ghostly hulks of the ruined, tumbling buildings. The township had suffered far greater damage than Salvation.

There was no evidence that it had been occupied for many years, and Ryan's hope of finding some sort of transport plunged. J.B. picked up the tracks of Strasser's arma wag, leaving the ville and turning south at the crossroads, heading down a winding trail that looked as if it were going to plunge straight into the river, way below.

"Think we'll ever see him again, lover?" Krysty asked.

Ryan rested the flat of his hand gently against the carved plane of her cheek, looking deep into her eyes. "What d'you think? What d'you see, lover?"

Her fingers, strong and capable, tangled with his. "Can't see. See only dark, lover. That's about all."

"Same here. I know he's got clear away, but I just have a feeling, like a shadow that sits at your shoulder."

"They don't work, boss." A tremor of naked terror shook the man's voice.

"Ah."

Rafe risked his own well-being again. "There was no way of knowing we'd want to use the wag so soon, or at night."

Strasser coughed. "And the bitching exhaust doesn't work. All right. The lights don't work and we're on a narrow trail, right by the river. What do we do? The slut here could get out and walk in front of us. How about that, Rosa?"

"Don't like walking, Cort, baby. Like sitting. You know that. Like the way I sit on your—"

He touched her soft lips with the muzzle of the Stechkin. "Take care, Rosa. Be real careful what you say."

"Could camp here. No way they can get around us, and there's only this track. Be easy to guard it. What d'you say, boss?"

"I didn't say a thing, Rafe. Let's go a mite farther." He nudged Rosa. "Out, bitch."

Mildred spotted the sign on the top floor of a row of weather-beaten stores. "Look," she said, pointing. "There."

Doc read the faded sign. Trail Riders. Off-Trail Bikes.

"Two-wheel wags you push with pedals," Ryan said. "Seen them around a couple of villes. Hard work. That what they are?"

"Let's go see." Mildred led the way up a dangerous, rotting flight of stairs, the treads painted in alternate strips of red, gold and green.

The door was gone, and the interior gaped silently in the semidarkness. Night had almost come, but they could still see the piles of tangled metal.

"Well, I'll be..." Doc said.

"Stop here for the night," Ryan decided. "If Strasser's gone, then he's gone. Be up at first light and then we can see what we got here."

Mendoza was dead.

When Rosa had come out of the night, tottering on her high heels, to announce that the road ahead was irrevocably blocked by a huge slide of red earth, the driver had turned to announce to his boss that he'd known that all along.

"You didn't let me tell you," the man had complained.

Strasser snapped his neck with a single, savage blow to his nape.

"Throw that in the river. And we'll camp here."

CHAPTER THIRTY-FOUR

FROM THE PILES of bicycles that were cluttered together, it took well over an hour to come up with enough serviceable machines for all six of them. Even then, to their mutual disgust, there were only four solo bikes, which left Mildred and Doc as the reluctant collaborators on an electric-blue tandem.

Breakfast had been some strips of tough jerky, washed down with water. Ryan was still worried that the devious Strasser might appear from some dark hole and strike at them. He couldn't believe that his enemy had truly gotten clear away.

Fortunately the tires on the bikes were a rot-proof plastic material and stood being pumped up without more than a couple going stubbornly flat. The store held a display of service manuals for the machines, so readying them presented few problems. Riding them was a different matter.

Jak took to the new skill with his customary ease, quickly discovering the excitement of wheelies. Ryan, Krysty and J.B. coped without too much difficulty. Back in Harmony ville, as a young girl, Krysty had ridden a beat-up old bicycle. The old truth held good. "Once you've done it, you never really forget how," she said.

The bikes had sixteen gears, and that took some mastering. But within a half hour all four could ride up and down the main street of the settlement, and turn, without falling.

Doc and Mildred didn't find it so easy.

First off there was the problem of who was going to ride up front and steer, and who would sit at the back and just provide the pedal power.

"I'm going at the front," Doc insisted. "As the senior partner—"

"No way, Doc. I'm younger, so I should be doing the steering."

Doc considered that. "Then I provide all of the power... Perhaps that is the best idea after all. Very well, madam, I agree."

Mildred had second thoughts. "No, wait a minute there. I'm not sure I want your nose up my ass."

Doc bridled. "I assure you that such a feeling is entirely mutual, madam!"

"Why's one part got a bar across it and the other doesn't?" J.B. asked.

It was a fair question, and it stopped the argument in midflow. Mildred coughed. "Well, from what I recall, never being a cyclist, the piece with the crossed bar is for men. One without is for ladies, to accommodate their skirts."

"So the man takes the lead!" Doc said, unable and unwilling to conceal his triumph.

"Looks that way," Ryan agreed.

"Well, now that I think about it, I have a feeling that most of these tandems were made this way. Suppose it was to spare the lady's dignity," Mildred said huffily.

Doc bowed to her. "Then let us both hazard our dignity, dear lady, and risk all on this velocipede? Shall we go?"

They went.

"Like drunk Siamese twins," Krysty commented, shaking her head and fighting to control her helpless laughter.

"Like gators with tails tied," was Jak's description.

"Like Doc and Mildred doing the best they can," Ryan said.

With Cort Strasser so far ahead of them, there was no longer any kind of pressure. No rush. No hurry. It wasn't until late morning that they'd mastered their machines enough to risk the steep descent down the switchback towards the tumbling spray of the invisible river.

Jak was in the lead, swerving confidently from side to side, often taking his hands off the faded chrome of the bars. The others watched him with mixed emotions.

"He sure is good on that machine," Krysty observed.

"I would personally take some pleasure in the cocky little devil falling off on his ass," Doc grated.

"Sounds like you're cut up, Doc," J.B. said, wobbling around a deep pothole.

"Cut up!" the old man squawked, standing on the pedals. "Not even Tomas de Torquemada and the finest brains of the Spanish Inquisition could have invented such a subtle instrument of torture as this knife-edged saddle."

"Shut up and work," Mildred panted. "At least we'll soon be going downhill."

"Is that going to be better?"

"Sure, Doc." Looking ahead she reached for the caliper brakes. "Hang on, everybody. Here we go!"

"The good news," Ryan said, "is that nobody's been seriously hurt."

The cycling expedition had eventually ground to a halt around two-thirds of the way down the vicious bends of the trail. Not all of them had made it that far.

Jak had gone first. Grinning over his shoulder, he'd never spotted the half-buried length of rusted girder. It had jammed his front wheel, and the boy had gone flying over the bars, turning a complete somersault in the air. Only his superb reflexes had enabled him to control his body, twisting so he broke the fall by landing half on his shoulder. He rolled with the impact, sliding in a cloud of dust, finishing perilously close to a sheer drop to the river.

J.B. came off next, skidding sideways and losing control. Stepping from the fallen bike, he brushed the dust off his pants. "The horse was easier," he said ruefully.

Krysty had a brake cable snap, sending her wheeling faster and faster down the steep hill, with Ryan pedaling at breakneck speed to catch up with her. He threw his arm out for her to hang on, both bicycles slewing sideways in a clatter of loose stones and sand.

Ironically it was Doc and Mildred who avoided an accident. Moving sedately downhill, the brakes squealing, they both leaned in on the sharp corners. Their slower pace left them well behind the others, but the chain of falls eventually caught them up with everyone.

Ryan brought them to a halt. "If we go on I reckon someone could get badly hurt."

Jak was trying to get the clots of crimson dust from his tangle of white hair, examining the graze on his elbow. "Bikes fun but fucking danger," he said. "Let's walk."

"Trail still shows that arma wag heading on," J.B. said. The deep ruts of the studded tires were unmistakable, following the winding track.

The Armorer had to shout to be heard above the noise of the river. Looking back upstream they could see the jagged remains of the locomotive and the carriages, still being pounded by the merciless water. Downstream it looked as though the gorge widened out a little and the fast-flowing current became a tad less lethal.

On level ground again, they were able to ride their bicycles. Everyone found the going much easier, though Jak was noticeably more cautious and didn't indulge himself in so many flash stunts.

"Looks like it might lead south," Ryan shouted, pedaling alongside Krysty.

"What?" She shook her head to show the sound of the rapids had drowned out his voice.

"Said river goes south!"

He took his left hand off the bars to point and nearly lost control of the bike.

"Shame these little boogers don't float," she yelled. "Could just drift along all the way to the Grandee."

The idea had already crossed Ryan's mind, and he'd been trying to scan the frothing edge of the river as they rode along, inviting the risk of a fall. But there'd been only an occasional piece of floating driftwood, chewed and splintered by the sharp-toothed boulders.

The cliffs loomed far above them, the orange and gray stone dappled with patches of bright green where small bushes had managed to establish themselves in narrow cracks.

A colony of swallows darted at the top of the ravine, etching crazy shadows against the blue of the morning sky. It was a beautiful place and Ryan let his thoughts wander, as they did with increasing frequency, to his future. A future that he liked to think of in terms of settling somewhere with Krysty.

Somewhere with a small house, well fortified. Good grass and sweet water.

"Ryan!"

Jak's breaking voice shrilled into the middle of his daydream, jerking him to the reality of where they were. And who they were chasing.

The boy had been pedaling a little ahead of the others, vanishing around one of the steep curves that followed the oxbow river. Moments after his disappearance, the boy came back, hair flowing over his shoulders like a torrent of incandescent fire, calling out a warning to the others.

The huge earth slip, two hundred yards across, made it obvious why Strasser had abandoned the arma wag. And the clear trail showed that he, with a woman and a man, had clambered over the obstacle.

What was infinitely more interesting was what lay on the far side of the mountain of earth.

CHAPTER THIRTY-FIVE

THE HUGE LANDSLIDE, combined with the barren isolation of the place, had kept it sacrosanct ever since the roiling black clouds of sky-dark. The few stragglers who'd made a home in the ville high above had never bothered to tackle the perilous descent to the raging waters. They didn't need to. From the old trestle bridge they could peer with a superstitious fear into the rainbowed gorge.

Before the missiles sang across the sky, that gorge had been one of the great tourist attractions of the Southwest. Not far away had stood the Best Western Running Rapids, a brand-new building with its four pools, atrium and leisure suites, each with individual redwood hot tub.

In Deathlands nobody except the hopelessly insane ever went walking anywhere for pleasure. The very idea would have been greeted with cackles of disbelieving laughter.

There was a warehouse that held half a dozen deflated rafts, a gas-powered generator linked to an air compressor, a changing room that held the rotted shreds of oilskins and orange life jackets. Another, smaller building had been used for administration, and contained a desk and some filing cabinets as well as a tiny word processor and a couple of radios.

The only thing that was interesting to Ryan and the others was the larger building—and the tracks that led from it down to the edge of the river. Deep scuff marks marred the ground as though something had been dragged down there, with the deeper imprints of three pairs of feet in the soft, pale sand.

Ryan, Jak and J.B. knelt alongside the tracks, staring intently at them. Jak touched the edges of the footmarks, looking at the way the sand crumbled in at his touch.

"Not long," he said finally.

"Yeah. Wind would've faded them more. I'd guess at less than two hours." Ryan looked questioningly at the Armorer.

"Maybe even less than two," J.B. replied.

Krysty called to them from the storage building. "Engine in here's still real warm! And there's a kind of boat, half blown up."

Ryan ran toward her, followed by the others, and entered the cool, damp-smelling concrete building.

J.B. had gone immediately to the little gas engine, laying his hand on the top. "Right," he said. "Can't be more than an hour. Could be less."

The big raft lay on one side, like a dying amphibian, its flanks streaked with mold, half-inflated.

"Obvious what happened," Ryan said. "Strasser got here, dumped his wag, found this place and started trying to blow up one of the boats. He got mostly through it and then...either got bored and picked a smaller one or realized it would be too big for three of them to handle.''

They spent ten minutes trying to get the stubborn gas generator to run, taking turns on the starting cord until it coughed into smoking life. Over the years Ryan had plenty of experience of trying to get prenuke machinery to work. It wasn't generally the best fun in the world.

"Join up that lead to the big raft. Jak, sort out enough paddles for us all, and a few spares. Mildred, see if any of those float jackets are of any use. Doc, find some lashing cord."

For a quarter of an hour there was a scene of organized chaos. An additional complication was the fact that the nozzle that connected the generator to the raft was faulty and kept slipping off in a violent hiss of escaping air.

It took the combined efforts of Ryan, J.B., Krysty and Jak to get enough air into the chambers of the big raft.

"We'll never get it full," J.B. panted.

"I guess this'll do," Ryan said. "Turn off the engine, Jak."

The sudden silence in the building was startling.

Ryan straightened, holding the small of his back where he could feel a kinked muscle. He looked around at the others. "Report," he said.

Mildred snapped to attention, clicking her heels. "Private Wyeth, Second Class, reporting, sir! Regret none of those life jackets would keep a gerbil afloat for thirty seconds. Sir!"

Doc straightened at her side. "Report that I took over paddle duty from Corporal Lauren, sir. Also found enough cord to bind an army. A dozen paddles all collected and ready to stow, sir."

Ryan returned the salute. "Well done, both of you. Put you in for a commendation when we get back to base."

"Thank you, sir," they chorused.

"Then I guess it's time we got this boat on the river."

The remains of a short jetty jutted into the river on the inside of a bend where the water flowed more slowly. All working together, the six friends managed to walk the big inflatable down to the edge, making sure that there was a stout piece of rope to tether it to a solid metal stanchion near the main building.

Before embarking, Ryan went and searched quickly through the small office, finding maps of the river that provided details of the various tours on offer to tourists: half-day morning, half-day afternoon, full day including packed lunch, overnight raft ride, with tent accommodation and an evening barbecue, two-day trip, all food included, and a three-day trip that would take you close to the Grandee.

"Three days." He took one of the brightly colored maps, even though it only gave sketchy details of the actual river journey, showing a number of rapids and one or two portage points "depending upon water conditions."

Whoever ran the raft operation had given exotic names to some of the more hazardous stretches of the river—Hell's Teeth, Dragon's Drop, Demon's Drop, Devil's Drop. Ryan thought that some of them showed a distinct lack of imagination. Bustagut was better. So was Piledriver.

From the map, and bearing in mind that it would have been drawn up before the nukes shattered the earth and altered the landscape, it didn't look an impossible journey. It seemed as if there were a couple of places where they'd have to get the unwieldy raft into the shore and manhandle it around particularly steep vertical falls.

"Right," Ryan said to himself, carefully closing the tumbledown door and stepping back into the bright sunlight.

Cort Strasser had also taken one of the maps, wishing within five minutes that he'd taken several of them. The spray was bad enough, but they were frequently hit by waves of solid white water. But his memory was crystal clear and he felt fairly confident that he could recall the more dangerous parts.

He'd taken the longer steering paddle and put himself in the stern of the clumsy yellow raft. A rope around his waist was tied to one of the mooring rings, though he had some doubt about whether he was really safer that way if anything happened. It was obvious that the material of this raft was somewhat frail, and if the craft went down it would take everyone with it.

Rosa was crouched in the middle, head down, face showing no expression at the tumbling and lurching as they went over the next set of rapids.

Rafe was kneeling in the bow, face streaming with water, trying to point out any particular hazards to Strasser, raising a right arm or a left. The speed of the racing river made it extremely difficult to control the direction of the raft.

In the quieter, slower passages of the river, Cort Strasser took time to stand up, balancing against the pitching of the craft, looking behind him for any sign of pursuit.

But there was nothing.

The blue-green water was calm in the eddying launch place, and they had no problems in getting the unwieldy craft safely afloat. Ryan still had worries about their failure to inflate all the sections fully. The material sagged wearily and there didn't seem very much freeboard. But he'd wanted to get moving and the plastic had seemed dangerously fragile.

"Tie on to the nearest metal ring," he said, "but make sure you use a knot that you can get untied real quick. If anything happens in this river you got seconds. No more."

"Take front," Jak said, clambering with his customary nimbleness to the rounded bow, perching himself there with one of the paddles.

Ryan chose to take the steering position in the stern himself. The other four split, J.B. and Mildred going on the starboard side, Krysty and Doc to port.

The stern mooring rope ran through a thick, rusted iron ring on the side of the jetty. Ryan looked around. "Ready?"

Everyone was.

He let go of the rope, allowing it to run through his fingers. The current tugged at the bow of the raft, nudging them into the main stream of the river.

And they were off.

CHAPTER THIRTY-SIX

RYAN LOST HIS MAP even more quickly than Cort Strasser. The very first bend on the river brought a vicious back swirl. A large white rock, slick and polished, caught the bow of the raft, lifting it before any of them could react to check it, and dropping the stern so that a wave of dark water broke clear over Ryan.

He felt himself heaved into the air, only the tugging rope around his waist keeping him attached to the raft. Arms and legs flailing, he was dumped hard in the bottom of the inflatable, mouth and nose filling with ice-cold water, choking him. The butt of the G-12 swung around and struck him on the side of the head, making him blink dizzily. The map dropped from his hand and whirled away into the white foam and vanished.

He managed to hold on to the paddle and fought his way upright, shaking his head to clear it. A quick glance told him his companions were still inside the raft, though everyone had been sent spinning by the massive force of the impact.

"Fireblast!" he gasped.

Krysty was next to recover, spitting out a mouthful of water and managing a grin. "If it's like this in the first hundred yards, then what the dark night'll it be like after a mile?"

Ryan was used to bumping, sickening journeys, locked into the stinking darkness of a rolling war wag. But he'd never in his entire life experienced anything to compare with that wild ride down the white water of that nameless river in what had once been South Texas.

During one of the quieter passages, Doc called out, "Reminds me of something I recall hearing a comedian once say about flying. This is very similar. He said that it was hours of boredom, interspersed with moments of stark terror."

Jak had started throwing up within a quarter mile of their start and continued being sick for the first hour and a half. Ryan would have thought it impossible for the albino teenager to look more pale than usual, but Jak achieved a greenish pallor of a frightening hue.

Much of their diminished supply of food went overboard at the same time as the map, but there was still enough to keep them going on reduced rations for several days.

"Least we won't die of thirst," J.B. yelled, after a particularly large wave had soaked them all to the skin.

"Thirst, no! Hypothermia, very possibly!" Mildred responded, digging in with her paddle to try to pull them from a sucking whirlpool.

Despite his lean build and his appallingly depraved style of living, Cort Strasser was a creature of almost endless strength. But as the afternoon light began to dim, filling the shadows between the high cliffs with an extra layer of darkness, even the ex-sec boss began to suspect he was coming to the end of his endurance.

Their small inflatable was much easier and lighter to handle than the big raft that Ryan and his group had commandeered. Yet even that needed constant vigilance and cunning to save it from being swamped or torn apart by the jagged rocks.

He'd taken the precaution of strapping extra paddles to the side of the clumsy craft. Twice during that endless day Strasser had to use one of them. One paddle snapped like a frail twig against a wall of rushing rock while the other simply started to disintegrate into splinters.

Rafe performed heroically, though his boss still screamed raging abuse at him for every jolt and spin of the raft.

Rosa had given up. Like Jak Lauren, miles behind, she was demolished by nausea.

Fortunately there was so much water swilling into and over the inflatable that her constant puking was washed away. Several times she wept, and once screamed at Cort Strasser to shoot her and take away the pitching misery. But he laughed, his thin lips peeling back off his gleaming teeth, his eyes like small pits of raging fire.

Ryan had tried to memorize the lost map, but he quickly discovered that it would have been precious little help. The land showed all the signs of lifting and shearing that typified overwhelming quake movement. There were long patches of oily calm, where he remembered some of the demonic drops from the brochure, and sudden falls where they had to stop and drag the inflatable along narrow paths, where he was sure the map had shown easy stretches.

One of the worries was that there were virtually no places along the endless southerly gorge where they could hope to safely land. Most of the time there was only the steep cliffs, towering up to five hundred feet high on either side, plunging clear down into the rushing water.

Occasionally they'd be the target for dozens of small, white-breasted blue birds that dived at them, whistling shrilly at the invasion of their territory. Once or twice they spotted fish, leaping upstream over the foaming rapids, with the silver glint of scales, iridescent in the rainbow spray.

As Jak recovered he began to take a more lively part in the adventure, standing balanced in the pitching bow of the raft, shrieking orders to Ryan at the steering paddle, his hand waving them to left or right.

Around midafternoon, they came down a great slide of rock and water, hopelessly out of control, trusting only to luck to get them through. Their luck nearly held.

But near the bottom a slicing piece of jagged boulder snagged one of the starboard flotation chambers and cut it open as neatly as a good steel knife. The inflatable immediately rode lower in the river, allowing waves to break in over Mildred and J.B. on that side.

The next mile or so was calmer, though the river still flowed fast, carrying them at a good twelve to fifteen miles an hour.

"Can we repair it?" Ryan called.

The Armorer shook his head. Despite the relative quiet, the water was still giving a constant soft roar, making conversation difficult. "No way. Even if we beached her we don't have anything that could mend a tear in this stuff."

"Still got freeboard," Doc said, trying to ring water out of the sleeves of his frock coat.

"As long as we don't lose another part," Mildred said, shaking her head so that the tiny, tight plaits all moved together, throwing off beads of water. "Any lower and we'll be sailing under this damned river, instead of on top of it."

Ryan looked at the bank. There was a gently shelving beach of golden sand, lined with clumps of sycamores and oaks, the wall of seamed rock rising steeply behind them. It would make a safe camping spot, but there were still hours of good daylight left and Strasser would be going on.

Even though the sun had gone behind the cliff to their right, the passage through the long canyon was still navigable.

"We keep going," he said. Nobody seemed to be at all surprised.

Rafe lay huddled in the bow, eyes squeezed shut, hands clasped between his thighs. He was trying to keep himself warm and stop the shuddering that racked his lean body. He'd reached the end of his limits of strength and then gone on even beyond that.

Strasser had given up trying to rouse his lieutenant with words and abuse. The river was never still and safe for long, so he was denied the opportunity to leave the steering position in the stern to go to flog Rafe with the steel-braided quirt.

The light was now fading fast. Ahead of them on the right he'd spotted a narrow strip of sand, but he lacked the power to beach the awkward raft. After the sandy stretch there was a jagged headland, which marked a sharp bend in the river. Strasser began to maneuver the inflatable closer to that bank. He'd noticed that there was often a small landing place on both sides of similar jutting crags, and he knew that he, too, was near to the end of his tether.

If they missed a chance to land and camp for the night, they might drift helplessly until they reached another of the sheer drops that they'd already portaged. But this time they would slide silently over the brink to their deaths.

"Coming in!" he shouted in a croaking voice.

Not all that far behind, Ryan was reaching the same conclusion. The day of rafting had been infinitely more tiring than he'd imagined. Everyone had pulled their weight to the best of his or her ability. But now the afternoon was near done, and it was time to get the raft out of the river for the night.

"Jak!"

"What?"

"Keep a good look out for someplace to pull in for the night."

The boy cupped his hand to his ear. "Can't hear, Ryan!"

"Place for the night!"

Jak waved a hand to show that he'd finally understood the message.

They'd just reached a point where huge earth slips had come down on both sides of the river, narrowing it to a hurtling, boiling cascade. Ryan steered the raft toward the center of the current, hoping that there was nothing around the next curve. They were now racing at twice their normal speed, and any sort of control was almost impossible.

Like a cork bursting from the neck of a bottle, the bright-colored inflatable shot through the gap, emerging into quieter waters.

"There!" Jak bellowed, right hand pointing like an accusing angel.

Ryan looked across to starboard, seeing that there was another rock slide jutting out into the stream from the right where the river made a sharp bend. There was a slender strip of sandy shore, but barely enough time to steer their inflatable toward it. Ryan was tempted to allow their craft to float on around the corner, with the hope of finding an easier landing place.

"Pull right!" Ryan shouted.

Krysty and Doc paddled furiously, bending all their strength into it, while Mildred and J.B. backed water, swinging the clumsy raft around and making it head with a grudging reluctance toward the sand.

"Take bowline!" Ryan called to Jak, who nodded his understanding.

Out of the center, the water flowed and eddied more slowly, and they managed to reach the shore without too much trouble. The bow came in with a soft, grating sound and Jak leaped with an eldritch agility, tying the rope around the stump of an old walnut tree.

Everyone climbed out and flopped on the sand, sighing with exhaustion. Ryan looked at them, wondering how long they'd be able to keep on rafting south. As far as he could judge they must now be close to halfway toward the Grandee.

"I'll get a fire going," J.B. offered, trying to wring water out of his battered fedora.

"How about Strasser?" Krysty asked. "He could be anywhere. Right around the next bend."

Ryan shook his head. "Doubt that. He had a good start on us. Likely he'll keep going till dark before he stops."

"Are we positive that the villain hasn't taken some backwater or side creek and is, e'en now, sneaking along behind us?"

Mildred looked pityingly at the old man. "I'm sure your brain's addled, Doc," she said. "Sometimes I reckon you're not even ten cents in the dollar."

"What?"

"First off there's been not even a stream where he could have gone. If you'd had your rheumy old eyes open you'd have seen that for yourself. And second I don't much see how anyone could come 'sneaking' along after us. Not on that river."

"Well, for your information, my good woman, I think you—"

Ryan stopped him. "Enough, you two. We'll need to dry out and get some food in us, mebbe see if there's any chance of catching a fish. Rest up. That most of all. Rest up."

Ryan had decreed that there was no need to keep watch. Nobody would risk navigating the river in the dark. It was perilous enough by daylight. And the cliffs behind them were so stark that nobody could hope to come down at them. Also, everyone was so bone weary that sleep was essential.

But Mildred had slept badly, finding that the ceaseless surge of the river kept her in a fitful, broken slumber. And the sand that had seemed so soft once they got off the raft now contrived to mold itself to the consistency of concrete, rubbing at her hips, knees, ankles and elbows.

The dreams had been the same as always—yellow flames against dried lawns; ropes, taut as iron bars, moving slowly against a starry, starry night; white hoods with small, piglike eyes that lurked behind them; knives, slick with spilled red blood; the taint of scorched flesh hanging over the richness of the magnolia.

She didn't know whether she'd cried out in waking. Looking around at the others, and knowing how lightly they slept, she guessed she couldn't have.

It wasn't even close to dawn yet, but the river seemed to give off a pale, phosphorescent glow. The stars above were like pinpoints of diamond, and the black woman shuddered at their coldness. Moving with infinite care, so as not to disturb the other five, she walked across the silent sand and stood for several minutes at the water's edge.

The noise of the rapids drowned out any sound. For a moment she thought she caught the faint scent of wood smoke from somewhere across the river, but then it vanished. She walked slowly toward the great bluff that dominated the bend in the deep canyon.

Mildred noticed that the level of the water had fallen a little, and there was now a path visible around the bottom of the earth slip that looked like it would take her clear around it. She glanced behind her, but nobody was stirring.

The water lapped at her sneakers, chilling her feet. By leaning against the cool rock Mildred was able to maintain her balance, picking her way over the slick pebbles. Halfway around she almost changed her mind and went back. But she was stubborn and kept going.

"Daddy didn't raise no quitters," she whispered to herself with a nostalgic smile.

Twice she stumbled and nearly fell into the nibbling water, but she kept angling her body toward the land. There were small plants growing in crevices in the dirt. Mildred crushed one of them between her fingers, holding its leaves close to her face and breathing in the sharp tang that smelled like a mixture of sandalwood and coriander.

The bend of the river was opening before her as she advanced, and she glimpsed the first sight of another stretch of beach, the sand glinting in the starlight. Now she could stand upright without any fear of falling into the water.

The shore was fringed with small trees and low scrub that eventually disappeared into the blackness. There was the momentary smell of wood smoke again that Mildred guessed must be from their own fire, whirled around between the high cliffs by convection currents.

The sand near the fringe of the water was furrowed and scuffed up, and Mildred walked along the beach to investigate, puzzled by the marks that looked so much like where they'd pulled their own large inflatable out of the river.

She never heard the steps close behind her, just the hateful, grinning voice in her ear. "Morning, bitch."

CHAPTER THIRTY-SEVEN

JAK WOKE from a vivid dream. He'd been sitting on a summer hillside in a field of cut wheat, looking up toward a farmhouse and a barn, both built in weathered wood. And there was a woman with him, her face turned away, wearing a thin dress of pink cotton, her hair drawn untidily into her nape. There'd been something not quite normal about her left foot.

Jak knew her name, but the waking and the booming of the river snatched it away from him.

He sat up, looking around him, sensing that dawn wasn't that far off, though the beach was in almost total darkness. A cloud had drifted across the face of the moon. There was time for an hour or so of sleep before they launched their raft onto the river again. Just as he was lying down, the boy noticed that someone was missing.

"Mildred."

He stood up and looked around. The obvious answer was that the woman had gone into the clump of trees to respond to a call of nature. The teenager had spotted soon after meeting the freezie how squeamish and delicate she was over things like that, which he figured came from not being used to life in Deathlands.

But there was no movement. Jak took a few hesitant steps across the beach, his foot nudging the end of a dried branch. Immediately both Ryan and J.B. sat up, Krysty a split second behind them.

Only Doc snored on.

"What is it, Jak?" Ryan whispered.

"Mildred. Gone."

Ryan uncoiled from the ground, looking toward the trees, turning back to Jak with the question on his lips.

But the teenager was quicker. "Could be. Don't think so."

The strip of beach was so narrow and the towering cliffs so close that it only took them a couple of minutes to search the area—and find that Mildred had indeed gone.

Krysty woke Doc, who rose mumbling from sleep. "Upon my soul that is... Oh, by the three Kennedys! Could the lady have been swallowed by the waters, do you think?"

Ryan looked around, glancing at the sky to try to judge how far off the dawn was, and guessed it was still an hour or more. "Could have done, but she'd only have gone to drink. And the sand shelves are gentle."

"Something out of the river? Mutie fish? Lizard?" J.B. suggested.

At that moment the clouds cleared the face of the moon and the deep wells of darkness became a little lighter.

Ryan spotted the tracks immediately, winding down through the soft sand toward the edge of the river, moving parallel, south toward the great bluff that forced the water into a sharp turn.

All five of them gathered there, looking at the narrow path, lapped by tumbling waves, that vanished around the base of the steep cliff.

"Why'd she go there?" J.B. asked.

Doc offered his own solution. "I would venture that it was merely the insatiable and endless curiosity of the species feminine, my dear John Barrymore. That and no more."

"So, we go after her?" Krysty suggested.

Ryan hesitated. "Don't like it. Don't like it at all."

It was a situation fraught with potential danger. The path was so narrow and dangerous that it would have to be taken slowly, and one at a time. The light came and went as ragged clouds scattered themselves over the moon, and if there was someone waiting on the far side...

"Come on, lover," Krysty prompted. "Mildred could be in trouble."

"No."

"No?"

"No." The flat syllable was repeated, louder this time. Ryan's face set like a marble mask, deep shadows cut around his mouth, highlighting the deep scar that slashed across his cheek.

"Danger for…" Jak began, the words faltering as he saw Ryan's anger.

"No. I'll tell you why. Woman shouldn't have gone off alone like this. Triple stupe! Two possibilities is all."

"Go on," Krysty said.

"She's safe. She'll come back. Can't yell. She'd never hear us above the river."

"But suppose the lady has encountered some peril beyond this cliff?" Doc offered. "Surely we should go and offer succor to her?"

Ryan's flaring rage had cooled. "Only real possibility is Strasser. Either he's got her or he hasn't. But if he has, then the first person around the point there gets chilled. Maybe the second and third. We can't get over and we can't get around. Not by land. Not in the dark. If Strasser's taken Mildred he's chilled her or, more likely, he'll try and hold her. There ain't a fucking thing we can do about that. Nothing!"

He turned on his heel and stalked back up the beach toward the smoldering remnants of their campfire.

"They aren't coming, boss," Rafe said nervously.

Cort Strasser had been waiting, flattened against the high wall of rock and earth, holding his Stechkin drawn and cocked. Over an hour had passed since the black woman had fallen into his hands, ready as a fresh apple. Now she sat near their inflatable, guarded by Rosa, who was using Mildred's own Czech revolver.

"I think you're right. Ryan Cawdor has his failings, but being a triple stupe isn't one of them. Ah, well, it was worth the try. Rafe, get the raft ready, and we'll move on. I'll cover you in case they suddenly come at us by land or water."

It wasn't yet full dawn. Jak had placed himself as near the earth slip as he could, making sure he had the best view possible of the sweeping bend of the river.

When his yell came, it was in a reedy, splintered voice that would have shattered crystal at fifty paces.

"Strasser!"

Ryan ran to join him, staggering as his boot heels slipped into a patch of softer sand. There they were, bobbing away in their craft, a smaller version of Ryan's inflatable.

"Four," Jak said. "Strasser, woman, man... Mildred. Four."

There was enough light for all of them to see that Jak was correct. Cort Strasser was in the stern of the yellow raft, his unmistakable skull-like face turned triumphantly toward them, his mouth gaped open in a terrible grin.

Over the river's roar, Ryan and the others clearly heard the screech of victory of the ex-sec boss, as harsh and raw as a hunting condor's.

Within seconds the frail craft had disappeared around the next tumbling bend.

Ryan clenched his fists in a moment of almost paralyzing anger, then he straightened and looked at his four friends.

"Get launched," was all he said.

CHAPTER THIRTY-EIGHT

THE CHASE CONTINUED during the long hot morning, with the two rafts never more than a mile apart. On the occasional calm stretches of the river, Ryan's inflatable with its extra paddling power, would narrow the gap. As soon as they came to the more dangerous rapids, the smaller and more maneuverable craft of Strasser's would ease its way ahead again.

Half a dozen times they were in sight of each other.

Once Strasser opened fired at them. They saw him kneeling and taking aim with his sniper rifle. But there was no sign of a muzzle-flash, and no bullet came anywhere near them. Ryan was tempted to try the G-12, but the risk of hitting Mildred was far too great.

Mildred managed to keep her fears under control, holding on to her courage and watching for the one snatched moment that could mean freedom.

The bobbing raft tossed and whirled down the gorge, waves constantly soaking everyone on board. Strasser had made sure everyone was tied on safely, taking the extra precaution of binding Mildred by the waist to Rosa's left wrist. The taciturn woman had Mildred's revolver stuck in her belt.

Despite the noise and turmoil, Strasser managed to keep up a running commentary on what he intended to do when Ryan and the others fell into his hands. Mildred succeeded in shutting her ears to most of the bloody filth, but she couldn't help hearing something of his plans for her.

Fortunately they reached her only in fragmented phrases, torn and whipped by the speed and noise of their passage.

But that was enough to sicken her.

His hissing, monotonous voice grated in her ears with its promises of the various ways he would inflict pain and degradation, the orifices of her body that he would enter and ravage, slice and burn, the instruments that he would use to cut and tear and scorch her, the senses that he would destroy, with agonizing slowness, one by one.

And the pleasure that he would take in all of it.

"You remember any of this from the map?" Krysty shouted in Ryan's ear, as his wrist chron showed they were nearing noon.

"Not much. There was a triple-red dangerous place somewhere way south. Satan's Scrambler, I think it was called. But the land's been pitched and changed so much, it don't mean a thing." Catching her eye, he said, "All right. It *doesn't* mean a thing."

"Going faster," J.B. observed.

The cliffs had begun to close in, shutting out the coppery sunlight, cramping the river and forcing it to run deep and fast. Land shakes, before the long winters began, had plucked massive boulders from the walls of orange stone and hurled them into the frothing torrent, bringing more hazard to the rafts, for there was now no possibility of landing to try a portage around the worst dangers.

Strasser's raft was in sight, appearing and then vanishing as the river's curves concealed it again.

Doc yelled out, throwing the shattered remnants of his paddle into the water where it had splintered against a submerged rock. He fumbled with the cords that secured their spare paddles, eventually freeing one. But a violent lurch threw him against the side before he could retie them, and all the spares went tumbling into the rapids.

"Hang on!" Ryan shouted, seeing the old man leaning out to try to retrieve the bobbing paddles.

The bends were getting sharper, and they could no longer see the small raft ahead of them. At one point the cliffs were so close together that their inflatable almost brushed both sides, riding on the wall of solid gray-green.

J.B. turned to shout something to Ryan, while simultaneously fending off the lunging walls of stone. But Ryan couldn't hear him above the thunder of the river.

Rosa was weeping. Fortunately for her, Strasser was too busy wrestling with the steering oar in the stern to reach her. He'd tried screaming, raging and threatening, but none of it had the least effect.

Rosa's shiny boots were dulled with the constant immersion in muddied water, and her trim riding skirt was torn and limp. The elegant ponytail was long gone. Her blankly beautiful eyes were swollen with weeping, and her quirt had been lost over the side of the raft.

But she was still gripping the butt of the ZKR 551, knuckles as white as carved bone.

Mildred watched, considering trying to untie herself and then slip into the water, but she could see that her chances of survival would be no better than by staying in the raft and taking her chances with Strasser. By now they were hurtling along at a fearful pace, spinning around blind corners at a speed that must have been close to thirty miles an hour. Mildred could feel herself becoming more and more dizzy.

Rafe cowered in the bow, having given up on trying to call out dangers to his boss in the stern. In any case, half the time the bow had become the stern as the inflatable whirled around uncontrollably.

As the raft shot out of yet another blind bend, Mildred glimpsed something, less than two hundred yards ahead, something so bizarre and incomprehensible that she closed her eyes and rubbed them. She opened them to find that her first startling impression had been right.

Her jaw dropped, and she began to scream.

Scant seconds later Ryan's larger raft came around the same corner, and they all saw what Mildred had seen.

Jak pointed, speechless, facing Ryan over his shoulder.

Then Ryan saw it.

The river vanished, disappearing into a great cloud of mist. Its edge was green and polished, like waxed oilcloth, seeming not to be moving. Ryan thought for a moment that they must somehow have reached the end of the world.

Nobody shouted. There was simply this grim fascination with the waterfall that was rushing toward them. It wasn't possible to guess how deep the drop was, or what lay at the bottom.

Satan's Scrambler, Ryan thought. It was his last coherent thought as the raft reached the brink of the roaring abyss.

There was a nanosecond of suspense. The inflatable hung in the singing, damp space, its own impetus holding it for a frozen fragment of time. Then it began to fold and tip at the front, and finally fell with a sickening, heart-stopping speed.

Ryan gave a grunt of shock, feeling his balls tighten with fear as they fell. Afterward, recollected in tranquillity, he guessed that the drop might have been barely eighty feet, less than two seconds from top to bottom.

They landed with a smashing force, right way up, water surging solid over every side. The impact burst five of the remaining buoyancy compartments, the aged fabric splitting apart, flooding immediately. Like a brain-shot animal, the raft made a quivering effort to reach the surface, just breaking clear, then subsiding lumpishly toward the bottom of the deep pool that lay at the foot of the teeming waterfall.

Krysty was thrown against J.B., cracking her head on his forearm. Fortunately the mat of fiery hair protected her from a broken skull.

Jak was thrown out over the bow, but the retaining cord around his midriff jerked him back in again, like a demented yo-yo.

Ryan had gone under with his mouth open, feeling liquid ice gush into his throat and fill his lungs. He choked, flailing in a moment of purest dark panic. Then he managed a grip on his senses and fumbled for the knot about his waist, knowing that the raft was sinking under him and dragging everyone down with it.

His chest was being squeezed in a gigantic vise of pain, and his eye bulged with the effort of fighting for freedom. The water had tightened the thin cord, and he finally reached for his panga, nearly dropping the slick hilt through his numbed fingers, eventually feeling the keen steel part the rope, which allowed him to kick his way to the distant, bleared surface.

Ryan burst into the fresh air with an instinctive whoop of indrawn air, filling his lungs with the cold dampness.

At his side he saw Jak, J.B. and Krysty, all treading water, trying to establish their bearings after the plummeting fall.

"Doc!" he managed to yell, hawking up a trickle of bile and river water.

Something nudged his ankle and he dived, reaching below the surface of the pool. His fingers tangled in something and he heaved, finding himself dragging up the head of Doc Tanner, the body trailing beneath it. As Ryan supported the old man, his eyes blinked open and he freed his silvery locks from Ryan's hand.

"You scalp better than the bloody Iroquois themselves, my dear friend!" he shouted feebly.

Despite the overwhelming noise of the falling water, the pool was comparatively calm. There was no strong undertow, and their drop had taken them a little to one side of the main current. All five bobbed close together, glancing around and trying to get their bearings. Ryan pointed, seeing the tatters of another inflatable raft, wrapped limply around a lichen-covered boulder to the left. That meant that Strasser had come the same course that they had, with what looked like the same result.

There was a shelf of low rock that thrust out from among trees on the right of the river. Ryan led the way toward it, moving in a slow sidestroke, kicking out strongly. The others followed him in a ragged, splashing line, Doc bringing up the rear, huffing like a world-weary grampus.

Krysty, last but one, suddenly screamed and vanished beneath the water, emerging a moment later, arms waving. "Something grabbed me," she said. "Something down in . . . Oh, Gaia!"

Beneath the oaks that fringed the pool, the noise of the fall was dimmed, the surface of the water calm and glassy. Just in front of Krysty, that stillness was broken by the eruption of a corpse.

It bobbed up, head first, clad in a torn blouse that revealed white breasts, the skin gashed into bloodless lips. Its eyes were wide open, staring blindly, protruding from their dark sockets. The mouth gaped, and the swollen, purpled tongue thrust obscenely between the thickened lips. As the corpse danced and swayed, everyone could see that there were marks, livid against the pallor of its throat. The hair of the woman, very dark, fringed the face.

"Someone strangled her," J.B. said, looking at the marks with a professional interest. "Did it real good."

Ryan stared at the dead woman, wondering if the fingers had belonged to Cort Strasser.

"Or Mildred," he murmured to himself, striking out for the shore.

CHAPTER THIRTY-NINE

STRASSER AND MILDRED had been the only two on their inflatable who'd seen the terrifying drop before plunging over. Rafe had been looking back toward his chief, staring past him to see if he could catch a glimpse of their inexorable pursuers.

Rosa, still gripping Mildred's revolver, lay on her face in the swilling water at the bottom of their raft, oblivious to everything.

Mildred saw the silken edge of the fall and was already starting to untie herself. Strasser also spotted the peril, and he began to laugh.

That was the last sound that Mildred heard as they dropped vertically, ending with a great wave of white foam.

In the smaller inflatable, the effect was even more devastating, with most of the strained panels bursting, and whole sections disintegrating. The mooring rings ripped away, releasing all four of them from the sinking vessel.

Mildred had untied herself from Rosa and was now completely free, trying to kick to the surface. She broke into the light and sucked in a great gulp of cold, wonderful air, when something snatched her ankle and pulled her under.

In the dark deeps, she realized that it was Strasser's woman, and, locked into blind panic, she was still holding Mildred's blaster!

Using all her strength, Mildred reached down the other woman's right arm, groping for the hand and the solid weight of the ZKR 551, feeling it and twisting with savage power. She was aware that she'd probably broken at least two of Rosa's fingers. She managed to wedge the pistol into the back of her belt, out of sight, but she was still pinioned below the water.

Mildred groped in the suffocating blackness, aware of the splintered emerald light far above, finding Rosa's long black hair and fumbling lower. The woman snapped at her, and Mildred barely jerked her fingers away in time.

Now she found the neck, her strong hands clamping around the slender throat, crushing the arteries and cutting off the supply of blood to the brain. For several startled, fearful seconds Rosa fought against the strangling grip. But Mildred's medical training had taught her precisely what to do.

Her own breath was fading, but she was inexorable, maintaining the brutal hold, forcing the other woman still deeper. She felt Rosa go limp, but she didn't relax, grimly counting off another twenty seconds, though her own lungs were bursting. She finally let go, kicking the corpse toward the bottom of the pool.

When she surfaced, Strasser was already kneeling on the gleaming rocks, the Stechkin steady in his fist. Rafe was on hands and knees at his side, coughing and spluttering.

"You chill her, bitch?" he shouted.

"She drowned." Mildred waited for the tearing shock of the bullet, but it never came.

Strasser laughed. "Saved me the trouble. Was going to chill the double-stupe little Mex gaudy today. Come on out. Let's haul ass!"

Ryan was agonizingly conscious that Cort Strasser could be waiting for them behind any of the thick grove of trees. There were clear tracks leafing off up the path from the river, one that was definitely Mildred's. Over the past few weeks Ryan had familiarized himself with her trail. He also spotted Strasser's footmarks, which meant that the third was the lieutenant, the man with the polished nunchaku sticks. Rafe.

Even with the former sec boss of Mocsin holding Mildred, unless she'd managed to break free after strangling the woman, the odds still favored Ryan and his friends. Whatever the cost in blood, the end of the trail was coming closer.

After the fatigue of the river passage, Strasser drove Rafe and Mildred along at a fearful pace.

There was a track from the river that wound up steeply for two hundred feet. There the trees began to thin out, and open spaces appeared. Twice Strasser called a halt, pausing and listening. But the noise of the river still filtered through, drowning out the noise of any pursuit. Mildred had succeeded in covering the butt of her revolver with her torn blouse. Knowing that she might only get one chance against Strasser and Rafe, she was content to wait for the right moment. As things went, it didn't seem like she was in any immediate danger.

Until her feet slipped and she slid backward, crashing into the skull-faced man. Strasser struck out at Mildred as she collided with him, but he was taken by surprise, having to grab at her to save himself. His hands went around her waist, and she felt the sudden tension as his fingers touched the concealed weapon in the small of her back.

He snatched the blaster, pushing her away from him with an almost orgasmic sigh of pleasure. "Aaah, what is... Clever, lady, clever. Drowned the slut *and* got your pretty pistol back, all at the same time. No wonder Cawdor has you along."

"I hope you develop penile cancer and die slowly and in the worst pain a man could imagine," she said calmly, though her heart fluttered with anger and with something that she knew was fear.

"If I do, bitch, you surely won't be around to do any gloating. You'll be dead. If not today, then very likely tomorrow. And if I have the time to enjoy your chilling..."

With a jerk of her blaster, the skull-faced man motioned her to start moving again, up toward the crest of the ridge.

They moved fast in a strung-out patrol line, Jak at point, with J.B. bringing up the rear. Blasters were drawn and ready, but from the teenager's reading of the trail, it looked as if Strasser was setting a very fast pace. They passed a point where there seemed to have been some sort of a scuffle, marks of skidding feet in the damp earth.

Ryan stared around, somehow expecting to find the corpse of Mildred spread out for them by the maniacal hatred of Strasser. But the spoor of the three pairs of feet still continued toward the top of the hill, where Jak had paused, waiting for them.

"Look" was all he said.

During his life in Deathlands, Ryan had seen plenty of evidence of what the mega-cull of the mass nuking had done to the earth, but he'd never seen a small area so devastated by quakes. It looked like the land had been trampled, then eaten up and spit out. You could clearly see where the waves of seismic force had turned solid rock into flowing jelly. From where they stood it was possible to make out the distant curve of the Grandee, bending around the tumbled remnants of a group of high peaks.

"There's some buildings there," Krysty said, brushing her crimson hair back off her forehead. "Look to be ruins."

"Could be the redoubt and the freezie center," Ryan said. "Or some kind of tourist motel or visitor center. Looks to be around six miles across the valley there."

"Doesn't look like any kind of a trail between hither and thither," Doc commented. "Just an awful lot of trees."

Below them there was a solid mass of pine trees, seemingly impenetrable. Though Ryan looked carefully he couldn't see any sign of Strasser.

The afternoon was already wearing on, though the sun was still above the range of low hills that stood, shrouded in haze, some forty miles to the east.

"What that?" Jak exclaimed. "Dogs?"

The mournful cry came from somewhere below them in the dark green ocean of forest, a rising, vibrating sound that chilled the bones.

"Not dogs," Ryan told him. "Wolves."

Rafe was leading, pushing between the close-packed trees, holding a small wrist compass in his hand. They'd taken a bearing on the group of buildings across the valley and were now making their best speed toward them. But the wood was so dense that Strasser had called a pause, binding Mildred's ankles together with a hobble, so that she could only take shortish steps.

"Stop you running, bitch." He grinned, easing his hand up the inside of her thigh as he stooped to tie her.

"I'm not running anyplace," she replied. "I truly want to be there and see you down and done. I want to spit in your eyeballs."

As he slowly lifted a brutal, careful fist, they all heard the dreadful howling of a wolf—from somewhere very close.

Ryan and the others also heard that dreadful baying sound. They'd just entered the fringes of the forest, heading on a compass bearing toward the distant mesa of tumbled rocks.

"Fireblast!" Ryan exclaimed. "That doesn't sound like any wolf I ever heard. Too deep. More like some sort of a cougar."

"Could be the trees muffling the noise," J.B. suggested.

Krysty shuddered and hugged herself. "Feels bad, lover. We have to go on?"

"There's no way we could get back up that gorge," Ryan told her. "And to strike out cross-country..." He allowed the sentence to fade away into the deep, pine-scented gloom around them.

Several times Mildred stumbled and nearly fell, but the skull-faced man was always at her elbow, seeming to sense her uncertainty, gripping her by the wrist to keep her going. Rafe was in the lead, moving in an easy hunter's lope, the steel chain on his fighting sticks jingling as he ran.

They reached a clearing in the forest, where lightning had felled a large tree, sending it crashing in flames. The fire had been localized but it had opened an area some fifty feet across. The scorched and blackened wood had been covered by tender ferns and the ubiquitous lichen. Rafe had paused at its center, looking around him, allowing his boss and Mildred to move past him toward the far side.

The wolf appeared out of the silent trees, a little behind them, the breath hissing in its throat.

"Oh, shit." Mildred sighed. Strasser didn't say anything.

The mutie animal was huge. Its eyes glittered like fire, and stinking froth hung in clusters from its steaming muzzle. Its lips were peeled back off ferocious teeth. Mildred guessed that it stood at least four feet high at the shoulder and that it must weigh close to five hundred pounds.

Rafe spun to face it, the nunchaku sticks whirring in his hands.

"Hold it, Rafe. Cover us." Strasser started to tug the woman toward the far side of the clearing.

"Sure, boss."

"It'll chill him," Mildred protested. "Why not shoot it?"

Strasser grinned at her. "Bring Ryan straight to me. Rafe can take his chances with the big mutie bastard."

He paused just beneath the first of the massive pines, looking back to watch his lieutenant. Mildred couldn't believe Strasser's coldhearted betrayal of his number one man.

Rafe was in a knife fighter's crouch, using the sticks to hold off the puzzled animal. Once it stepped in close and he whacked it across the snout, drawing a trickle of blood and a roar of pain. The creature backed off and crouched a moment, its eyes fixed on the man who faced it.

For a moment Mildred actually started to believe that Rafe's skill and undeniable bravery would be enough to win the day.

Then two more of the gigantic animals came loping into the clearing.

"Boss?" Rafe said, half turning toward Strasser.

"Bye, Rafe," the former sec boss said, dragging Mildred with him into the trees.

"You can't—" she panted.

"I can," he replied. "I have."

For several seconds she heard nothing, conscious only of the cold iron grip of Strasser's fingers biting into her arm just above the elbow.

Then she heard the noises—the clean, hard sound of the polished rosewood striking flesh; a yelp of pain and then a triple growling; a scream that started high and rose higher, until it was cut off in a brief, bubbling moan of terror and agony; the hideous sound of crunching bone, and finally the blood-chilling noise of a pack of wolves that have successfully completed their kill.

As Strasser ran on, pulling Mildred with him, he began to laugh, louder and louder.

CHAPTER FORTY

THE NOISE HAD WARNED Ryan and the others of the threat from the wolves. They moved on more cautiously, eyes raking the late-afternoon darkness around them for any sign of the animals. Jak spotted the mutie creatures in the clearing and waved to Ryan to cut around to the left. The wolves were too busy at their meal to notice the five shadows that flitted past them among the pine trees.

Ryan glimpsed the ragged remnants of the corpse, with enough remaining of the clothing for him to see, with relief, that the body could only be Strasser's lieutenant. Mildred and the skull-faced man must have gotten away and gone on ahead toward the remains of the distant building.

"You don't have a chance, you murdering bastard! You against Ryan and the others. No fucking chance at all."

Strasser slapped her across the face, hard enough to rattle her teeth in her jaw. His voice was calm and gentle.

"Lady, I've been alone all of my life, found in the outhouse of a frontier gaudy. That was how I started, and it's been downhill all the way ever since. Alone is what I like."

It was a quarter of a mile from the edge of the forest to the main entrance to the old redoubt, up a steep, zigzagging pathway, its edges crumbled by the earthquakes of a century ago.

At some point during the past hundred years the whole region had been submerged under water. It could have been the Grandee, blocked off somewhere south of the Mex border, or one of the other rivers, rerouted after the nuking. It had left great areas of soft sand, treacherous to walk on, piled in the low places all around.

Mildred now walked ahead of Strasser. He'd freed her from the hobbles once they were away from the trees, making her keep ten paces in front of him. Her revolver was in his belt, the Stechkin machine pistol in his right hand.

Once she stumbled into a patch of the yellow sand, finding it suddenly sucking at her feet, drawing her into its cool embrace. Luckily it was only a small area of quicksand and Mildred was able to throw herself quickly forward, breaking the suction by pulling herself onto solid, bare rock.

"Better watch where you put them dancing feet, bitch." Strasser laughed.

They reached the main gate to the abandoned fortress, with the skull-faced man constantly looking back over his shoulder, watching for any sign of Ryan and the others emerging from the forest. But the waving fringe of trees was undisturbed. To the west, the sun was already well down, showing only half its brazen disk.

"Soon be dark," Strasser said.

"So what?" Mildred replied, conscious of how bone weary she felt.

"So, the night makes things level," he told her. "You'll see. Or, rather, you won't see."

Moving more slowly, worried about the possibility of an ambush, Ryan and the other four didn't reach the edge of the trees until dusk. The sun was gone, leaving only the fading golden glow over the western mountains. It had become much cooler, and their breath feathered out when any of them spoke.

They could see the trail as it snaked above them, vanishing over the lip of the hill, in among the cold ruins. There was no sign of Strasser, though Ryan was uncomfortably aware of the Russian rifle that his enemy was so skilled at using. If it had come safely through the waterfall it could be trained on them from the shadows above.

"We stop or go on?" J.B. asked, moving a drooping branch with his hand and peering up at the towering wreckage of the redoubt.

"The longer we wait, the longer that triple bastard has to get around whatever's left up there. Be full dark in a half hour. We'll move then."

From what Mildred had learned about the huge military fortresses that had been built in secret during the 1990s, she'd imagined them as impenetrably vast and indestructible. The Russian missiles had certainly damaged some of them, but that had been nothing compared to what the Earth itself had done.

The massive sec-steel doors that had once guarded the front entrance were buckled and twisted, lying in rusting, mangled heaps in the dirt. Mildred couldn't imagine that anything remained of value in the ruined complex.

If there had ever been a cryo-center linked to the redoubt, the chance of any freezies surviving looked hopelessly remote.

"Now, bitch, we'll find us somewhere snug and warm. Somewhere that One-Eye won't come creepy-crawling after us. Get moving."

Even Cort Strasser was nearing the far edge of ragged exhaustion. His gleaming boots were now cracked and muddied. His white ruffled shirt was torn and stained with trail dirt. The leather pants had several long tears in them. In the dusky light, Mildred could see the lines of tiredness carved deep in the wind-washed bone of the skeletal face, but his inexorably ruthless drive hadn't weakened for a moment. She knew that the first sign of rebellion, or any attempt to escape, would earn her a bullet through the head.

She began to pick her way through the tumbled rubble.

The trail took the five companions above the valley, with its insidious patches of patient quicksand. They reached what had been the main entrance to the redoubt at least an hour after Strasser and Mildred had walked there. There was a silver segment of moon floating far above them, giving enough light for them all to wonder at what seemed to be total devastation.

"I fear that little can have survived within this maelstrom of fallen rocks," Doc said. "And if there should be a freezie center, I cannot believe it would have fared any better. Our journey has proved fruitless."

"What fruit?" Jak asked, puzzled. But nobody explained. Everyone was locked into their own private thoughts.

Ryan had two worries. If the redoubt had ever had a gateway, could it possibly still be functioning? And a wilderness of concrete and rusted iron like this was made for an ambush.

"Where's Strasser?" he said, hardly even aware that he'd spoken out loud.

Mildred was afraid to breathe. The thin cord was knotted tightly around her ankles, then brought up her back to bind her wrists together. The whipcord finally was looped around her neck on a running slipknot, so that if she tried to move to get away she would garote herself.

Strasser had tied her with the religious pleasure of the true sadist, pulling each knot as tight as he could. The thin cord cut deep into her skin, making blood seep around her nails. After she was completely helpless he'd started to fondle her breasts, digging his long nails into the tender skin.

"I'm a freezie, Strasser," she whispered through dry lips. "Back where I come from I tested HIV positive. Means I could have AIDS. You heard about the AIDS epidemic of 1994? Have you, Strasser? Chilled one person in eleven in Chicago. One in fourteen in New York. One in nine in some districts of San Francisco." His hand stopped moving. "Any kind of sexual contact, Strasser. All it takes. How come you stopped? Afraid of dying if you fuck me?"

He slapped her hard across the side of the face and moved away from her, curling up against a broken wall of gray stone, deep in the recesses of the long empty redoubt.

Eventually, despite the cramp and the discomfort, Mildred managed to snatch a few restless minutes of sleep.

Six hundred yards away Ryan and the others had been readying themselves for the night. Despite the fact that all of them were gut weary, Ryan insisted on a watch.

"Strasser could be anywhere around here, like a rat in a ruined ville. We got a place here that he can only come one way. Can't overlook us, 'cause we're high. So we do an hour on and four off. Me first. Then Jak, then Krysty, then Doc and then J.B. And then me again. Through the night."

But nothing happened. Once Ryan came awake, jerked from sleep by the distant howling of the giant mutie wolves. But it was far away, and he quickly slipped back again into the dark, dreamless world.

Doc touched his shoulder, finally waking him to the first pallid light of near dawn. "I heard nothing and saw less," said the old man.

Ryan stood and stretched, easing the night's stiffness from cracking muscles. Around him the others were waking, wiping a heavy dew from their coats.

"Saw an old vid once about a ruined city with lots of temples," Krysty said. "That's what this place reminds me of. Think we'll find any freezies around here?"

"Or a gateway?" J.B. added, yawning and furiously polishing his glasses.

"Most places have the gateway buried deep. Always a chance. Have to get a real lucky ace on the line to find any live freezies."

"What think Strasser do?" Jak asked, trying to bring some sort of order to his mane of snowy hair.

Ryan shook his head. "Don't know, Jak. I've been thinking about it. Way I see it, there doesn't look like there's anywhere to run. He's tough enough to go cross-country and work back north. We could do it, if we really had to."

"I fear that the future looks bleak for poor Mildred."

"Can't argue with that, Doc. Place like this... The bastard could hide up."

"Good tracking," J.B. said. "All this sand all over. Strasser can run, but he sure can't hide from us forever."

Ryan looked around in the dawn's pearly light. "Best get moving and see if we can find some way inside the redoubt."

It was a world of destruction. As soon as there was the first hint of pinkish-yellow light in the east, Strasser roused Mildred, quickly cutting through the cords with his ivory-hilted knife, pasting on his feral grin as she rolled on the floor, moaning with the pain of restored circulation.

"Keep the noise down or I'll slit your throat," he whispered, kneeling at her side. "Cawdor can't be far away."

Once she could stand, he was off and running, pushing her ahead of him. He followed some crazed logic of his own, winding and doubling between the ruins, climbing over tottering gantries and bridges of rusting metal, across chasms filled with quicksand. She realized that he was trying to find a way into the complex, but every gate and door was long blocked or fallen.

He hardly spoke to her, apart from the occasional curse, generally accompanied by a slap or a kick. Once they stopped and he allowed her to sip from a canteen of warm, stale water. The rest of the time they moved at dizzying speed.

"Bastard fast," Jak said, waiting for the others to catch up to him.

They were on the edge of an open space. All around them rose the wreckage of the massive military complex. Some walls still stood, forty to fifty feet high, some with slitted ob-ports, shadowed slashes of blackness against the sun-washed concrete.

It made the skin crawl to know that Cort Strasser might be behind any of the windows, squinting through the sniperscope of his SVD.

The tracks were easy to follow, Mildred's sneakers and Strasser's boots. They were wide spaced, showing the pair was often running. Occasionally they'd vanish on bare stone, but the albino teenager would always pick them up again.

"Way he's spinning around...we're closing in." J.B. pointed at a deep heel mark, with some water still seeping into it. "Minutes is all."

Ryan had a sudden sense that an ending was coming near.

CHAPTER FORTY-ONE

BEFORE THEY FOUND Cort Strasser, they stumbled over the remnants of what had once been the cryo-center. Ryan's fears proved right. The buildings hadn't been built as solidly as those of the redoubt, and the effects of the nuking and subsequent quakes had proved totally ruinous.

Only one part had been freakishly preserved, where a roof had fallen at an angle and had protected one of the inner chambers. The five friends stood by the canted concrete roof, trying to make out what lay beneath it. There was the glint of glass.

Doc straightened. "I do not imagine anything can have survived beneath that, Ryan."

"No."

The disappointment was considerable.

"Want to go take a look, lover?" Krysty asked, sensing his disappointment. She touched him gently on the arm.

"Yeah."

Jak and J.B. remained outside the tumbled building, on watch against the appearance of Cort Strasser.

"Watch that roof," the Armorer warned. "I've seen better on pesthole outhouses."

The fallen roof kept the interior in shadow. Ryan led the way, crawling on hands and knees under the lowest part, managing to straighten after a few feet, looking around him. Krysty was at his side, Doc also standing up, knees cracking.

"Gaia!"

The single word said it all. The two other freezie centers that they'd entered had been in good shape, more or less fully functioning. Here there was no suspended life, only death.

Old death.

The pods that had held the cryogenically treated bodies were smashed, torn apart by the angry, shifting earth. Cables and life-support systems had been ripped away and lay like a nest of torpid reptiles, all around the cracked floor.

As Ryan moved he heard a deep rumble, as something shifted far within the complex. The roof creaked, and a light dust filtered down across his head and shoulders. He shrugged it off.

"Don't take too long, partner," J.B. called.

"Be out in a minute."

Protected from sun and rain and from the attacks of voracious animals, the interior of the large cryo-chamber was surprisingly untouched. But the purpose that it had been built for had vanished in a single microsecond, a century ago.

Ryan leaned over one of the broken capsules, looking into the shadowed inside, and saw the torn ends of several tubes, and the plastic shroud that had once held a human being in frozen, suspended animation. The body was gone, rotted down to a distorted skeleton, the bones all wrapped in a layer of dark brown gristle and sinew. The flesh had melted away and dried into black dust.

He reached in and took a handful, holding it out at arm's length and letting it trickle through his fingers to the floor.

"There's God's plenty," Doc Tanner said quietly. "Such was man."

It was good to scramble back out into the morning sun.

"Fuck this."

Mildred stopped, surprised by the sudden flatness in Strasser's voice. They'd reached the far side of the devastated complex, moving through various open spaces between fallen buildings. The ex-sec boss had tied her hands again and had taken the lead, dragging on a length of thin rope.

Now he'd halted, having just stepped over a low wall. Behind and below him, the woman wasn't able to see what it was that had brought him to a standstill.

"What's wrong?" she asked cautiously. Over the last hour or so Strasser had become even more taciturn, snarling and muttering to himself.

"Come and look, bitch!" He jerked on the line so hard that she nearly fell flat on her face.

Mildred hopped clumsily over the wall and stood alongside Strasser. "Jesus."

There was nothing in front of her feet.

Six feet of seamed concrete and then space. The whole building ended as if a gigantic cleaver had sliced through it, carving down past the bedrock, leaving a hacked cliff that dropped sheer and smooth for three hundred feet.

"I'm not going to fuck around any more. No more running or hiding from that bastard, Cawdor! No, this is it."

"You going to jump?" Mildred asked, rewarded by a lipless smile of utter venom.

"This is a good day to die, bitch. Before it's done there'll be some chilling. Mebbe me. Mebbe you. Ryan. The other bastard grave eaters! This is enough!" He pulled at the rope, leading her back over the parapet toward the sprawling remnants of the redoubt.

"Where we going?"

"To find Cawdor. And chill him."

Krysty found the entrance. They'd gone a long way through the sprawling ruins finding more and more of the perilous patches of soft, clinging sand, filling every hollow and dip. Jak had been leading, still trailing the marks of Mildred and her captor, when the flame-haired woman called him to halt.

"Hold it, there, Jak."

"What?"

She looked around her. "I felt... I *saw* something. In here." She tapped her forehead. "There *is* a way in, and there is part untouched."

"The gateway?" Ryan asked.

"I don't know, lover. Might be. I can feel deeps around us. There's a doorway over..." She looked around and pointed to a shattered corner of a wall. "Just around there."

It had been the main weapons complex, which meant it had been built with extra reinforcements. And there was a massive sec door, standing slightly ajar. Ryan put his face to the gap and tried to see inside, but it was full dark. The air smelled stale and dusty, but he'd tasted worse.

He touched the cool metal and it moved, feather-balanced, despite the damage all around it. Ryan eased it open a couple of feet to give them room to squeeze inside.

There was a crackle of sound and a string of ceiling lights flickered on, showing a corridor ahead, totally bare. On the wall to his right there was a large annotated map of the redoubt.

He whistled to himself. Generally the mat-trans units would be hidden far below the safest and most secure areas of the redoubts. If the gods smiled on them, then they could be all right.

"Looks promising," he called over his shoulder. "I'll take a look at this plan. Keep watch for Strasser out there."

"Want us to come in with you?" Krysty asked, peering around the sec door, her hair catching the fire of the sun.

Ryan moved out to stand in the doorway at her side, looking around the ruins of the big redoubt, watching, from instinct, for the glint of light off metal or glass. But he could see nothing moving. Away to the south there was the stump of a tall tower. A frail bridge ran from it to a similar tower, dominating the only part of the fortress that they hadn't yet moved to explore. As far as he could see, the space below the rusted gantry was brimming with leprous yellow sand.

"Leave one on watch and the rest can come inside with—"

The crack of the bullet interrupted him.

CHAPTER FORTY-TWO

TRASSER PUNCHED Mildred in the stomach, bending her over like a cringing courtier in an old Holly vid. She puked as she fell to her knees and fought for breath. But the skull-faced man wasn't finished. He swung the butt of his rifle round in a hissing arc, smashing it against her shoulder, narrowly missing his target, her head, in his rage. Then he kicked her, his boots thudding into her ribs.

Mildred rolled sideways, trying to protect herself, struggling to breathe.

"Bitch! Bitch! I had him straight down the cross hairs! Put him down and the rest'd fucking run."

He stopped as quickly as he'd started, turning away from her and slinging the rifle over his shoulder. Strasser glanced through the window, but the wide square below the ob-port was deserted. At the impact of the bullet, a yard to the left of Ryan's head, they'd all taken cover.

"You really came close to the big chill, bitch," he said, steadying his breathing. "Knock into me like that and—" He shook his head. "Now the game's all changed."

"Least we know Skullface's still around," J.B. commented, flattened against the inside wall of the redoubt. He pushed back the brim of his fedora and looked around,

smiling a little to himself. Now that the trigger had be
squeezed, the Armorer was at home in his own world.

Ryan looked around the corner of the door, trying
work out where the shot had come from, quickly decidi
it could only have come from the farther of the two tower
From there Strasser could dominate the whole area, rea
to pick off anyone that tried to make a move.

The one thing that genuinely puzzled Ryan was how h
old enemy could possibly have missed him at that range. H
knew the Russkie rifle and what it could do. The sh
couldn't have been more than two hundred yards, mayl
less. Yet the bullet had gone well wide. The most likely e
planation had to be that Cort Strasser was injured, dar
aged a wrist or a shoulder when his raft crashed over the fa

Behind him, Doc was looking at the main sectioned pla
for the redoubt. "This brings back so many splinters of n
poor old memory," he said. "It appears that the fortress wa
abandoned before Armageddon and the opening of the la
seal that brought the silence. The silence between heave
and earth."

"Is there a gateway shown, Doc?" Ryan asked.

"Project Cerberus," the old man whispered in his dee
resonant voice. "A part of the Overproject Whisper.
small segment of the brutish, terminal Totality Concept."

"Doc," Ryan said, smothering his own impatience at th
old man's rambling.

"Yes?"

"The gateway. Is there anything on the map showing
gateway?"

He continued to look for any sign of Strasser, while be-
ind him Doc was tracing his bony forefinger around the
lan.

"Ah, here we are. 'Mat-trans Department. Closed red.
Entry forbidden to this section to all but B sixteen cleared
ersonnel.' That's it, my friends, and it appears to be al-
nost directly beneath us. Just two, no, three floors below."

"Better check," Jak said, starting to move toward a
losed door to their far right.

"Better chill Strasser first," Ryan replied.

"Yeah," the teenager agreed.

Mildred couldn't decide whether any of her ribs had been
roken. Breathing hurt, but the blood that flooded her nose
lidn't make it any easier. She coughed and spit out a clot of
ed-black blood onto the pale stones near her face.

"Shut the fuck up," Strasser growled, turning from the
b-slit to face her. "I'm trying to think."

"What's to think about?" she asked. "One way or the
ther it's time for the last train to the coast, isn't it?"

He sighed and knelt down, touching her face, his voice
ike a fingertip over black velvet. "Yes, madam, I think it
robably is. But I'll not make that ride alone."

He stood up again, the riding crop dangling from his belt.
here was still no sign of movement from below him.
lightly to his left he could see the spider-thin bridge of tilt-
ng iron over the drop to the quicksand lake.

"Yeah," he muttered. "That'll do fine."

The voice was familiar and echoed around the long
abandoned fortress. Ryan, just within the heavy sec door
could hear every word.

"Cawdor! I know you're there. I'm real tired of this run
ning."

"What're you suggesting, Strasser?" Ryan shouted, sti
hoping to bring the other man out into the open, where h
could put one of his scarce caseless rounds through the an
gular skull.

"You and me. End it. One time pays all. What d'you say'
You got the balls for this, Cawdor?"

J.B. touched Ryan lightly on the shoulder. "Agree. Ge
him in the open and I'll chill him. Best way to end it."

Ryan nodded. "Yeah. Yeah, I guess so."

Krysty was on his other side, looking at his face in th
semidarkness. "No. No, lover. Please don't do it!"

"What?"

For a moment he thought the woman was going to sla
him.

"Don't fuck with me, lover!" She spoke with cold, bit
ter anger. "You're going to go out and face him, aren't you'
Just because he challenged you. Said you didn't have th
balls for it. Why do it? Do what J.B. suggests and end i
safe."

"No," Ryan said with utter finality.

The shouted exchange didn't take very long to establis
the terms that Ryan and Strasser would meet on.

Both men took the greatest care to avoid revealing them
selves, the former sec boss in his high tower and Ryan be
hind the screening door within the ruined redoubt.

No blasters. Only blades. Mildred would check Strasser for hidden firearms. Ryan gave his word that there would be no treachery from his side. The men would meet in one hour on the bridge that ran across the lake of quicksand. One would start from each end, and only one of them would walk away.

"Once he's in the open, I'll take him with your G-12," J.B. told him.

"No. Not this time. It goes down my way or not at all. After it's done, if he chills me, then you do what you want. Until then, we stick to what we've agreed."

Strasser pushed Mildred ahead of him, her hands still bound, and knotted the end of the whipcord to a rusted rail. He laid his rifle and the Stechkin carefully against the wall, near the door, pointing to them.

"There." He held out his arms and pirouetted to demonstrate to her that he had no other blaster concealed on him. "Just the knife." He showed her the ivory-hilted blade.

"Why do it this way?" she asked.

Cort Strasser took a step closer, so that his bony face was against hers. "Because I'm *really* tired of all this."

"But what . . ."

He shook his head and stroked her cheek, making her wince. "I know they could go back on their word, one of the others chill me with a long gun. Of course I know that. I'd do it that way. I don't think Cawdor will. Mebbe I'm wrong. But if I'm right, I at least get a good ace on the line at him. Him alone. That's why."

"I still—"

Again Strasser shook his head. "Lady," he said, "I don'
have the time."

While Ryan readied himself, warming up muscles, famil
iarizing himself with J.B.'s Tekna knife, Doc and Krysty had
gone exploring. They discovered that the interior of the
fortress, in that area, was relatively untouched by the
quakes. They got within a floor of the gateway site befor
returning.

"Looks clear, lover," she said.

"Good. Once this is done, we go. Make the jump. Tha
okay with everyone?"

For a moment he thought that Jak was going to say
something, but the boy finally nodded.

Ryan glanced at his wrist chron. "Time."

Krysty looked at him. "I've said it before, lover. I'll no
say it again. Just take care."

"Sure. I'll be back. If not, get the fuck out of here. Good
luck everyone."

J.B. and Jak both grinned at him. Doc shook him firml
by the hand. "Fare you well, my dear friend."

Ryan moved to the edge of the door. "Strasser!" h
yelled.

"Yeah?"

"Let's get to it."

"Sure. I got your word about the blaster?"

"Yeah. Let me hear from Mildred." He could see her, tied
to the gantry. "Mildred! He just got a blade with him?"

"Yeah. The SVD's here. And his Stechkin. As far as I ca
see he's clean."

"I'm coming out."

Having Mildred there made Ryan feel a whole lot safer, knowing that the skeletal figure of Strasser couldn't make a play for a blaster without her giving some kind of warning. He reached the tower and climbed the dusty steps, boots grating in the stillness.

Down below him Ryan could just make out the barrel of the G-12, held by J.B., covering him against last-second treachery.

The bridge was at least a hundred feet long, its handrail corroded and partly missing. The drop to the lake of sand was around fifty feet. In the dark doorway of the far tower, Ryan saw the tall figure of Cort Strasser, a knife glinting in his right fist.

It was time for the ending.

CHAPTER FORTY-THREE

"FIREBLAST!" The moment that Ryan set his foot on the narrow bridge, he realized that Strasser wasn't the only threat he faced.

The supports, century-old, had crumbled under the assault of the initial earth movements and the subsequent harsh weather. Now it trembled and creaked, as if it was straining to plummet into the depths beneath.

At the far end Strasser had simultaneously made the same discovery. He shouted with harsh laughter, waving the knife in the air. "Looks like mebbe neither of us is walking away, One-Eye!"

Ryan didn't answer him, concentrating on his own balance. The knife hilt, with its distinctive circular holes, was warm to his fingers. He held the Tekna with its sharp blade uppermost, ready for the lethal upward cut of the experienced fighter.

Far above the two men, riding a dying thermal, a bronze-winged hawk gazed unblinkingly down.

Ryan edged on, not trusting to the rail, passing a section of twenty feet where there was no support at all. The bridge, no more than three feet wide, was made of steel strips. A cool breeze blew around them, making the ragged wires sing. Ryan took care not to look down into the waiting mixture of sand and water, a mixture that lay waiting for the loser of the fight. Or, perhaps, for the winner as well.

Both men had covered half the distance between them, which left only about twenty feet separating them.

Down below, J.B. peered through the scope of the G-12, finger light on the trigger. But Krysty was at his elbow, the muzzle of her own P7A 13 in his ribs. "Don't do it, J.B., please."

"Not yet," he replied.

The gap had narrowed to ten feet, and both men had paused. Ryan had his first close look in months at his most bitter enemy, but time didn't seem to have changed Cort Strasser that much. The familiar riding crop still dangled from his belt; drooping, narrow mustache concealed the crushed mouth; the stump of the missing finger was against the ivory hilt. His eyes were as cold and dead as ever, the wisps of hair pasted to the goatlike skull.

"Had a good look, Cawdor?"

"Enough."

"Got anything to say? Last words? That sort of thing."

"No."

Strasser nodded slowly. "Good."

If you're good with a blade and you're against someone who isn't, you aim to finish it fast and clean. If the other man's also good, then you don't. Or it's you looking puzzled with your intestines looped around your knees.

But on the swaying, creaking old bridge, things were a little different. There was no safe footing, and the handrail peeled away like the skin off a ripe orange.

For a half minute they fenced with each other, the tips of the two knives weaving and darting, occasionally clashing lightly. But neither man would take the initiative, aware that the counterattack could lead to the winning thrust.

There was a sharp clanging sound from behind Ryan, and a snapped cable hissed to the sand, rust spurting from its flailing length. The center of the bridge dipped, and both Strasser and Ryan broke away, fighting for balance.

The skull-faced man was smiling. "Like I said, One-Eye...both together."

It was now perilously clear to Ryan that Strasser had picked the place cleverly. Subtle skills were of little use. To bring the matter to a conclusion meant one of them taking a chance and closing in.

With Ryan, to think in a fight was to act.

He stamped hard, pitching himself violently from side to side, hearing the twanging of other cables snapping. The bridge dipped and swayed.

And he attacked.

Strasser was one of the most violent and dangerous men in a violent and dangerous world. He saw the threat and tried to counter it, bringing up the bone-hafted knife, aiming it at Ryan's stomach. But the one-eyed man was quicker, blocking the blow by parrying it with his forearm, accepting the flame of pain along it, below the elbow. He felt instant warmth dripping off the fingers of his left hand.

But his right hand held the old Tekna knife, driving it in beneath Strasser's arm, feeling it plunge deep under the ribs. Ryan gave it the classic knifeman's twist as he withdrew it, tearing open Strasser's lean stomach and feeling more sticky warmth flood over his right hand. But this time the blood belonged to Cort Strasser.

The wound was serious, but not mortal.

And both men knew it.

"Useless, you blind bastard!" Strasser sneered, backing away on the wildly pitching bridge. "Fucking useless!"

"Ryan!" Mildred screamed from behind the skull-faced man. "It's going!"

The sudden movements of the fight had been enough to complete the ruination that had been going on since 2001. More cables snapped and the whole thing slithered sideways, the entire handrail unrolling, snapping all its connections.

There was no time to do anything very positive. No time for retreat, no time to do anything but rely on instinct and self-preservation. The bridge was tumbling from the end behind Strasser, crashing down toward the huge pit of soft sand. Ryan had a moment to drop the Tekna knife, seeing it fall away, glinting and blood-slick.

Then he threw himself flat, fingers locking on to one of the rusted slats.

Strasser was motivated by something more bloodily potent than self-preservation.

Hatred.

Mouth wide open he lunged toward Ryan, grinning his triumph as he saw his enemy's own blade spinning to the sand below.

Ryan drew up his knees, taking his legs out of reach of the questing steel. The point of the ivory-hilted knife grated horribly on the step of the bridge just below Ryan's boots.

By taking that last desperate shot, Strasser deprived himself of the microsecond needed to grab on to a secure hold as the bridge unwrapped itself into the sand.

It struck bottom about a third of the way along and immediately broke up, though the end tethered to Ryan's starting point remained solid. And there it hung, trailing into the greedy sand.

Despite the force of the fall, Ryan was able to keep his grip, rolling on one side, his legs slipping into the sand.

Strasser was less lucky. The impact jarred him off the tumbled tangle of wires and steel, landing him in an awkward, crouched position, about ten feet away from where Ryan clung to the slats.

Once the metallic grinding and pinging noises had stopped, there was a sudden, shocked silence.

"Ryan! You okay there?"

It was Mildred, leaning over the edge of the drop, still tied to the railing. Ryan could also hear footsteps, toward the edges of the great pit of sand. All around his legs he could feel the cold, sucking embrace, folding him into itself. He clung to the dangling cables and fought to pull himself free.

"Give me a hand, One-Eye," Strasser said in a calm, conversational voice.

With a bubbling noise, Ryan heaved himself from the sand onto the relative safety of the fallen bridge, taking a moment to turn around and look at his enemy.

Strasser had already sunk to the waist, the sand rippling around him as he tried to kick himself free. But the sludge was neither liquid nor solid, and it resisted all his efforts. He still gripped the knife.

"Help me. Pull me out."

"No."

Out of the corner of his eye, Ryan could see that Krysty and the others were watching, unable to help him. The only way out was up the hanging half of the bridge. It would be dangerous, but it could be done.

But first there was Strasser.

Now the sand was almost to the man's armpits, rising inexorably. He'd stopped kicking, and his face was turned to Ryan with a look of resignation.

"Not this way," he said, head strained back to avoid the quicksand, the tendons in his throat standing out like steel cords.

"Good as any," Ryan panted, beginning to work his way a little higher.

"Chill me. Bullet in the head, now, before it's too late."

Ryan shook his head, ignoring the quiet request. "Man gets what he deserves, Strasser. You're the most swift and evil bastard I ever knew. Nothing's bad enough for you."

"Don't preach. Don't do that to me."

"So long."

Strasser's animal scream of pure rage made him turn back. The former sec boss of Mocsin heaved himself upright, teeth grinning at Ryan with an obscene ferocity. He drew the edge of the knife deep across his own throat, opening the arteries, and, in a continuation of the same movement, hurled the bloodied dagger at Ryan.

It sliced across Ryan's upper arm, cutting a small nick in the skin, then rang off the red metal and hissed harmlessly into the sand.

Strasser, bright crimson fountaining from the severed artery, opened his mouth for a last shriek of helpless rage, but blood filled his throat and he choked on it. He slumped into the moist fingers of the quicksand.

Ryan perched on the fallen bridge and watched the ending, watched the bubbles of blood that discolored the yellow sand, watched the head sink slowly despite Strasser's last, agonized struggle, head back in a rictus of terror, watched the skull vanish.

Last to disappear was the right hand, the four fingers clenched in a spasm of death.

After that there was only stillness.

CHAPTER FORTY-FOUR

THE SUN WAS SETTING out of a sky that flamed with purple chem clouds. The six friends, reunited, had reached the mat-trans part of the complex and found it in good functioning order. Now they stood together outside the gateway, ready to make the next jump.

The ruined cryo-center had been a disappointment, particularly to Ryan, but he was philosophical about it. There would always be other highways to travel.

"Everyone ready?" he asked.

They all nodded.

Except for Jak. "No."

Somehow, Ryan had been expecting it. He faced the teenager. "End of the line, Jak?"

"Yeah. Had good times. Good friends. Never forget it. Never forget any of you. But . . ."

"Not Sharon Vare, surely?" Doc said. "You aren't going back for that vapid little moppet, are you, Jak?"

Ryan answered for the boy. "It's Christina Ballinger, isn't it?"

Jak nodded. "Yeah. Asked me if ever out her way again and sort of promised."

"Man should keep his promises," J.B. said solemnly.

"Anytime any you around spread we'd...you know."

Ryan hated long farewells. He offered his hand to the slim, white-haired boy, who gripped it firmly. "Good luck, Jak, I liked her. Liked her a lot. You'll have good times. And...yeah, we'll come by that way, one of these days."

Krysty embraced Jak, kissing him gently on each cheek. "Respect each other, and respect the kids when you get them. Bye, Jak."

Mildred, her face still swollen from Strasser's brutal treatment, also hugged the boy. "Been good to know you," she said. "And you be careful."

J.B. took off his fedora and shook the boy by the hand. "Always keep your back to the sun," he told him. "And keep your weapons right. Good luck, kid."

It was the only time that Jak Lauren ever let any of them call him "kid" and get away with it.

Doc was last, eyes glistening with unshed tears. "Look after yourself, my dear young friend. A great singer and writer once said something about keeping your dreams as clean as silver. If this is the last hurrah, young fellow, then let it be a prelude to good days. I, too, promise that I will one day visit you and your lovely wife. One day."

Jak stepped back, nodding to each of them. "One day," he echoed and turned on his heel.

They watched him go, out through the main control room with its whirring consoles and dancing lights, his white hair flaring like a beacon.

Ryan finally broke the long silence. "Let's go."

The chamber was the usual design of silver-tinted arma glass. Everyone arranged themselves as comfortably as possible around the floor, avoiding the inset metal plates. Ryan stood by the entrance looking around, making sure everyone was comfortable. He closed the door firmly and sat down next to Krysty, reaching out to hold her hand.

There was the familiar faint humming sound and the feeling of power building up. The disks in floor and ceiling began to glow, and the first delicate tendrils of mist began to appear. Ryan could feel the numbness settling over his brain.

Krysty squeezed his fingers. "This the ending, lover?"

"No. Like they say, 'it ain't over till it's over.'"

The darkness came, and Ryan Cawdor closed his eye.

An action-packed new series from Gold Eagle!

FUSE POINT
David North

For Two Brothers-in-Arms, Time is no Barrier

BLACK JACK HOGAN:

A counter-insurgency specialist left for dead by the Khmer Rouge, he was miraculously given new life. Now, Hogan finds that his survival leaves the U.S. government with two choices: to kill him ... or keep him.

BROM:

A ferocious, primitive warrior, he was mortally wounded after a bloody clash with the Warrior Queen. Like Hogan, he is one more man the Devil didn't want to take, and so he was reborn.

TIME WARRIORS:

Kicked out of Hell, they travel back and forth through time, joining forces to battle evil in two worlds.

Available now at your favorite retail outlet, or order your copy by sending your name, address, zip or postal code along with a check or money order for $4.25 (includes 75¢ postage and handling) payable to Gold Eagle Books to:

In the U.S.
3010 Walden Ave.
P.O. Box 1325
Buffalo, NY 14269-1325

In Canada
P.O. Box 609
Fort Erie, Ontario
L2A 5X3

Please specify book title with your order.
Canadian residents please add applicable federal and provincial taxes.

TW-1A

THE MEDELLÍN TRILOGY

THE EXECUTIONER

Message to Medellín: The Executioner and his warriors are primed for the biggest showdown in the cocaine wars—and are determined to win!

Don't miss The Medellín Trilogy—a three-book action drama that pits THE EXECUTIONER, PHOENIX FORCE and ABLE TEAM against the biggest narco barons and cocaine cowboys in South America. The cocaine crackdown begins in May in THE EXECUTIONER #149: *Blood Rules*, continues in June in the longer 352-page Mack Bolan novel *Evil Kingdom* and concludes in July in THE EXECUTIONER #151: *Message to Medellín*.

Look for the special banner on each explosive book in The Medellín Trilogy and make sure you don't miss an episode of this awesome new battle in The Executioner's everlasting war!

Available at your favorite retail outlet or order your copy now:

THE MEDELLÍN TRILOGY	
BOOK I: Blood Rules (THE EXECUTIONER #149)	$3.50 ☐
BOOK II: Evil Kingdom (352-page MACK BOLAN)	$4.50 ☐
BOOK III: Message to Medellín (THE EXECUTIONER #151)	$3.50 ☐
Total Amount	_____
Plus 75¢ postage ($1.00 in Canada)	_____
Total Payable	_____

Please send a check or money order payable to Gold Eagle Books:

In the U.S.
3010 Walden Ave.
Box 1325
Buffalo, NY 14269-1325

In Canada
P.O. Box 609
Fort Erie, Ontario
LZA 5X3

Canadian residents add applicable federal and provincial taxes.

Please Print

Name: _____

Address: _____

City: _____

State/Prov.: _____

Zip/Postal Code: _____

MT-1

AGENTS

The action-packed new series of the DEA.... Sudden death is a way of life at the drug-enforcement administration—in an endless full-frontal assault on America's toughest war: drugs. For Miami-based maverick Jack Fowler, it's a war he'll fight to the end.

TRIGGER PULL

PAUL MALONE

In TRIGGER PULL, a narc's murder puts Fowler on a one-man vengeance trail of Miami cops on the take and a Bahamian king-pin. Stalked by Colombian gunmen and a hit team of Metro-Dade's finest, Fowler brings the players together in a win-or-lose game where survival depends on the pull of a trigger.

Available in May at your favorite retail outlet, or order your copy by sending your name, address, zip or postal code along with a check or money order for $4.25 (includes 75¢ postage and handling) payable to Gold Eagle Books to:

In the U.S.	In Canada
Gold Eagle Books	Gold Eagle Books
3010 Walden Ave.	P.O. Box 609
Box 1325	Fort Erie, Ontario
Buffalo, NY 14269-1325	L2A 5X3

Please specify book title with your order.
Canadian residents please add applicable federal and provincial taxes.

AGI-1A